MYSTERY OF THE AMBER ROOM

ORDER OF THE BLACK SUN—BOOK 13

PRESTON WILLIAM CHILD

Edited by
ANNA DRAGO

HEIKEN MARKETING

Operation Hydra

The Genesis Project

The Alcázar Code

The Louisiana Files

Bones in the Bayou

Mystery of the Swamp

Louisiana Blues

PROLOGUE

land Islands, Baltic Sea – February

TEEMU KOIVUSAARI HAD *his hands full with the illegal product he was trying to fence, but once he managed to get a buyer it was all worth the trouble. It had been six months since he had left Helsinki to join two of his associates on the Aland Islands where they pursued the lucrative venture of counterfeit gems. They flogged anything from cubic zirconia to blue glass as diamonds and tanzanite, sometimes passing off – quite skillfully – base metals as silver and platinum to unsuspecting amateurs.*

"What do you mean, there is more?" Teemu asked his associate, a corrupt African silversmith by the name of Moola.

"I need another kilogram to fill the Minsk order, Teemu. I told you that yesterday," Moola complained. "You know, I have to face the clients when you screw up. I expect another kilogram by Friday or else you can go back to Sweden."

"Finland."

"What?" Moola scowled.

"I'm from Finland, not Sweden," Teemu corrected his partner.

Wincing, Moola stood up from his desk, still wearing his thick cutting glasses. "Who gives a damn where you are from?" The glasses magnified his eyes to a ridiculous fish eye shape that had the Fin screaming with laughter. "Piss off, man. Go get me more amber and I need more raw materials for emeralds. That buyer will be here by the weekend so move your ass!"

Laughing aloud, the scrawny Teemu walked out of the hidden makeshift factory they operated.

"Oi! Tomi! We have to get to the coast for one more haul, pal," he told their third associate who was busy chatting up two Latvian girls on holiday.

"Now?" Tomi wailed. "Not now!"

"Where are you going?" the more extrovert girl asked.

"Uh, we have to," he hesitated, looking at his friend with a pitiful face. "Need to get some work done."

"Really? What work do you do?" she asked, suggestively sucking spilled Cola off her finger. Tomi looked at Teemu again with his eyes rolling back in his head from sheer lust, surreptitiously begging him to abandon work for now so that they both could score. Teemu smiled at the girls.

"We are jewelers," he bragged. The girls were instantly intrigued, conversing excitedly in their mother tongue. They locked hands. Teasingly they begged the two young men to take them with. Teemu shook his head profusely, and whispered to Tomi, "There is no way we can take them!"

"Come on! They can't be older than seventeen. Show them some of our diamonds and they will give us anything we want!" Tomi growled in his friend's ear.

Teemu looked at the gorgeous little kittens, and it took him all but two seconds to reply, "Okay, let's go."

With cheer Tomi and the girls slipped into the backseat of the battered old Fiat the two drove on the island to stay inconspicuous while they transported stolen precious stones, amber, and chemicals for the production of their counterfeit treasures. At the local harbor, there was a small business that stocked imported silver nitrate and gold dust among other things.

The crooked owner, an obsessed old sailor from Estonia, normally assisted the three con men in reaching their quotas and hooking them up with prospective clients for a generous cut of the profits. When they skipped out of the small car they saw him rush past them, shouting zealously, "Come boys! It is here! It is here right now!"

"Oh my God, he is in one of his crazy moods again today," Tomi sighed.

"What is here?" the quieter girl asked.

The old man briskly glanced back, "The ghost ship!"

"Oh geez, not that again!" Teemu moaned. "Listen! We have some business to discuss with you!"

"Business is not going to run away!" the old man clamored as he headed for the docks' edge. "But the ship will vanish."

They ran after him, amazed at his swift and spryer movement. When they caught up with him, they all stopped to catch their breath. It was an overcast day, and the icy ocean breeze chilled them to the bone as the looming storm drew nearer. Every now and then the sky flashed with lightning accompanying distant growls of thunder. Every time the lightning pulsed through the clouds, the young people recoiled a little, but their curiosity kept the upper hand.

"Look, now. Look," the old man said with glee, pointing toward the shallows off the bay to the left.

"What? Look what?" Teemu said, shaking his head.

"Nobody knows about this ghost ship but me," the retired sailor told the young women with old world charm and a glint in his eye. They seemed interested, so he told them about the apparition. "I see it on my radar, but sometimes, it is gone, just," he said in a mysterious voice, " – just gone!"

"I see nothing," Tomi reported. "Come, let's go back."

The old man looked at his watch. "Soon! Soon! Don't go. Just wait."

The thunder clapped, startling the girls into the arms of the two young men, at once making it a very welcome storm. With the girls wrapped in their arms, they watched in stunned shock as suddenly a sizzling magnetic charge was hovering over the waves. From it, the bow of a shipwreck appeared, barely visible above the surface of the water.

"See?" the old man screamed. "See? It is low tide, so this time, you can finally see that godforsaken vessel!"

The young people behind him stood in awe at what they were seeing. Tomi got his phone out to take a picture of the phenomenon, but a particularly vicious bolt of lightning shot down from the clouds, sending them all cowering. Not only did he not capture the scene, but they also did not see the bolt clash with the electromagnetic field around the ship, which caused an infernal crash that almost popped their ear drums.

"Jesus Christ! Did you hear that?" Teemu screamed against the cold gust. "Let's get away from here before we get killed!"

"What is that?" the extroverted girl cried and pointed to the water.

The old man crept closer to the edge of the jetty to investigate. "It's a man! Come help me get him out, boys!"

"He looks dead," Tomi said with a spooked expression.

"Nonsense," the old man disagreed. "He is floating face up, and his cheeks are red. Help me, you deadbeats!"

The young men helped him pull the man's limp body from the crashing waves to keep him from getting smashed against the pier or sinking. They carried him back to the old man's workshop and laid him on the work bench in the back where the old man had been melting down some amber for reshaping. After they had ascertained that the stranger was indeed alive, the old man covered him with a blanket and left him until he was done concluding his business with the two young men. The back room was delightfully warm from the melting process. Finally, they departed for their little flat with their two friends and left the old man in charge of the stranger's fate.

CHAPTER 1

*E*dinburgh, Scotland – August

ABOVE THE STEEPLES, the sky had turned pale, and the weak sun was immersing everything in a yellow glow. Like a scene from the looking glass of a harbinger of ill omen, the animals seemed restless, and the children fell silent. Sam wandered aimlessly through veils of silk and cotton, hung from somewhere he could not determine. Even when he raised his eyes and looked up, he could not see any anchor point for the whipping fabric, no railing, no thread and no wooden supports. It was as if they were hung from an invisible hook in the air, stirred by a wind that only he could feel.

Nobody else who passed him on the street seemed to be subjected to the dusty gusts carrying desert sand. Their frocks and the hems of their long skirts were only moved by the movement of their legs when they walked, none by the wind that drowned his breath every now and then and tossed his wild dark hair into his face. His throat was dry and

7

his stomach burned from days without food. He was heading for the well in the middle of the town square where all the citizens gathered for market days and to catch up on news from the past week.

"God, I hate Sundays here," Sam mumbled inadvertently. "I hate those crowds. I should have come two days ago when it was quieter."

"Why didn't you?" he heard Nina ask from his left shoulder.

"Because I was not thirsty then, Nina. There is no use coming here to drink when you are not thirsty," he explained. "People will find no water in the well until they need it, didn't you know?"

"I did not. Sorry. But it is strange, don't you think?" she remarked.

"What?" he frowned as the whipping sand grains stung his eyes and dried his tear ducts.

"That everyone else can drink from the well, except you," she replied.

"How so? Why would you say that?" Sam snapped defensively. "No-one can drink until they are parched. There is no water."

"There is no water for you. For others there is plenty," she chuckled.

It infuriated Sam that Nina was so nonchalant about his suffering. To add to the blow, she continued to rouse his fury. "Maybe it is because you do not belong here, Sam. You are always interfering with things and end up drawing the shortest straw, which is fine, had you not been such an insufferable whiner."

"Listen! You have...," he started his retort, only to find that Nina was gone from his side. "Nina! Nina! Vanishing will not win you this argument!"

By now Sam had reached the salt-weathered well, pushed

and shoved by the people congregated there. Nobody else wanted to drink, but they all stood like a wall to block off the gaping hole where Sam could hear the splashing water in the dark below.

"Excuse me," he muttered as he pushed them out of the way one by one to peek over the edge. Deep inside the well, the water was dark blue, even in the blackness of the depth. The light from above refracted in glittering white stars on the rippling surface as Sam was yearning for a mouthful.

"Please, can you give me a drink?" he asked no-one in particular. "Please! I am so bloody thirsty! The water is right there, and yet I cannot reach it."

Sam stretched out his arm as far as he could, but with every inch his arm won forward, the water seemed to recede deeper keeping the distance, eventually lying farther down than before.

"Oh, for fuck's sake!" he shouted furiously. "Are you kidding me?" He recovered his stance and looked around the strangers who were still unperturbed by the incessant sandstorm and its dry onslaught. "I need a rope. Does anybody have a rope?"

The sky grew lighter. Sam looked up at the burst of light that shot from the sun, barely disturbing the perfect roundness of the star.

"A solar flare," he mumbled perplexedly. "No wonder I'm so bloody hot and thirsty. How can you people not feel the unbearable heat?"

His throat was so dry that it refused his last two words and they came out as nothing but whispered grunts. Sam hoped that the raging sun would not dry up the well, at least not until he had had a drink. From the darkness of his desperation, he resorted to violence. If nobody paid attention to a polite man, perhaps they would take note of his plight if he was acting out.

Wildly throwing urns and breaking pottery as he went, Sam screamed out for a cup and a rope; anything that could help him get the water. In his gut, the lack of liquid felt like acid. Sam felt his entire torso course with burning pain as if every organ in his body had been sunburned to blisters. He fell to his knees, keening like a banshee in the throes of agony, gripping the loose yellow sand in his clawing fingers as the acid spurted up into his throat.

He grabbed their ankles, but they only kicked carelessly at his arm without paying much attention to him. Sam wailed in pain. Through narrowed eyes, somehow still pelted by the sand, he looked up at the sky. There was no sun, no clouds. All he could see was a dome of glass from horizon to horizon. All the people with him stood in awe of the dome, frozen in fascination before a loud clap blinded them all – all but Sam.

A wave of invisible death pulsed from the sky under the dome and turned all the other citizens to ash.

"Jesus, no!" Sam cried at the sight of their horrific demise. He wanted to take his hands off his eyes, but they would not move. "Let my hands go! Let me be blind! Let me be blind!"

'Three...'

'Two...'

'One.'

Another clap like the pulse of destruction echoed in Sam's ears as his eyes shot open. His heart raced uncontrollably as he surveyed his surroundings with widened eyes filled with terror. Under his head was a thin pillow and his hands were gently restrained, testing the strength of the light rope.

"Great, *now* I have a rope," Sam noted when he looked at his wrists.

"I suppose the call for a rope was your subconscious mind recalling the restraints," the doctor speculated.

"No, I needed a rope to get water from a well," Sam countered the theory as the psychologist freed his hands.

"I know. You were telling me everything as you went, Mr. Cleave."

Dr. Simon Helberg was a forty-year veteran of the sciences, with a particular affinity for the mind and its trickery. Parapsychology, Psychiatry, Neuroscience and oddly enough a special inkling for Extra Sensory Perception floated the old man's boat. Thought by most to be a quack and a shame to the science community, Dr. Helberg did not allow his tainted reputation to faze his work in any way. An anti-social scholar and reclusive theorist, Helberg thrived only on information and practice of theories typically perceived as myth.

"Sam, why do you think you did not die in the pulse, while all the others did? What was it that set you apart from the others?" he asked Sam, sitting down on the coffee table in front of the couch where the journalist was still lying down.

Sam gave him a borderline juvenile scoff. "Well, it is rather obvious, isn't it? They were all of a similar race, culture, and country. I was a complete outsider."

"Yes, Sam, but that should not exempt you from suffering an atmospheric catastrophe, should it?" Dr. Helberg reasoned. Like a wise old owl, the overweight, bald man stared at Sam with his huge pale blue eyes. His glasses rested so far down his nasal bridge that Sam felt compelled to shove them back up before they would fall off the tip of the doctor's nose. But he kept his urges restrained to consider the points laid out by the old man.

"Aye, I know," he admitted. Sam's large dark eyes scanned the floor as his mind searched for a plausible answer. "I reckon it was because it was my vision, and those people were merely extras in the scene. They were part of the story I was watching," he frowned, unsure of his own theory.

"That makes sense, I suppose. However, they were there

for a reason. Otherwise you wouldn't have seen anybody else there. Perhaps you needed them to understand the effects of the death pulse," the doctor suggested.

Sam sat up and ran his hand through his hair. He sighed, "Doctor, what does it matter? I mean, really, what is the difference between seeing people disintegrate and just watching an explosion?"

"Simple," the doctor answered. "The difference is the human element. Without witnessing the atrocity of their deaths, it would be but an explosion. It would be nothing more than an event. Yet the presence, and ultimately the loss of human life is meant to impress upon you the emotional or moral element of your vision. You are meant to perceive the destruction as a loss to life, not just a victimless cataclysmic occurrence."

"I'm too sober for this," Sam groaned, shaking his head.

Dr. Helberg laughed and slapped his own leg. He pressed his hands down on his knees and pushed himself up laboriously, still chuckling away as he went to stop his recorder. Sam had agreed to be recorded during his sessions for the interest of the doctor's research into psychosomatic manifestations of traumatic experiences – experiences that originated from paranormal or supernatural sources, ludicrous as it may sound.

"*Poncho's* or *Olmega*?" Dr. Helberg grinned as he opened his cleverly hidden liquor cabinet.

Sam was surprised. "I never took you for a tequila man, doc."

"I fell in love with it when I was in Guatemala a few years too long. Sometime in the seventies I lost my heart to South America and do you know why?" Dr. Helberg smiled as he poured the shots.

"Nope, do tell," Sam urged.

I became obsessed with obsession," the doctor said. And

when he saw Sam's most befuddled look he explained. "I had to know what caused this mass hysteria people usually refer to as religion, son. Such a powerful ideology to have subjected so many over so many eons, yet yielded no concrete excuse to exist but for the power of men over others, was indeed a good reason to probe."

"Slainte!" Sam said, lifting his glass to meet his shrink's. "I have been privy to that same kind of observation myself. Not only religion but unorthodox methods and downright illogical doctrines that had masses under their thrall as if it was almost…"

"Supernatural?" Dr. Helberg asked, lifting one eyebrow.

"*Esoteric*, I believe, would be a better word," Sam said, downing the shot and wincing at the nasty bitterness of the clear substance. "Are you sure this is tequila?" he stammered, catching his breath.

Ignoring Sam's trivial question, Dr. Helberg didn't stray from the subject. "Esoteric subjects encompass the phenomena of which you speak, son. The supernatural is but an esoteric theosophy. Are you perhaps referring to your recent visions as one of those perplexing mysteries?"

"Hardly. I see them as dreams, nothing more. They hardly constitute mass manipulation, like religion does. Look, I am all for spiritual belief or some sort of trust in a higher intelligence," Sam explained. "I am just not convinced that these deities can be appeased, or persuaded by prayer to give people what they wish for. Things will be what they will be. Hardly anything throughout time came about by man's pity-party begging a god."

"So you believe that what will happen will happen regardless of any spiritual interference?" the doctor asked Sam, having pressed the record button in secret. "So you are saying our fate is already set out."

"Aye," Sam nodded. "And we're fucked."

CHAPTER 2

*B*erlin was finally calm again after the recent assassinations. Several high commissioners, members of the *Bundesrat* and various well-known financiers had fallen victim to the killings that were as yet unclaimed by any organization or individual. It was a conundrum the country had never had to deal with before, as the reasons for the attacks were beyond speculation. The men and women targeted had little else in common than being wealthy or well-known, though mostly in the political arena or the business and financial sectors of Germany.

Press releases had confirmed nothing and journalists all over the world flocked to Germany to look for some sort of secret report somewhere in the city of Berlin.

"We believe it was the work of an organization," Gabi Holtzer, ministerial spokeswoman, had told the press during a formal statement issued by the *Bundestag*, Germany's parliament. "The reason we believe that is because there was more than one person responsible for the deaths."

"Why is that? How can you be so sure it was not the work of one individual, Frau Holtzer?" one reporter asked.

She hesitated, letting out a nervous sigh. "It is only speculation, of course. However, we believe that many are
involved because of the different methods that were used to
murder those elite citizens.

"Elite?"

"Wow, elite, she says!"

The exclamations of several reporters and onlookers
repeated her ill-chosen words in exasperation while Gabi
Holtzer tried to correct her formulation.

"Please! Please, allow me to explain…" she tried to
rephrase, but the crowds outside were already roaring in
upset. Headlines were bound to reflect the unsavory
comment in a worse light than it had been intended. When
she did finally manage to get the journalists in front of her to
calm down, she explained her choice of words as eloquently
as she could, struggling, since her English-skills were not
particularly strong.

"Ladies and gentlemen of the international media, I beg
your pardon for the misunderstanding. I am afraid I
misspoke - my English, well… M-my ap-pologies," she stuttered slightly and took a deep breath to compose herself. "As
you all know, these terrible acts were committed on highly
influential and prominent people of this nation. While these
targets had seemingly nothing in common and did not even
move in the same circles, we have reason to believe that their
financial and political status had something to do with the
attackers' motives."

That was almost a month ago. It had been a difficult few
weeks since Gabi Holtzer had to deal with the press and their
vulture mentality, yet she still felt sick to her stomach when
she thought about the press conferences. Since that week the
attacks had ceased, but all over Berlin and the rest of the
country, there prevailed a dark, uncertain peace, fraught
with apprehension.

"What did they expect?" her husband asked.

"I know, Detlef, I know," she sneered as she looked out the window of her bedroom. Gabi was undressing for a long hot shower. "But what nobody understands outside of my line of work is that I have to be diplomatic. I cannot just say things like *we think it is a well-funded bunch of hackers in cahoots with a shadowy club of evil landowners just waiting to topple the German government*, can I?" she frowned, struggling to unclip her bra.

Her husband came to her aid and opened it, slipping it off, and then unzipping her beige pencil skirt. It dropped to her feet on the thick, soft carpeting, and she stepped out of it, still in her Gucci platform heels. Her husband kissed her neck and rested his chin on her shoulder as they looked over the floating lights of the city in a sea of darkness. "Is that what is really going on?" he asked in muffled words as his lips explored her collar bone.

"I think so. My superiors are very apprehensive. I believe it's because they're all thinking the same. There is information we did not reveal to the press about the victims. That's the disturbing facts that tell us it is not the work of one person," she said.

"What facts? What are they hiding from the public?" he asked as he cupped her breasts. Gabi swung around and looked at Detlef with a stern scowl.

"Are you prying? Who do you work for, Herr Holtzer? Are you actually trying to seduce me for information?" she barked at him, playfully shoving him backward. Her blonde locks danced on her bare back as she followed him every step he retreated.

"No, no, I am just showing interest in your work, darling," he protested meekly and fell backward on their bed. The powerfully built Detlef had a personality quite the opposite of his physique. "I did not mean to interrogate you."

Gabi stopped in her tracks and rolled her eyes. "Um Gottes willen!"

"What did I do?" he asked apologetically.

"Detlef, I know you are not a spy! You were supposed to play along. Say stuff like 'I am here to get information from you, at all costs' or 'if you don't tell me everything I will fuck it out of you!' or anything else you can think of. Why are you so goddamn sweet?" she lamented, thrashing down her sharp heel on the bed right between his legs.

He gasped at the close vicinity to his family jewels, freezing in position.

"Ugh!" Gabi grunted and pulled her foot away. "Light me a cigarette, will you?"

"Of course, darling," he replied downheartedly.

Gabi opened the taps in the shower to let the water get hot in the meantime. She pulled off her panties and walked into the bedroom to get her cigarette. Detlef sat down again, looking at his stunning wife. She was not very tall, but on those heels, she towered over him, a kinky goddess with a Karelia blazing between her full red lips.

THE CASINO WAS the epitome of lavish luxury and only allowed the most privileged, wealthy, and influential patrons into its sinfully exuberant embrace. The MGM Grand stood majestically in its azure façade that reminded Dave Purdue of the surface of the Caribbean Sea, but it was not the billionaire inventor's final destination. He looked back at the concierge and staff who waved goodbye clutching their $500 tips tightly. An unmarked black limousine picked him up and drove him to the closest airstrip where Purdue's aircrew awaited his arrival.

"Where to this time, Mr. Purdue?" the head stewardess

asked as she accompanied him to his seat. "The Moon? Orion's Belt, perhaps?"

Purdue laughed with her.

"Denmark Prime, please James," Purdue commanded.

"Right away, Guv," she saluted. She had something he valued very much in his staff members – a sense of humor. His genius and inexhaustible wealth had never changed the fact that Dave Purdue was a fun-loving and daring individual, first and foremost. Since most of the time he was working on something somewhere for some reason, he elected to use his time off to travel. In fact, he was heading for Copenhagen for some Danish extravagance.

Purdue was exhausted. He had not been up for over 36 hours straight since he had designed a laser generator with a group of friends from the British Institution of Engineering and Technology. When his private jet took off, he kicked back and opted for some well-deserved sleep after Las Vegas and its crazy nightlife.

As always when he traveled alone, Purdue left the flat screen on to soothe him to sleep with whatever boredom it broadcast. Sometimes it was golf, sometimes cricket; other times a nature documentary, but he always chose something unimportant to give his mind some reprieve. Above the screen, the clock showed half past five when the stewardess served him an early dinner so that he could go to sleep with a full stomach.

Through his slumber, Purdue heard the monotonous voice of a news reporter and the debate that followed to discuss the assassinations that had been haunting the political sphere. While they argued on the low volume television screen, Purdue fell blissfully asleep without a care for the dumbfounded Germans in the studio. Every now and then turbulences would shake his mind to consciousness, but soon he would doze off again.

Four stops for refueling on the way gave him some time to stretch his legs between naps. Between Dublin and Copenhagen, he caught the last two hours of deep, dreamless sleep.

AFTER WHAT FELT LIKE AGES, Purdue woke to the gentle urging of the stewardess.

"Mr. Purdue? Sir, we have a slight problem," she cooed. At the sound of the word, his eyes sprang open.

"What is it? What's the matter?" he asked, still slurring in his daze.

"We have been denied permission to enter Danish or German airspace, sir. Shall we redirect to Helsinki, perhaps?" she asked.

"Why were we den..." he muttered, rubbing his face. "Alright, I'll sort this out. Thank you, dear." With that, Purdue rushed to the pilots to figure out what the problem was.

"They did not give us a detailed explanation, sir. All they told us was that our registration identifier was blacklisted in both Germany and Denmark!" the pilot explained, looking as puzzled as Purdue. "What I don't understand is that I requested preclearance, and it was granted, but now we are told we can't land."

"Blacklisted for what?" Purdue frowned.

"It sounds like bullshit to me, sir," the co-pilot chimed in.

"I wholeheartedly agree, Stan," Purdue replied. "Alright, do we have enough fuel for go anywhere else? I'll make the arrangements."

"We still have fuel, sir, but not enough to take too many chances," the pilot reported.

"Try Billord. If they don't let us in, head north. We can land in Sweden until this is sorted out," he ordered his pilots.

"Roger that, sir."

"Air traffic control again, sir," the co-pilot said suddenly. "Listen."

"They are directing us to Berlin, Mr. Purdue. What do we do?" the pilot asked.

"What else can we do? I suppose we would have to adhere for now," Purdue reckoned. He called the stewardess and asked for a double rum on the rocks, his choice of libation when things didn't go his way.

Touching down at Dietrich Private Airstrip on the outskirts of Berlin, Purdue prepared for a formal complaint he wanted to lodge against the authorities in Copenhagen. His legal team would not make it to the German city anytime soon, so he called the British Embassy to arrange an official meeting with a government liaison.

Not a man of hot temperament, Purdue felt rather livid about the sudden so-called *blacklisting* of his private aircraft. For the life of him, he could not figure out what on earth he could be blacklisted for. It was ridiculous.

The following day, he entered the Embassy of the United Kingdom.

"Good day, my name is David Purdue. I have an appointment with Mr. Ben Carrington," Purdue told the receptionist in the fast-paced surroundings of the Embassy on Wilhelmstrasse.

"Good morning, Mr. Purdue," she smiled cordially. "Let me take you to his office right away. He has been waiting to see you."

"Thank you," Purdue replied, too confused and irritated to even force a smile for the receptionist.

The doors to the British representative's office were open as the receptionist showed Purdue in. At the desk sat a woman with her back to the door, chatting to Carrington.

"Mr. Purdue, I presume," Carrington smiled as he rose from his seat to welcome his Scottish visitor.

"That is correct," Purdue affirmed. "Good to meet you, Mr. Carrington."

Carrington gestured to the seated woman. "I contacted a spokesperson from the German international press office to assist us."

"Mr. Purdue," the stunning woman smiled, "I hope I can help you. Gabi Holtzer. Pleased to meet you."

CHAPTER 3

*G*abi Holtzer, Ben Carrington, and Dave Purdue discussed the unexpected landing ban over tea in the office.

"I have to assure you, Herr Purdue, that this is unprecedented. Our legal department, as well as Mr. Carrington's people, has checked your background intensively for anything that could merit such a claim, but we found nothing on your records that could possibly explain the refusal of entry for Denmark and Germany," Gabi reported.

'Thank God for Haim and Todd!' Purdue thought as Gabi mentioned his background check. *'If they knew what a score of laws I have broken in my explorations they would lock me away right now.'*

Jessica Haim and Harry Todd were Purdue's anything but legal computer analysts, both freelance computer security experts he had on retainer. While they were responsible for Sam, Nina, and Purdue's exemplary criminal record sheets, Haim and Todd had never been involved in any financial tampering. Purdue's own affluence was more than adequate. Besides, they were not greedy people. Just as with Sam

Cleave and Nina Gould, Purdue surrounded himself with people who had integrity and propriety. They were often operating outside the law, yes, but they were far from common criminals, and that was something most authorities and moralists would simply not comprehend.

In the pale morning sun that pierced through the blinds in Carrington's office, Purdue stirred his second cup of Earl Grey. The fair beauty of the German woman was electrifying, yet she did not wield her charisma or looks as he would have expected. On the contrary, she seemed to really want to get to the bottom of things.

"Tell me, Mr. Purdue, have you ever had any dealings with Danish politicians or financial institutions?" Gabi asked him.

"I have done extensive business deals in Denmark, yes. But I do not move in political circles. I am more academically inclined. Museums, research, investing in higher learning institutions, but I keep away from political agendas. Why?" he asked her.

"Why do you think that is relevant, Mrs. Holtzer?" Carrington inquired, looking positively curious.

"Well, that is quite obvious, Mr. Carrington. If Mr. Purdue has no criminal record, he must be a threat to these countries - including mine - in some other way," she informed the British liaison confidently. "If the reason is not based on crime then it has to be due to his reputation as a businessman. We are both aware of his financial status and his reputation as a bit of a celebrity."

"I see," Carrington said. "In other words, the fact that he had been involved in countless expeditions and is well known as a philanthropist makes him a menace to your government?" Carrington laughed. "That is absurd, Madam."

"Wait, are you saying that my investments in certain

countries may have caused other countries to distrust my intentions?" Purdue scowled.

"No," she replied calmly. "Not countries, Mr. Purdue. Institutions."

"I'm lost," Carrington shook his head.

Purdue nodded in agreement.

"Let me explain. I am in no way saying that this is the case for my country or any other. Like you, I am just speculating and what I am thinking is that you, Mr. Purdue, might be unwittingly caught in the middle of a dispute between..." she paused to find the right English word, "... certain bodies?"

"Bodies? Like organizations?" Purdue asked.

"Ja, precisely," she said. "Maybe your financial standing with various international institutions has caused you to be antagonized by bodies opposing those you are involved in. Matters like that can easily spill over on a global level, ending in your ban from certain countries; not by the governments of those countries, but instead by someone with influence on the infrastructure of those countries."

Purdue gave it some serious thought. The German lady had a valid point. In fact, she was more correct than she could ever know. He had previously been seized by companies who felt his inventions and patents could be of tremendous value to them but feared their opposition could make better offers. This sentiment had often before turned into industrial espionage and trade boycotts that kept him from securing business with his international affiliates.

"I have to concede, Mr. Purdue. This makes a lot of sense if you consider your presence in powerful conglomerates of the science trade," Carrington acceded. "But as far as you know, Mrs. Holtzer, this is not an official entry ban, then? It is not on the part of Germany's government, right?"

"Correct," she confirmed. "By no means is Mr. Purdue in any trouble with the German government... or the Danish I would guess. I believe this is done by more under wraps, um, under—," she struggled for the right term.

"You mean covert? Secret organizations?" Purdue prodded, hoping that he was misinterpreting her flawed English.

"That is correct. Underground groups that want you to stay out of their way. Is there anything you are currently involved in that could prove a threat to the competition?" she asked Purdue.

"No," he answered swiftly. "As a matter of fact, I have been taking some time off. I am actually on holiday right now."

"That is a bother!" Carrington cried, shaking his head amusedly.

"Hence the frustration, Mr. Carrington," Purdue smiled. "Well, at least I know that I'm not in any trouble with the law. I will sort it out with my own people."

"Good. Then we have discussed all we can with the little information we have on this unusual occurrence," Carrington concluded. "Off the record, though, Mrs. Holtzer," he addressed the attractive German envoy.

"Yes, Mr. Carrington," she smiled.

"On CNN the other day you officially represented the Chancellor regarding the assassinations, yet you did not disclose the reason for it," he asked with a very interested tone. "Is there something amiss that the press is not supposed to get hold of?"

She looked extremely uncomfortable while trying her utmost to maintain her professionalism. "I'm afraid," she looked at both men with a nervous expression, "that is highly sensitive information."

"In other words – *yes*," Purdue probed. He approached Gabi Holtzer with care and soft spoken respect and sat down right next to her. "Madam, does it perhaps have something to do with the recent targeting of the political and social elite?"

There was that word again.

Carrington looked utterly spellbound in his anticipation of her answer. With fumbling hands he poured more tea, keeping all his attention on the German liaison.

"Everyone has their own theory, I suppose, but as an official spokesperson, I am not permitted to voice my own views, Mr. Purdue. You know this. How can you think I could discuss this with a civilian?" she sighed.

"Because I get concerned when secrets run on a governmental level, my dear," Purdue replied.

"It is Germany's business," she said plainly. Gabi flashed her gaze toward Carrington. "May I smoke on your balcony?"

"Of course," he agreed and got up to unlock the lovely glass doors that led from his office onto a beautiful balcony overlooking Wilhelmstrasse.

"I can see the whole city from here," she remarked as she lit her long, slender cigarette. "Out here, one would be inclined to speak freely, away walls that may have ears. There is something brewing, gentlemen," she told Carrington and Purdue as they flanked her to enjoy the view. "And it is an age-old demon that has woken up; a long forgotten rivalry... no, not a rivalry. It is more like a conflict between factions that had been presumed dead for a long time, but they have woken up and are ready to strike."

Purdue and Carrington exchanged rapid glances before taking note of the rest of Gabi's message. Not once did she look at them, but she talked as she sucked on the thin smoke between her fingers. "Our Chancellor was taken already before the killings began."

Both men gasped at the bomb Gabi had just dropped on them. Not only was she sharing privileged information, but she had just admitted that Germany's head of government was missing. It smelled like a coup, but it sounded like something far darker was behind the abduction.

"But that was over a month, ago, maybe more!" Carrington exclaimed.

Gabi nodded.

"And why has it not been made public?" Purdue asked. "Surely alerting all neighboring countries would be of great benefit before this kind of insidious plot moves to the rest of Europe."

"No, it has to be kept under wraps, Mr. Purdue," she disagreed. She turned to face the billionaire with eyes that emphasized the seriousness of her words. "Why do you think those people, those *elite members* of society, were murdered? It was all part of an ultimatum. The people behind all this threatened to kill influential German citizens until they got what they wanted. The only reason our Chancellor is still alive is that we are still within their ultimatum," she informed them. "But when we approach that deadline and the Federal Intelligence Service has not delivered what they demand, our country will be…," she laughed bitterly, "… under new management."

"Good God!" Carrington said under his breath. "We have to get MI-6 involved, and -"

"No," Purdue interrupted him. "You cannot risk turning this into a huge public show, Mr. Carrington. If this leaks out, the Chancellor is dead before dusk. What we need to do is get someone to investigate the origin of the attacks."

"What do they want from Germany?" Carrington fished.

"That part I do not know," Gabi lamented, blowing her smoke up into the air. "What I do know is that it's a very wealthy organization with basically unlimited resources and what they want is nothing short of world domination."

"And what do you suppose we do about this?" Carrington inquired, leaning on the banister to look at both Purdue and

Gabi. The wind disturbed his thinning straight gray hair as he waited for a suggestion. "We cannot let anybody find out about this. If it becomes public, hysteria will spread all over Europe, and I am almost certain that would be the death sentence for your Chancellor."

From the door, Carrington's secretary beckoned him to sign off on a visa discrepancy, leaving Purdue and Gabi in awkward silence. Each contemplated their role in this matter, even though it was none of their business. They were just two good citizens of the world, eager to help fight the dark souls who had brutally ended innocent lives for the pursuit of greed and power.

"Mr. Purdue, I hate to admit this," she said, quickly glancing back to see if their host was still occupied. "But I was the one who arranged for your flight to be rerouted."

"What?" Purdue uttered. His pale blue eyes were full of questions as he stared at the woman in astonishment. "Why would you do that?"

"I know who you are," she said. "I knew you would not tolerate being turned away from Danish airspace, and I had some - let's call them associates - hack into the air traffic radio control to send you to Berlin. I knew I was going to be the person Mr. Carrington would call in on the matter. I had to meet you in an official capacity. People are watching, you see."

"My God, Mrs. Holtzer," Purdue frowned, looking at her with great concern. "You certainly went through a lot of trouble to speak to me, so what is it you want from me?"

"That Pulitzer-winning journalist, your companion on all your hunts," she started.

"Sam Cleave?"

"Sam Cleave," she repeated, relieved that he knew to whom she was referring. "He must look into the kidnapping and the attacks on the wealthy and powerful. He should be able to figure out what the hell they are after. I am not in a position to expose them."

"But you know what's going on," he said. She nodded as Carrington joined them again.

"So," Carrington said, "have you told anyone else in your office about your ideas, Mrs. Holtzer?"

"I have archived some information, of course, but, you know," she shrugged.

"Clever," Carrington remarked, sounding deeply impressed.

Gabi added with conviction. "You know, I am not supposed to know anything at all, but I am not asleep. I tend to make things like this, things that would impact the well-being of the German people, and all others for that matter, my business."

"That is very patriotic of you, Mrs. Holtzer," Carrington said.

He pressed the barrel of the silencer against her jaw and blew her brains out before Purdue could blink. As Gabi's mutilated body fell over the banister from where Carrington had flung her, Purdue was promptly overpowered by two embassy bodyguards who knocked him unconscious.

CHAPTER 4

*N*ina bit down on the mouthpiece of the snorkel, wary of breathing *wrongly*. Sam had insisted that there was no such thing as wrong breathing, that she could only be breathing in the wrong place - like underwater. Pristine and at a pleasant temperature, the water enveloped her floating body as she propelled forward over the reef, hoping that she would not be ravaged by a shark or any other sea creature having a bad day.

Below her, the twisted corals decorated the pale and barren ocean floor, livening it up with bright and beautiful colors in hues Nina did not even know existed. A great assortment of fish species joined her in her exploration, darting across her way and swirling in rapid movements that made her a bit nervous.

'What if something hides among these bloody schools and lunges out at me?' Nina scared herself. *'What if right now I am being followed by a kraken or something and all the fish are actually racing like this because they want to get away from it?'*

With a jolt of adrenaline courtesy of her overactive imagination, Nina kicked faster, pressed her arms tightly at her sides and speared her way past the last large rocks to get to the surface. Behind her, a wake of silver bubbles marked her progress and a rush of shimmering little beads of air jetted from the top end of her snorkel.

Nina broke the surface just as she felt her chest and legs begin to burn. With her wet hair swept back on her head, her brown eyes looked especially big. Her feet found the sandy floor and she started to wade her way back to the beach inlet between the hillocks formed by rocks. Wincing, she pushed hard against the current, goggles in hand.

Behind her, the tide started swelling for the flow, a very dangerous time to be in the water around here. The sun had thankfully disappeared behind the gathering clouds, but it was too late. It was Nina's first time in the tropical climes of the world and already she was suffering for it. Sore shoulders punished her every time the water hit her red skin. Her nose had started to peel already from the sunburn of the day before.

"Oh God, can I just get to the shallows already!" she sneered in frustration at the constant onslaught of the waves and sea spray that spattered salty surf against her reddened body. As the waist deep water became knee deep, she hurried to find the closest shelter, which just happened to be a beach bar.

Every single boy and man crossing her path turned to stare as the petite beauty strutted onto the loose sand. Nina's dark eyebrows, perfectly shaped over large dark eyes, only accentuated her marble skin; even if now it was quite reddened. All eyes immediately fell on the three emerald green triangles that barely covered the parts of her that men coveted most. Nina's physique was by no means perfect, but it was the way she carried herself that drove others to admire and desire her.

"Have you seen the man who was with me this morning?"

she asked the young bartender who was aptly sporting an unbuttoned flower shirt.

"The man with the obsessive lens?" he asked her. Nina had to smile and nod.

"Aye. That would be the very one I am looking for," she winked. She collected her white cotton tunic from the corner chair where she had left it and pulled it over her head.

"Have not seen him recently, ma'am. Last I saw he was on his way to meet with some elders of the neighboring village to learn about their culture or something," the barman added. "Drink?"

"Um, run me a tab?" she charmed.

"Of course! What will it be?" he smiled.

"Sherry," Nina decided. She doubted they would have liqueur. "Ta."

The afternoon dulled into a smoky coolness as the tide brought with it a saline mist that drifted onto the beach. Nina sipped her drink, clutching her goggles, while her eyes surveyed her surroundings. Most of the people had left, save for a group of students from Italy making a drunken racket on the other side of the bar and two strangers hovering quietly over their respective drinks by the counter.

When she had finished her sherry, Nina realized that the sea had come much closer, and the sun was sinking quickly.

"Is there a storm coming or something?" she asked the barman.

"I don't think so. There are not nearly enough clouds for that," he replied, leaning forward to peek upward from under the straw roof. "But the cold will be coming in soon, I think."

Nina laughed at the thought.

"And how could would that be?" she giggled. At the bartender's puzzled frown, she filled him in why she found their idea of chill amusing. "Oh, I'm from Scotland, see?"

"Ah!" he laughed. "I see! That is why you talk like Billy

Connelly! And why you," he frowned sympathetically at her red skin with specific attention, "lost a fight against the sun on your first day here."

"Aye," Nina agreed, pouting at the defeat as she looked her arms over once more. "Bali hates me."

He laughed and shook his head. "No! Bali loves beauty. Bali loves beauty!" he cried and ducked under the counter, only to emerge with the sherry bottle. He poured her another glass. "On the house, compliments of Bali."

"Thank you," Nina smiled.

The new-found relaxation unquestionably served her mood well. Not once since she and Sam had arrived two days before had she lost her temper, except of course when she had cursed the sun that had lashed her. Away from Scotland, away from her home in Oban, she felt as if more profound matters could simply not reach her. Especially here, where the Equator was north of her instead of south, for once, she felt well out of the reach of any kind of mundane or serious matter.

Bali was hiding her securely. Nina enjoyed the strangeness, how unlike Europe the islands were, even if she loathed the sun and the incessant waves of heat that turned her throat into a desert and made her tongue stick to the roof of her mouth. Not that she had anything specific to hide from, but Nina needed a change of pace for her own good. Only then would she be on top of her game when she returned home.

After learning that Sam was alive and seeing him again, the feisty academic had promptly decided to make the most of his company now that she knew he was not lost to her after all. Seeing him step out of the shadows at Dave Purdue's estate, *Wrichtishousis*, taught her to appreciate the present and nothing else. When she had thought he was dead, she had learned the meaning of finality and regret and vowed to never endure that pain again – the pain of not knowing. His absence from her life had convinced Nina that she loved Sam, even if she could not imagine being tied down in a serious relationship with him.

These days Sam was different to some extent. Naturally, he would be, having been spirited away on board a devilish Nazi ship that had imprisoned his very being in its bizarre webbing of unholy physics. How long he had been flung from wormhole to wormhole was unclear, but one thing was clear – it had altered the world renowned journalist's view of the improbable.

Nina listened to the dwindling conversation of the patrons, wondering what Sam was up to. Having his camera with him only assured her that he would be away for a while, probably getting lost in the beauty of the islands and not keeping track of the time.

"Last one," the bartender smiled and offered to pour her another.

"Oh, no, thanks. On an empty stomach this stuff is like Rohypnol," she chuckled. "I think I will call it a day."

She hopped off her bar stool and gathered up her amateur snorkeling gear, slinging it over her shoulder as she waved goodbye to the bar staff. At the room she shared with Sam, there was no trace of him yet, which was to be expected, yet Nina could not help but feel ill at ease about Sam wandering off. She brewed herself a cup of tea and waited, looking out through the wide glass sliding door where the gauzy white drapes rippled in the sea breeze.

"I can't," she groaned. "How can people just sit around like this? Jesus, I'll lose my mind."

Nina closed the windows and got dressed in her khaki cargo pants, hiking boots and packed her small satchel with a switchblade, compass, towel and a bottle of fresh water.

Determined, she set off toward the thickly forested area behind the holiday resort where a hiking trail led to a local village. At first, the overgrown sandy path meandered through a glorious cathedral of jungle trees, full of colorful birds and crisp, clear streams. For several minutes, the bird calls were almost deafening, but eventually, the chirps diminished as if they were restricted to the vicinity she had just emerged from.

Before her, the path ran straight uphill, and the plant life here was far less lush. Nina realized that the birds had stayed behind and that she was now trudging through an eerily quiet place. Far in the distance, she could hear the voices of people in heated debate echo across the flat terrain that stretched from the edge of the hill where she was standing. Down below in the small village, women wailed and cowered while the men of the tribe were shouting defensively at one another. In the middle of it all, one man sat in the sand – an intruder.

"Sam!" Nina gasped. "Sam?"

She began to walk down the hill toward the settlement. The distinct smell of fire and meat filled the air as she came closer, keeping her eyes on Sam. He sat with his legs crossed and had his right hand on the crown of another man, repeating one word over and over in a foreign language. The disturbing sight scared Nina, but Sam was her friend, and she hoped to assess the situation before the mob became violent.

"Hello!" she said as she entered the center clearing. The villagers reacted with raw hostility, immediately shouting at Nina and waving their arms wildly to chase her off. With arms outstretched she tried to gesture that she was not an enemy.

"I'm not here to cause any harm. That," she pointed to Sam, "is my friend. I will take him away, alright? Alright?"

Nina sank to her knees to exhibit a submissive body language, moving toward Sam.

"Sam," she said as she reached out to him. "My God! Sam, what is wrong with your eyes?"

His eyes had rolled back in their sockets as he chanted one word over and over.

"Kalihasa! Kalihasa!"

"Sam! Dammit, Sam, wake the hell up! You're going to get us killed!" she shouted.

"You cannot wake he," a man, who must have been the chief of the tribe told Nina.

"Why not?" she frowned.

"Because he dead."

CHAPTER 5

*N*ina felt her hair stand on end in the dry heat of the late afternoon. Above the village, the sky turned into a pallid yellow, resembling the highly pregnant skies of Atherton, where she had once visited as a child during an electrical storm.

She scowled in disbelief, looking sternly at the chief. "He is not dead. He is alive and breathing... right there! What is he saying?"

The old man sighed as if he had seen the same scene one too many times in his life.

"Kalihasa. He tells man under he hand to die in he name."

The other man next to Sam started convulsing, yet the raging onlookers did not take one step forward to help their fellow. Nina shook Sam violently, but the chief pulled her away in alarm.

"What?" she shouted at him. "I will stop this! Let me go!"

"Dead gods talking. You must listen," he warned.

"Are you all out of your minds?" she cried, throwing her hands up in the air. "Sam!" Nina was terrified, yet she kept reminding herself that it was Sam – *her* Sam and that she had to keep him from killing the native. The chief held her by the wrist to stop her from interfering. His grip was unnaturally strong for such a frail-looking old man.

In the sand in front of Sam, the native man screamed in agony as Sam kept repeating his iniquitous chant. Blood trickled from Sam's nose and dripped on his chest and thighs, prompting the villagers to voice a chorus of terror. Women wept, and children screamed, upsetting Nina to tears. Shaking her head profusely, the Scottish historian let out a hysterical scream, gathering her strength. She bolted forward with all her strength, breaking the hold of the chief's grasp.

With fury and fear, Nina raced towards Sam with her water bottle in her hand, trailed by three villagers sent to stop her. But she was too fast. When she reached Sam, she poured the water onto his face and head. Her shoulder dislocated as the village men tackled her, their momentum proving too strong for her small frame.

Sam's eyes closed under the drops of water running down his forehead. His chanting ceased instantly, and the native in front of him was delivered from his anguish. Exhausted and crying he rolled in the sand, crying out to his gods in thanked them for their mercy.

"Get off me!" Nina screamed, using her good arm to wallop one of the men. He slapped her hard across the face, sending her down on the sand.

"Take your evil prophet away from here!" Nina's attacker roared in a heavy accent, holding his fist up, but the chief stopped him from committing more violence. The other men got up from the ground at his command and left Nina and Sam alone, but not before spitting on the intruders as they passed.

"Sam? Sam!" Nina screamed. Her voice quivered in shock and rage as she held his face in her hands. Painfully she pressed her injured arm to her chest as she tried to pull a dazed Sam up to his feet. "Jesus Christ, Sam! Get up!"

For the first time, Sam blinked. He frowned as confusion overtook him.

"Nina?" he groaned. "What are you doing here? How did you find me?"

"Listen, just get the fuck up and let's go before these people barbecue our pale asses for dinner, okay?" she said under her breath. "Please. Please, Sam!"

He looked up at his beautiful friend. She appeared to be rattled.

"What's that bruise on your face? Nina. Hey! Did someone…" he realized that they were in the middle of a rapidly growing crowd, "…did someone *hit you*?"

"Don't get all macho now. Let's just get the fuck out of here. Now," she whispered with firm urgency.

"Alright, alright," he slurred, still thoroughly dazed. His eyes swam from side to side as he surveyed the spitting onlookers who were barking insults and motioned him and Nina away. "Christ, what is their problem?"

"Doesn't matter. I'll explain everything if we get out of here alive," Nina panted in agony and panic as she dragged Sam's unsteady body with her toward the top of the hill.

They moved as fast as they could, but Nina's injury kept her from running.

"I can't, Sam. You go ahead," she cried.

"Absolutely not. Let me help you," he replied, fumbling clumsily at her stomach.

"What are you doing?" she frowned.

"Trying to put my arm around your waist to that I can pull you along, love," he huffed.

"You are not even close. I am right here in plain sight," she moaned, but then something occurred to her. Waving an open hand in front of Sam's face, Nina noticed that he did follow the movement. "Sam? Can you see?"

He blinked rapidly and looked frustrated. "Not much. I see you, but it's hard to tell distances. My depth perception is fucked, Nina."

"Okay, okay, let's just get back to the holiday resort. Once we are safe in the room we can figure out what the hell happened to you," she suggested sympathetically. Nina took Sam's hand and navigated for the both of them all the way back to the hotel. Amidst stares from guests and staff, Nina and Sam hurried to their room. When they got inside, she locked the door.

"Go lie down, Sam," she said.

"Not until we get you a doctor for that nasty bruise," he protested.

"How can you see the bruise on my face, then?" she inquired as she looked up a number in the hotel's phone directory.

"I can see you, Nina," he sighed. "I just cannot tell how far things are away from me. I have to admit this is far more annoying than not being able to see if you can believe that."

"Oh yeah. Of course," she answered as she punched in the number for a taxi service. She booked a car to the nearest emergency room. "Take a quick shower, Sam. We have to figure out if your vision is damaged permanently -right after they pop this back into the rotator cuff, that is."

"Your shoulder is out of the socket?" Sam asked.

"Aye," she replied. "Came out when they tackled me to keep me away from you."

"Why? What were you going to do that they wanted to protect me from you?" he half-smiled in amusement, but he could tell Nina was keeping the details from him.

"I was just going to wake you up, and they did not seem to want me to, that's all," she shrugged.

"That is what I want to know. Was I asleep? Was I out cold?" he asked sincerely, shifting to face her.

"I don't know, Sam," she said unconvincingly.

"Nina," he tried to pry.

"You have less than," she looked at the bedside clock, "twenty minutes to shower and get ready for our taxi."

"Okay," Sam yielded as he got up to get to the shower, slowly groping his way along the edge of the bed and the table. "But this is not over. When we come back, you are telling me everything, including whatever you are hiding from me."

At the hospital, the on-duty medical professionals took care of Nina's shoulder.

"Do you want something to bite on?" the sharp-looking Indonesian doctor asked. He reminded Nina of one of those promising young hipster Hollywood directors with his dark-skinned features and wisecracking personality.

"Your nurse, perhaps?" Sam chipped in, leaving the unsuspecting nurse stunned.

"Ignore him. He can't help it," Nina winked at the surprised nurse who was scarcely halfway through her twenties. With effort, the girl forced a smile, darting an uncertain eye towards the handsome man who had come to the ER with Nina. "And I only bite men."

"Good to know," the charming doctor smiled. "How did you do this? And don't say you did heavy lifting."

"I fell during a hike," Nina replied without flinching.

"Okay, here we go. Ready?" the doctor asked.

"No," she whined for a split second before the doctor pulled her arm with a powerful hold that sent her muscles into a cramp. Nina screamed in agony at the burning ligaments and stretched muscle fibers that sent a devastating jolt of pain through her shoulder. Sam jumped up to come to her side, but the nurse gently pushed him back.

"It's over! It's done," the doctor comforted her. "It's back in, okay? It will burn for another day or two, but then it will be better. Keep it in the sling. Not too much movement for the next month, so no hiking."

"Jesus! For a moment I thought you were ripping my fucking arm off!" Nina scowled. Her brow glistened with sweat, and her clammy skin felt cold to the touch when Sam came to hold her hand.

"You alright?" he asked.

"Aye, I'm golden," she said, but her face told a different story. "We have to get your eyes checked now."

"What is wrong with your eyes, sir?" the charismatic doctor asked.

"Well, that is the thing. I have no idea. I...," he looked suspiciously at Nina for a moment, "fell asleep, you know, outside while getting a tan. And when I woke up I had trouble focusing on the distance of objects."

The doctor stared at Sam, locking his eyes dead on Sam's as if he wasn't buying a word of what the tourist had just reported. He dug around in his coat pocket for his pen light as he nodded. "You say you fell asleep tanning. Do you tan with a shirt on? There is no tan line on your chest, and unless you reflect sunlight with your pale skin, my Scottish friend, there is little indication that your story is true."

"I don't think it matters why he was sleeping, doc," Nina defended.

He looked at the petite firecracker with the big dark eyes. "Actually, it makes all the difference, ma'am. Only if I know where he was and for how long, what he was exposed to, et cetera, will I be able to determine what may have caused the problem."

"Where did you study?" Sam asked, completely off topic.

"Pre-med Cornell and four years at Beijing University, sir. I was working on my masters at Stanford, but I had to interrupt it to come and help out with the flood of 2014 in Brunei," he explained while he examined Sam's eyes.

"And you are hidden away in a small place like this? Almost a pity, I would say," Sam remarked.

"My family is here, and it is where my skill is needed most, I think," the young doctor said, keeping things light and personal because he wanted to cultivate a close rapport with the Scotsman, especially considering what he suspected was wrong. It would be impossible to have a serious discussion about such a condition even with the most open-minded of people.

"Mr. Cleave, why don't you come with me into my office so that we can speak in private," the doctor suggested with a serious tone that worried Nina.

"Can Nina come with?" Sam asked. "I want her with me in private conversations about my health."

"Very well," the doctor said, and they accompanied him to a small room off the short hallway of the ward. Nina looked at Sam, but he seemed calm. In the sterile environment, Nina felt queasy. The doctor closed the door and gave the two of them a long, hard look.

"Were you up in the village off the beach, perhaps?" he asked them.

"Aye," Sam said. "Is it a local infection?"

"Is that where you got hurt, ma'am?" He addressed Nina with a tinge of apprehension. She affirmed with a nod, looking somewhat embarrassed for her clumsy fib earlier.

"Is it a disease or something, doctor?" Sam pressed for an answer. "Do those people have some illness…?"

The doctor took a deep breath. "Mr. Cleave, do you believe in the supernatural?"

CHAPTER 6

*P*urdue woke up in what felt like a freezer, or a coffin made to preserve a corpse. His eyes could not make out anything in front of him. Darkness and silence were akin to the frigid atmosphere that was burning his exposed skin. His left hand reached for his right wrist, but he found that his watch had been removed. Every breath was a rattle of torment as he panted from the cold air coming in from somewhere in the blackness. It was then that Purdue discovered that he was completely nude.

'Oh my God! Please don't tell me I am lying on a slab in some morgue. Please don't tell me that I have been mistaken for dead!' his inner voice pleaded. *'Stay calm, David. Just stay calm until you know what is going on. No use panicking prematurely. Panic only clouds the mind. Panic only clouds the mind.'*

Carefully he moved his hand down his body and moved them along his sides to feel what was underneath him.

'Satin.'

'Could it be a coffin?', he wondered but thought that a coffin would be anything but cold. Sporadic muscle twitches eventually turned into full-fledged cramps, especially in his feet. In pain Purdue wailed into the darkness, clutching his feet. At least this meant that he was not confined to a casket or a morgue fridge. Still, knowing this brought him no solace. The cold was unbearable, even more so than the solid dark around him.

Suddenly, the silence was broken by footsteps approaching.

'Is this my salvation? Or my doom?'

Purdue listened carefully, fighting the urge to hyperventilate. No voices filled the place, only the incessant footfalls. His heart raced at the myriad of thoughts at what it could be – *where* he could be. A switch flicked and white light blinded Purdue, stinging his eyes.

"There he is," he heard a high-pitched male voice that brought to mind Liberace. "My Lord and Savior."

Purdue could not open his eyes. Even through shut eyelids, the light pierced into his skull.

"Take your time, Her Purdue," the voice advised in a heavy Berlin accent. "Your eyes must first adjust, or you will go blind, darling. And we don't want that. You are just too precious."

Uncharacteristic of Dave Purdue, he elected to respond with a well pronounced "Fuck you."

The man giggled at his profanity, sounding rather amused by it. A clapping of hands cut through Purdue's ears, and he winced.

"Why am I naked? I don't swing that way, mate," Purdue managed to say.

"Oh, you will swing any way we push you, my dear. You will see. Resistance is very unhealthy. Cooperation is just as important as oxygen as you will soon realize. I am your host, Klaus, and you are naked for the simple reason that nude men are easy to detect when they escape. There is no need to restrain you when you are naked, you see. I believe in simple but effective methods," the man explained.

Purdue forced his eyes to adjust to his bright environment. Contrary to every image he had had in his head while lying in the darkness, the chamber where he was held captive was large and luxurious. It reminded him of the décor in the chapel of Glamis Castle in his home country, Scotland. Renaissance-style paintings adorned ceilings and walls, all in colorful oils and gilded framing. Golden chandeliers were hanging from the ceiling and stained glass windows decorated the window panes that peeked through from behind lavish drapery in dark purple.

Last his eyes found the man of whom he had only heard the voice until that moment, and he looked almost exactly as Purdue had pictured him. Not very tall, the slim and elegantly dressed Klaus stood attentively with his hands neatly folded in front of him. Deep dimples formed on his cheeks when he smiled, and his dark beady eyes appeared to glow occasionally under the bright light. Purdue noticed that Klaus wore his hair in a way that reminded him of Hitler's – dark side parting, very short from the top of the ear down. But his face was clean shaven, and there was no trace of the detestable clump of hair under the nose that the demonic Nazi leader had sported.

"When can I get dressed?" Purdue asked, trying to be as polite as possible. "I am really cold."

"You cannot, I'm afraid. As long as you are here you will be naked for practical as well as," Klaus' eyes examined Purdue's tall, lean physique with shameless delight, "*esthetic* purposes."

"Without clothing, I will freeze to death! This is ludicrous!" Purdue objected.

"Please, control yourself, Herr Purdue," Klaus replied evenly. "Rules are rules. However, the heating will be turned on as soon as I command so that you will be comfortable. We only chilled the room to wake you."

"Couldn't you just wake me the old fashioned way?" Purdue sneered.

"What is the old fashioned way? Calling your name? Pouring water on you? Sending a pet cat to paw your face? Please. This is a temple of unholy gods, my dear man. We are certainly not about kindness and pampering," Klaus reported in a cold voice that did not fit his smiling face and blazing eyes.

Purdue's legs were shivering, and his nipples hardened from the cold while he stood beside the silk cloth covered table that had served as his bed since he was brought here. His hands covered his manhood, revealing his dropping body temperature by the purple look of his nails and lips.

"Heizung!" Klaus ordered. He took a gentler tone, "Within a few minutes, it will be much more comfortable for you, I promise."

"Thank you," Purdue stuttered through clattering teeth.

"You may sit if you wish, but you will not be allowed to leave this room until you are taken out – or carried out – depending on the degree of your cooperation," Klaus informed him.

"About that," Purdue said. "Where am I? A temple? And what will you need from me?"

"Slowly!" Klaus exclaimed with a big smile, clapping his palms together. "You just want to get to the details. Relax."

Purdue felt his frustration mounting. "Listen, Klaus, I am not a bloody tourist! I am not here for a visit, and I am certainly not here to entertain you. I want the details so that we can conclude our unfortunate business and I can go home! You seem to assume that I *am fin*e being here in my goddamn birthday suit jumping through your hoops like a circus animal!"

Klaus' smile disappeared rapidly. After Purdue had finished his rant, the slight man leered at him, unmoving. Purdue hoped that his point got through to the obnoxious idiot who was playing games with him on one of his not-so-good days.

"Are you quite done, David?" Klaus asked in a low, sinister voice that was barely audible. His dark eyes stared straight into Purdue's while he dropped his chin and locked his fingers. "Let me clarify something for you. You are not a guest here, you are right; neither are you a master. Here you do not possess any power because here you are naked, and that means you have no computer access, gadgets or credit cards to perform your magic tricks."

Klaus slowly approached Purdue while he continued his clarification. "Here you will have no permission to question or have an opinion. You will comply or die, and you will do so without question, am I clear?"

"Crystal clear," Purdue answered.

"The only reason I am even treating you with a tiny measure of respect is that you have once been *Renatus* of the Order of the Black Sun," he told Purdue as he circled him. Klaus displayed a distinct expression of utter contempt for his captive. "Even though you were a bad king, a treacherous turncoat who elected to destroy the Black Sun instead of using them to reign the new Babylon."

"I never applied for the position!" he defended his case, but Klaus kept on talking as if Purdue's words were but creaks and squeaks in the wooden panels of the room.

"You had the most powerful beast in the world at your beck and call, Renatus, and you chose to shit on it, sodomize it and almost caused the total collapse of ages of power and wisdom," Klaus preached. "If that had been your plan from the start I commend you. It shows a talent for deception. But if you did it because you were afraid of the power my friend, you are worthless."

"Why do you defend the Order of the Black Sun? Are you one of their minions? Did they promise you a place in their throne room once they have destroyed the world? If you trust them you are a fool of special proportions," Purdue bit back. He felt his skin relax under the soft warmth of the changing room temperature.

Klaus scoffed, smiling bitterly as he stood in front of Purdue.

"I suppose the moniker of fool depends on the object of the game, don't you think? To you, I am a fool to pursue power by any means necessary. To me you are the fool for throwing it away," he said.

"Look, what do you want?" Purdue seethed.

He walked to the window and pulled the curtain aside. Behind the curtain, set flush into the wooden frame, was a keypad. Before he used it, Klaus looked back at Purdue.

"You have been brought here to be programmed so that you can serve a purpose again," he revealed. "There is a particular relic we want, David, and you are going to find it for us. And do you want to know the best part?"

Now he smiled as before. Purdue said nothing. He preferred to bide his time and use his observational skills to find a way out as soon as the madman left. For now, he did not want to entertain Klaus anymore, but instead just acted along.

"The best part is that you will *want* to serve us," Klaus chuckled.

"What relic is it?" Purdue asked, pretending to be interested in knowing.

"Oh, something truly special, even more special than the Spear of Destiny!" he disclosed. "Once called the *Eighth Wonder of the World*, my dear David, it was lost during the Second World War by a most baleful force that spread across Eastern Europe like a crimson plague. Due to their interference it is lost to us, and we want it back. We want every surviving part of it reassembled and restored to its former beauty to decorate the main room of this temple in its golden glory."

Purdue choked. What Klaus insinuated was absurd and impossible, but that was typical for the Black Sun.

"Are you seriously hoping to locate the *Amber Room?*" Purdue asked, astonished. "It was destroyed by British air raids and never made it out of Königsberg! It does not exist anymore. Only shards of it are scattered all over the ocean floor and under the foundations of old ruins obliterated in 1944. It is fool's errand!"

"Well, let's see if we can change your mind about that," Klaus smiled.

He turned to enter a code on the keypad. A loud hum followed, but Purdue could see nothing out of the ordinary until the exquisite paintings of the ceiling and walls faded into their canvas. Purdue realized that it had all been an optical illusion.

LED screens made up the surfaces inside the frames, capable of changing the scenes like windows to a cyber-universe. Even the windows were just depictions on flat screens. Suddenly, the monitors all displayed the dreaded symbol of the Black Sun before switching to one giant image that spread across all the screens. Nothing was left of the initial room. Purdue was no longer in a lavish castle drawing room. He stood inside a cavern of fire, and although he knew it was merely a projection, he could not deny the discomfort of the rising temperature.

CHAPTER 7

The television's blue light gave the room an even more somber atmosphere. Against the walls of the room, the movement on the news cast a plethora of shapes and shadows in black and blue, flashing like lightning and only momentarily illuminating the ornaments on the tables. Nothing was where it belonged. Where glass shelves on the sideboard used to hold glasses and plates, there was only a gaping frame with nothing inside. On the floor in front of it as well as on top of the drawer compartment lay scattered the large jagged pieces of the smashed crockery.

Smears of blood colored some of the flinders and floor tiles, taking on a black hue in the light of the television. The people on the screen seemed to speak to no-one in particular. There was no audience for them in the room, although someone was present. On the sofa, the slumbering mountain of a man filled all three seats as well as the arm rests. His blankets had fallen to the ground, leaving him exposed to the chill of the night, but he did not care.

Since his wife had been killed, Detlef wasn't feeling

anything. Not only had his emotions abandoned him, but his senses had become numb, too. Save for sorrow and mourning Detlef did not want to feel. His skin was cold, so cold that it burned, but the widower felt only numbness when his blankets had slipped off and piled on the carpet.

Her shoes were still lying on the side of the bed where she had tossed them the day before. Detlef could not bear to take them away because then she would really be gone. Gabi's fingerprints were still on the leather of the strap, the dirt from her soles still there and when he touched the shoes he could feel her. If he put them in the closet, the traces of his last moments with Gabi would be forever lost.

The skin had come off his broken knuckles, and scurf was covering the raw flesh now. Detlef did not feel that either. He only felt the cold that killed the pain in the aftermath of his rampage and of the lacerations left behind by jagged edges. Sure he knew that he would feel the burning gashes the next day, but for now, he only wanted to sleep. When he slept, he would see her in his dreams. He would not have to face reality. In sleep, he could hide from the reality of his wife's death.

'This is Holly Darryl at the scene of the heinous incident that took place this morning at the British Embassy in Berlin,' the American reporter on the television babbled. 'It was here where Ben Carrington of the British Embassy witnessed the horrific suicide of Gabi Holtzer, ministerial spokesperson of the German Federal Chancellery. You might remember Mrs. Holtzer as the representative who addressed the press with regards to the recent killings of politicians and financiers in Berlin, now dubbed by the media as the 'Midas Offensive'. Sources report that there is still no clarity on Mrs. Holtzer's motive for taking her own life after assisting in the investigation into those murders. It remains to be seen if she was possibly targeted by the same assassins or if perhaps she was even affiliated with them."

Detlef growled in his half-sleep at the audacity of the

media to even insinuate that his wife would have anything to do with the killings. He could not decide which of the two lies vexed him more – the alleged suicide or the absurd misrepresentation of her involvement. Disturbed by the unfair speculation of the know-it-all journalists, Detlef felt a welling hate for those who besmirched his wife in the eyes of the world.

Detlef Holtzer was not a coward, but he was a serious loner. Maybe it was his upbringing or perhaps just his personality, but he had always been suffering around people. Diffidence had always been his cross, even in his childhood. He could not imagine that he was important enough to have an opinion and even while he was a man in his mid-thirties married to a stunner known to all of Germany, Detlef still tended to withdraw.

Had he not had extensive combat training in the military, he would never have met Gabi. During the 2009 elections, there was widespread violence due to rumors of corruption that had sparked protests and boycotts against candidates' appearances at certain venues throughout Germany. Gabi, among others, had played it safe by hiring personal security. When she had first met her bodyguard, she had instantly fallen in love with him. How could she not love a soft-hearted, gentle giant of a man such as Detlef?

He never understood what she saw in him, but that was all part of his low self-esteem, so Gabi had learned to take his modesty lightly. She never forced him to appear in public with her after his contract as her bodyguard had ended. His wife respected his inadvertent reservation, even in the bedroom. They were quite opposite in matters of inhibition, but they had found a comfortable middle ground.

Now she was gone, and he was all alone. His *longing* for her crippled his heart, and he wept incessantly in the sanctuary of the couch. Ambivalence prevailed in his thoughts.

He was going to do whatever was necessary to find out who killed his wife, but first, he had to get over his self-imposed obstacles. That was the hardest part, but Gabi deserved justice, and he simply had to find a way to grow more confident.

CHAPTER 8

Sam and Nina had no idea how to respond to the doctor's question. With all the things they had witnessed during their adventures together, they had to concede that inexplicable phenomena existed. Although most of what they had experienced could be chalked up to abstruse physics and undiscovered scientific principles, they were open to other explanations as well.

"Why do you ask?" Sam asked.

"I need to be sure that neither you nor the lady here will not see me as some superstitious idiot at what I am about to tell you," the young physician admitted. His eyes darted back and forth between them. He was deadly serious, but he was uncertain about trusting the strangers enough to explain such an apparently far-fetched theory to them.

"We are very open-minded when it comes to such things, doctor," Nina assured him. "You can tell us. Honestly, we have seen some weird stuff ourselves. There is very little than can still surprise Sam and me."

"Ditto," Sam added with a juvenile chuckle.

The doctor took a moment to figure out how to convey

his theory to Sam. His face betrayed his unease. Clearing his throat, he shared what he thought Sam had to know.

"The people in the village you visited had a very strange encounter a few hundred years ago. It is an account that had been passed on verbally through the ages, so I am not sure how much of the original story is left in today's legend," he conveyed. "They tell of a gem stone that was picked up by a young boy and brought to the village to give the chief. But because the stone looked so unusual the elders thought it to be the eye of a god, so they covered it in fear of being watched. Long story short, everyone in the village died three days later because they had blinded the god and he poured out his wrath on them."

"And you think my eye problem has something to do with that story?" Sam frowned.

"Look, I know it sounds crazy. Believe me, I know how it sounds, but hear me out," the young man insisted. "What I think is a little bit less medical and leaning more towards the... um... the kind of..."

"Weird side?" Nina asked. Her skepticism seeped through her tone.

"Wait now," Sam said. "Go on. What does it have to do with my sight?"

"I think something happened to you up there, Mr. Cleave; something you cannot remember," the doctor speculated. "I'll tell you why. Because this tribe's forefathers blinded a god, only a man harboring a god would go blind in their village."

Overwhelming silence enveloped the three, while Sam and Nina stared at the doctor with the most unintelligible looks he had ever seen. He had no idea how to clarify what he was trying to say, specifically because it was so utterly ludicrous and quixotic.

"In other words," Nina slowly started to make sure she got it right, "you mean to tell us that you believe the old wives tale, right? So, this has nothing to do with a solution. You just wanted to let us know that you buy into this crazy shit."

"Nina," Sam frowned, not too pleased that she was so snappy.

"Sam, the guy is practically telling you that you have a god inside you. Now, I am all for ego and can even handle a bit of narcissism here and there, but for Christ's sake, you cannot possibly believe this bullshit!" she admonished him. "My God, that is like saying if you have an earache in the Amazon Basin you are part unicorn."

The foreign woman's ridiculing was too much and too rude, forcing the young doctor to reveal his course of diagnosis. Facing Sam, he turned his back on Nina to ignore her in return for her disregard of his intelligence. "Look, I know how this sounds. But you, Mr. Cleave, have conducted an alarming amount of concentrated heat through your organon visus in a short amount of time and although it should have made your head explode, it left you with only mild damage to your lens and retina!"

He glanced at Nina. "*That* was the basis of my diagnostic conclusion. Do with it what you will, but that is just a little too weird to dismiss as anything but supernatural."

Sam was dumbstruck.

"So that is the reason of my crazy vision," Sam said to himself.

"The excessive heat caused minor cataracts, but those can be removed by any ophthalmologist once you return home," the doctor said.

Remarkably, Nina was the one who prompted him to elaborate on the other side of his diagnosis. With more respect and curiosity in her tone of voice, Nina asked the doctor about Sam's vision problem from an esoteric perspective. At first reluctant to entertain her query, he agreed to give Nina his take on the peculiarity of what had happened.

"All I can say is that Mr. Cleave's eyes suffered a temperature similar to that of lightning and came off with minimal damage. That alone is unnerving. But when you know the villagers' stories, such as I do, you remember things, especially things like an angry blind god that killed the entire village with sky fire," the doctor recounted.

"Lightning," Nina said. "So that's why they insisted that Sam was dead while his eyes were rolled back into his skull. Doctor, he was having a seizure when I found him."

"Are you sure it was not just a byproduct of the electrical current?" the doctor asked.

Nina shrugged, "Could be."

"I remember none of that. When I woke up, I only remember being hot, half blind and extremely confused," Sam admitted with a very perplexed frown on his forehead. "I know even less now than I did before you told me all this stuff, doc."

"None of this was supposed to be a solution to your problem, Mr. Cleave. But this was nothing short of a miracle, so I at least owed you a bit more insight as to what might be happening to you," the young man told them. "Look, I don't know what caused this ancient…" he looked at the skeptical lady with Sam, not wanting to provoke her derision again. "I don't know what mysterious anomaly caused you to cross the rivers of the gods, Mr. Cleave, but if I were you, I would keep it a secret while seeking the help of a witchdoctor or a shaman."

Sam laughed. Nina did not find it at all funny, but she held her tongue about the more unsettling things she had seen Sam do when she had found him.

"So, I am possessed by an ancient god? Oh, sweet Jesus!" Sam guffawed.

The doctor and Nina exchanged looks, having a silent accord between them.

"You have to remember, Sam, that in ancient time, forces of nature that can be explained by science today were referred to as gods. I think that is what the doctor is trying to make clear here. Call it what you will, but there is no doubt that something extremely bizarre is happening to you. First the visions, and now this," Nina clarified.

"I know, love," Sam appeased her, with a chuckle. "I know. It just sounds so fucking crazy. Almost as crazy as time travel or man-made wormholes, you know?" Now he looked bitter and broken through his smile.

The doctor gave Nina a frown at Sam's mentions of time travel, but she only shook her head dismissively and waved it off. As much as the physician believed in the weird and wonderful, she could hardly explain to him that his male patient had suffered a nightmarish few months as involuntary captain of a teleporting Nazi ship that defied all laws of physics just a while back. Some things were just not meant to be shared.

"Well, doctor, thank you so much for the medical – and mystic – help," Nina smiled. "Ultimately you have been of far greater help than you will ever know."

"Thanks, Miss Gould," the young doctor smiled, "for finally believing me. You are both welcome. Please take care, okay?"

"Aye, we are tougher than a hooker's…"

"Sam!" Nina interrupted him. "I think you need some rest." She raised an eyebrow at the amusement of both men who were laughing it off as they said their goodbyes and left the doctor's office.

LATE IN THE EVENING, after well-deserved showers and

tending to their respective injuries, the two Scots went to bed. In the dark, they listened to the rush of the nearby ocean, when Sam pulled Nina closer.

"Sam! No!" she protested.

"What did I do?" he asked.

"My arm! I cannot lie on my side, remember? It is burning like hell and it feel as if the bone is rattling around in the socket," she complained.

He was quiet for a bit as she recovered her spot on the bed with effort.

"You can still lie on your back, right?" he flirted playfully.

"Aye," Nina replied, "but my arm is bound over my tits, so, sorry Jack."

"*Only* your boobs, right? The rest is fair game?" he teased.

Nina scoffed, but what Sam did not know was that she was smiling in the dark. After a brief pause, his tone was far more serious but relaxed.

"Nina, what was I doing when you found me?" he asked.

"I told you," she shielded.

"No, you gave me the synopsis," he refuted her answer. "I saw how you held back at the hospital when you told the doctor in what state you found me. Come on, I might be daft and silly sometimes, but I am still the world's best investigative journalist. I have gotten through insurgent deadlocks in Kazakhstan and followed a lead to a terrorist organization hideout in the heated wars of Bogota, baby. I know body language, and I know when sources are holding out on me."

She sighed. "How would knowing the details profit you at all? We still don't know what is going on with you. Hell, we don't even know what happened to you the day you disappeared on board the *DKM Geheimnis*. I am really not sure how much more far-fetched shit you can handle, Sam."

"I understand that. I do, but this concerns me, so I have to know. No, I am *entitled* to know," he argued. "You have to tell me so that I have the whole picture, love. Then I can put two and two together, see? Only then will I know what to do. If there is one thing I have learned as a journalist, it is that half of the information…no, even 99% of the information is sometimes not sufficient to implicate a culprit. Every detail is necessary; every fact has to be assessed before drawing a conclusion."

"Okay, okay, already," she interrupted him. "I get it. I just don't want you to deal with too much so soon after you came back, understand? You have been through so much and miraculously braved all of it against all odds, honey. All I am trying to do is to spare you some of the bad shit until you are better equipped to deal with it."

Sam laid his head on Nina's shapely stomach, starting her into a fit of giggles. He could not lay his head on her chest because of the sling, so he wrapped his arm around her hip and slipped his hand under the small of her back. She smelled like roses and felt like satin. He felt Nina's free hand rest on his thick dark hair as she held him there and she began to speak.

For over twenty minutes Sam listened to Nina recount the whole incident, not sparing any details. When she told him about the native man and the strange voice Sam had spoken words in an obscure language in, she could feel his fingertips twitching on her skin. Apart from that, Sam handled the tale of his frightening condition pretty well, but neither of them slept until the sun came up.

CHAPTER 9

The incessant hammering on the front door had driven Detlef Holtzer to the point of despair and rage. It had been three days since his wife had been killed, but contrary to what he had been hoping, his feelings had only gotten worse. Every time yet another reporter knocked at his door he would cringe. The shadows of his childhood came creeping from his memories; those dark times of abandonment that had caused his aversion to the sound of someone knocking at the door.

"Leave me alone!" he shouted, regardless of the caller.

"Mr. Holtzer, it is Hein Mueller from the funeral home. Your wife's insurance company contacted me to sort some matters out with you before they can go ahead..."

"Are you deaf? I said get lost!" the forlorn widower spat. His voice was unsteady from the alcohol. He was on the verge of a full-fledged breakdown. "I want an autopsy! She was killed! She was killed, I tell you! I will not bury her until they have investigated that!"

No matter who showed up at his door, Detlef refused them access. Inside the house, the reclusive man ineffably crumbled to next to nothing. He had stopped eating and barely moved away from the sofa where Gabi's shoes kept him anchored to her presence.

"I will find him, Gabi. Don't you worry, sweetheart. I will find him and throw his carcass off a cliff," he growled softly as he rocked with eye frozen in place. Detlef could not deal with the sorrow anymore. He got up and walked through the house, heading for the blacked-out windows. With his index finger, he picked away at a corner of the refuse bags he had taped over the glass. Outside, two cars were parked in front of his home, but they were vacant.

"Where are you?" he sang softly. Sweat meandered over his forehead and ran into his burning eyes, red from lack of sleep. His massive body had shrunk by several pounds since he had stopped eating, but he was still a tank of a man. Barefoot in his pants and a creased long sleeve shirt that hung loosely over his belt, he stood waiting for someone to appear by the cars. "I know you are here. I know you are at my door, little mice," he winced as he sang the words. "Mousy, mousy! Are you trying to get into my house?"

He waited, but nobody knocked at his door, which was a great relief even though he still did not trust the peace. He dreaded that knocking that sounded like a battering ram to his ears. During his teenage years, his father, an alcoholic gambler, would leave him home alone when he fled loan sharks and bookies. The young Detlef would hide inside, curtains drawn, while the wolves were at the door. Hammering on the door was synonymous with a full-blown attack on the young boy and his heart would slam inside him, terrified for what would happen if they got in.

On top of the knocking, the angry men would shout threats and swear at him.

'I know you're in there, you little fuck! Open the door or I'll burn your house down!' they would scream. Some threw bricks

through the windows, while the teenager sat cowering in his bedroom corner, covering his ears. When his father came home conveniently late, he would find his son in tears, but he only laughed and called the boy a pussy.

To this day Detlef would feel his heart jump when someone knocked at his door, even though he knew the callers were harmless and had no bad intentions. But now? Now they were once again knocking *for him.* They wanted *him.* They were like the angry men outside back in his teenage years, insisting he came out. Detlef felt hunted. He felt threatened. It did not matter why they came. The fact was that they tried to force him out of his sanctuary, and that was an act of war to the sensitive emotions of the widower.

For no apparent reason, he went to the kitchen and took the paring knife from the drawer. He was perfectly aware of what he was doing but relinquished control. Tears filled his eyes as he sank the blade into his skin, not too deep, but deep enough. He had no idea what drove him to do it, but he knew he had to. By some order of a dark voice inside his head, Detlef ran the blade a few inches from one side of his forearm to the other. It burned like a gigantic paper cut, but it was bearable. When he lifted the knife, he watched the blood ooze quietly from the line he had drawn. As its little red line became a trickle on his white skin, he took a deep breath.

For the very first time since Gabi died, Detlef felt at peace. His heart slowed to a mellow rhythm, and his worries drifted out of reach – for now. The tranquility of the release fascinated him, making him grateful for the knife. For a while, he looked at what he had done, but despite his moral compass' protests, he did not feel guilty for doing it. As a matter of fact, he felt accomplished.

"I love you, Gabi," he whispered. "I love you. This is a blood oath for you, my baby."

He wrapped a dish cloth around his arm and washed the knife, but instead of replacing it he tucked it into his pocket.

"You just stay right there," he whispered to the knife. "Be there when I need you. You are safe. You make me feel safe." A twisted smile played on Detlef's face as he reveled in the serenity he felt all of a sudden. It was as if the act of cutting himself had cleared his mind, so much that he felt positive enough to put some work into finding his wife's killer with some proactive investigation.

Detlef walked over the broken glass of the sideboard without caring to bother. The pain was just another layer of agony piled on to that which he already was already suffering, making it somehow trivial.

As he *had just known* to cut himself to feel better, he *also knew* that he had to find his late wife's appointment book. Gabi was old-fashioned that way. She believed in physical notes and calendars. Even though she had used her phone to remind her of her appointments, she had also put everything down in writing, a most welcome habit now that it could serve to point out her possible killers.

Rummaging through her drawers, he knew exactly what he was looking for.

"Oh God, I hope it was not in your purse, baby," he muttered through his frantic searching. "Because they have your purse, and they will not give it back to me until I go out this door to talk to them, you see?" He kept talking to Gabi as if she was listening, the privilege of the lonely to keep them from losing their mind, something he had learned by watching his abused mother when she endured the hell she had married into.

"Gabi, I need your help, baby," Detlef moaned. He sank down on a chair in the small room that Gabi had used as her office. Looking at the books piled everywhere and her old cigarette box on the second shelf of the wooden cabinet she used for her files. Detlef took a deep breath and composed himself. "Where would you have put a business diary?" he asked in a low voice as his mind flipped through all the possibilities.

"It has to be someplace where you could easily access it," he frowned, deeply in thought. He stood up and imagined it was his office. "Where would be convenient?" He sat behind her desk, facing her computer monitor. On her desk, she had a calendar, but it was blank. "I suppose you would not write it here because it is not for the world to see," he remarked, going over the objects on the surface of the desk.

A porcelain cup with her old rowing team's logo held her pens and a letter opener. A flatter bowl contained several flash drives and trinkets like hair elastics, a marble and two rings she had never worn because they were too big. To the left, an open packet of throat lozenges sided with the foot of her desk lamp. No diary.

Detlef felt the misery take him again, distraught at not finding the black leather-bound book. Gabi's piano stood in the far right corner of the room, but the books there had only sheet music in them. Outside he heard the rain fall, befitting his mood.

"Gabi, any help?" he sighed. The phone on Gabi's file cabinet rang and startled him half to death. He knew better than to pick it up. It was them. It was the hunters, the accusers. It was the very people who saw his wife as some suicidal weakling. "No!" he screamed, shivering in rage. Detlef grabbed an iron bookend from the shelf and hurled it at the phone. The heavy bookend mowed the phone off the cabinet with immense force, leaving it smashed on the floor. His reddened watery eyes leered at the broken device and then moved to the cabinet he had damaged with the heavy bookend.

Detlef smiled.

On top of the cabinet, he found Gabi's black diary. It had been lying under the telephone all along, obscured from view. He went to pick up the book, laughing manically. "Baby, you are the best! Was that you? Huh?" he mumbled affectionately as he opened the book. "Did you call me just now? Did you want me to see the book? I know you did."

He flicked through it impatiently, looking for the appointments she had written down on the date two days ago when she died.

"Who did you see? Who saw you last besides that British fool? Let's see."

With dried blood under his nail, he ran his index finger from the top downward, carefully perusing every entry.

"I just need to see who you were with before you…" he swallowed hard. "They say you died in the morning."

8.00 – Meeting with intelligence people

9.30 – Margot flowers bh plotC

10.00 – David Purdue Ben Carrington office abt flight divert Milla

11.00 – Consulate remember Kiril

12.00 – Call for Detlef's dentist appointment

Detlef's hand reached up to his mouth. "The toothache is gone, you know, Gabi?" His tears obscured the words he tried to read and he slammed the book shut, held it tightly against his chest, and collapsed in a heap of woe, sobbing his heart out. Through the blacked-out windows, he could see the flashes of lightning. Gabi's small office was almost completely dark now. He just sat there, weeping until his eyes dried up. The sadness was overwhelming, but he had to pull himself together.

'Carrington office,' he thought. *'The last place she visited was Carrington's office. He told the media he was there when she died.'* Something prodded at him. There was more to that notation. Quickly he reopened the book and slammed on the desk

lamp switch to see properly. Detlef gasped, "Who is Milla?" he wondered out loud. "And who is David Purdue?"

His fingers could not move fast enough as he paged back to her contacts list, roughly scribbled on the hard inner cover of her book. There was nothing for a 'Milla', but at the bottom of the page, there was the web address of one of Purdue's businesses. Detlef immediately went online to see who this Purdue was. After reading through the 'About' section, Detlef clicked on the 'Contact' tab and smiled.

"Gotcha!"

CHAPTER 10

*P*urdue closed his eyes. Resisting the urge to watch what the screens displayed, he kept his eyes shut and ignored the sounds of screams that shrieked out of the four loud speakers in the corners. What he could not ignore was the elevated temperature, gradually escalating. His body was sweating from the onslaught of the heat, but he tried his best to follow his mother's rule of not panicking. She had always said that Zen was the answer.

'Once you panic you are theirs. Once you panic your mind will believe it and all emergency reactions will take hold. Keep calm or else you are done for,' he told himself over and over as he stood still. In other words, Purdue employed upon himself a good old mindfuck that he hoped his brain would buy. Even moving, he feared, would increase his body temperature even more and he did not need that.

The surround sound was tricking his mind into believing that it was all real. Only by keeping himself from looking at the screens could Purdue prevent his brain from consolidating the perceptions and turning them into reality. During his study of basic NLP in the summer of 2007, he had learned small tricks of the mind to influence comprehension and reasoning. He never thought his life would depend on it.

For hours, the deafening sound blared from all sides. Screams of abused children would be replaced by a choir of gunfire before turning into a constant rhythmic clank of steel on steel. The noise of hammer on anvil would slowly morph into the cadence of sexual moans before it was drowned out by the yelps of seal pups being beaten to death. The recordings were played in an endless loop for so long, that Purdue could predict which sound would follow the current.

To his dismay, the billionaire soon realized that the horrible noises no longer sickened him. Instead, he became aware that certain segments aroused him, while others provoked his odium. In his refusal to sit down his feet had begun to ache, and his lower back was killing him, but the floor had started to heat up too. Remembering a table that would provide refuge, Purdue opened his eyes to find it, but while he had had his eyes shut, they had removed it, leaving him nowhere to go.

"Are you trying to kill me already?" he screamed, jumping from one foot to the other to give his feet reprieve from the burning hot surface of the floor. "What do you want from me?"

But no-one answered him. After six hours, Purdue was exhausted. The floor had not grown any hotter, but it was enough to burn his feet if he dared put them down for longer than a second at a time. What was worse than the heat and having to keep moving was the fact that the audio clip kept playing nonstop. Every now and then he couldn't but open his eyes to see what had changed in the time that had elapsed. After the table had disappeared, nothing else had changed. To him, that fact was more unnerving than the other way round.

Purdue's feet started to bleed when the blisters on his soles burst open, but he could not afford to stop for even a moment.

"Oh, Jesus! Please make it stop! Please! I'll do what you want!" he screamed. Trying not to lose it was no longer an option. Otherwise, they would never buy that he was suffering enough to believe their mission successful. "Klaus! Klaus, for God's sake, please tell them to stop!"

But Klaus did not answer, nor did he stop the torment. The detestable audio-clip was repeated in an endless loop until Purdue screamed over it. Even just the sound of his own words presented some relief over the repetitive noises. It was not long before his voice failed him.

"Well done you idiot!" he uttered in nothing more than a hoarse whisper. "Now you cannot call for help, and you don't even have a voice to surrender with." His legs buckled under his weight, but he was afraid to fall to the floor. Soon he would not be able to take one more step. Crying like a child, Purdue begged. "Mercy. Please."

Suddenly the screens died, leaving Purdue in pitch darkness again. The audio stopped instantly, leaving his ears ringing in the sudden silence. The floor was still hot, but within a few seconds, it cooled down, allowing him to finally sit down. His feet throbbed in excruciating pain and every muscle in his body twitched and cramped.

"Oh thank God," he whispered, grateful that the torture had come to an end. He wiped his tears with the back of his hand and did not even mind the burn of his sweat in his eyes. The silence was sublime. He was finally able to hear his heartbeat, which was racing from the exertion. Purdue took a deep breath of relief, relishing in the blessing of oblivion.

But Klaus did not have oblivion in mind for Purdue.

Exactly five minutes later the screens came back on, and the first shriek blasted through the speakers. Purdue felt his soul shatter. In disbelief he shook his head, feeling the floor heating up once again and his eyes welled up in despair.

"Why?" he grunted, punishing his throat with his attempts at screaming. "What kind of bastard are you? Why don't you show your face, you son of a whore!" His words - even if they were audible - would have fallen on deaf ears because Klaus was not there. In fact, nobody was there. The torture machine was set on a timer to switch off just long enough to get Purdue's hopes up, a lovely Nazi-era technique to increase the psychological torture.

Never trust hope. It is as fleeting as it is cruel.

When Purdue woke up, he was once more in the lavish castle room with its oil paintings and stained glass windows. For a moment he thought it had all been a nightmare, but then he felt the agonizing sting of burst blisters. He could not see well since they had taken his glasses along with his clothing, but his vision was good enough to examine the details of the ceiling – not the paintings, but the framework.

His eyes were dry from the desperate tears he had shed, but it was nothing compared to the splitting headache he was suffering from the acoustic overload. Trying to move his limbs, he discovered that his muscles held taken the strain better than he had anticipated. Finally, Purdue looked down at his feet, fearing what he would see. As expected his toes and sides of his feet were covered in burst blisters and crusty blood.

"Don't worry about those, Herr Purdue. I promise you will not be forced to stand on them for at least another day," a snide voice swam through the air from the direction of the door. "You slept like dead, but it is time to wake up. Three hours is enough sleep."

"Klaus," Purdue sneered.

The slight-built man strode leisurely toward the table where Purdue was lying with two cups of coffee in his hands.

Tempted to chuck it into the German's mousy mug, Purdue elected to resist the urge on to quench his terrible thirst. He sat up and grabbed the cup from his tormentor, only to find that it was empty. Furious, Purdue hurled the cup to the floor where it smashed into smithereens.

"You really have to mind that temper of yours, Herr Purdue," Klaus advised in his cheerful voice, sounding more amused than surprised.

'This is what they want, Dave. They want you to act like an animal,' Purdue thought to himself. *'Don't let them win.'*

"What do you expect me to do, Klaus?" Purdue sighed, appealing to the German's personable side. "What would you have done in my position? Tell me. I guarantee you would have done the same."

"Ouch! What happened to your voice? Would you like some water?" Klaus asked cordially.

"So that you can deny me again?" Purdue asked.

"Maybe. But maybe not. Why don't you give it a try?" he replied.

'Mind games.' Purdue knew the game all too well. Instill confusion, and leave your opponent in the dark whether to expect punishment or reward.

"May I have some water, please," Purdue tried. After all, he had nothing to lose.

"Wasser!" Klaus shouted. He gave Purdue a warm smile that bore the authenticity of a lipless corpse as a woman brought in a sturdy container with pure, clean water. Had Purdue been able to stand on his feet, he would have run to meet her halfway, but he had to wait for her. Klaus set the empty mug in his hand down next to Purdue and poured some water.

"Good thing you bought two cups" Purdue grated out.

"I brought two mugs for two reasons. I assumed you were going to smash one of them. So I knew you would need the second one to drink the water you'd be begging for from," he explained while Purdue grabbed the bottle to get to the water.

Ignoring the cup at first, he stuck opening of the bottle between his lips so violently that the heavy container hit his teeth. But Klaus took it away and offered Purdue the cup. Only when he had finished two cups did Purdue catch his breath.

"One more? Please," he begged Klaus.

"One more, but then we talk," he told his captive, and filled his cup again.

"Klaus," Purdue gasped after finishing it to the last drop. "Could you please just tell me what you want from me? Why did you bring me here?"

Klaus sighed and rolled his eyes. "We have been through this. You are not supposed to ask questions." He gave the bottle back to the woman, and she left the room.

"How can I not? At least let me know what I am being tortured for," Purdue implored.

"You are not being tortured," Klaus insisted. "You are being reconditioned. When you got first got in touch with the Order, it was to entice us with your *Holy Lance* that you and your friends had found, remember? You invited all of the high-level Black Sun members a secret meeting on Deep Sea One to show off your relic, yes?"

Purdue nodded. It was true. He had been using the relic as leverage to get into the Order's good graces for possible business.

"When you played with us that time, our members got into a very dangerous situation. But I am sure you meant well, even after you departed with the relic like a coward to leave them to their fate when the water came rushing in," Klaus lectured with flamboyance. "We want you to be that man again; to work with us to obtain what we need so that

74

we can all thrive. With your genius and wealth, you would be the perfect candidate, so we are going to… *change your mind.*"

"If you want the *Spear of Destiny* I'll be more than happy to give it to you in exchange for my freedom," Purdue bartered, and he meant every word.

"Gott im Himmel! David, have you not been listening?" Klaus exclaimed with juvenile disappointment. "We can have anything we want! We want you to come back to us, but you offer a trade and want to negotiate. This is not a business deal. It is an orientation and only once we are convinced that you are ready, you will be allowed to leave this room."

Klaus looked at his watch. He got up to leave, but Purdue tried to hold him up with a triviality.

"Um, can I have more water, please?" he croaked.

Without stopping or looking back, Klaus hollered, "Wasser!"

As he closed the door behind him, an enormous cylinder with a radius almost the size of the room lowered from the ceiling.

"Oh God, what now?" Purdue cried out in utter panic as it locked into the floor. The center panel of the ceiling slid open and started releasing a stream of water into the cylinder, drenching Purdue's sore, nude body and muffling his cries.

What terrified him more than the fear of drowning, was the knowledge that they did not intend to kill.

ina had finished packing while Sam had been taking one last shower. They were due at the airstrip in an hour, bound for Edinburgh.

"You done yet, Sam?" Nina asked loudly outside the bathroom.

"Aye, just giving me ass one more foaming. Be right out!" he answered.

Nina laughed and shook her head. Her phone rang in her purse. Without looking at the screen, she answered.

"Hello."

"Hello, uh, Dr. Gould?" the man on the phone asked.

"This is she. Who am I speaking with?" she frowned. She was being addressed by her title, which meant that it was business or some insurance salesman.

"My name is Detlef," the man with the heavy German accent introduced himself. "Your number was given to me by one of Mr. David Purdue's assistants. I am actually trying to get hold of him."

"So why did she not give you *his* number?" Nina inquired impatiently.

"Because she has no idea where he is, Dr. Gould," he replied in a gentle, almost timid manner. "She told me you might know?"

Nina was stumped. That made no sense. Purdue was never off the radar to his assistant. His other employees, perhaps, but never his assistant. It was pivotal, especially with his impulsive and adventurous nature, that one of his people always knew where he was going, in case something went wrong.

"Listen, Det-Detlef? Right?" Nina asked.

"Yes, ma'am," he said.

"Give me a few minutes to locate him and I'll call you right back, alright? Give me your number, please."

Nina did not trust the caller. Purdue would not just vanish like that, so she reckoned it was a shady businessman trying to get Purdue's personal number by bullshitting her. He gave her his number and she hung up. When she called Purdue's mansion, his assistant answered.

"Oh, hi Nina," the woman greeted her when she heard the familiar voice of the pretty historian Purdue always kept company with.

"Listen, did a stranger just call you to speak to Dave?" Nina asked. The answer caught her completely by surprise.

"Aye, he called a few minutes ago, asking for Mr. Purdue. But truth be told, I have not heard from him today. Maybe he was gone for the weekend?" she speculated.

"He did not check in with you about going somewhere?" Nina pushed. It worried her.

"The last I had him in Las Vegas for some time off, but he was going to travel to Copenhagen on Wednesday. There was a posh hotel he wanted to visit, but that's all I know," she reported. "Should we be worried?"

Nina sighed hard. "I don't want to start a panic, but just to be sure, you know?"

"Aye."

"Was he traveling with his own jet?" Nina wanted to know. It would give her a place to start looking. On affirmation from the assistant, Nina thanked her and ended the call to try Purdue's cell phone. Nothing. She rushed to the bathroom door and stormed in, catching Sam just wrapping his towel around his waist.

"Hey! If you wanted to play, you should have said so before I got all cleaned up," he grinned.

Ignoring his jest, Nina rambled, "I think Purdue might be in trouble. I'm not sure if it is *Hangover 2* kind of trouble or real trouble, but something is off."

"How so?" Sam asked, following her into the room to get dressed. She filled him in on the mysterious caller and the fact that Purdue's assistant have not heard from him.

"I suppose you have tried his cell?" Sam suggested.

"He never switches off his phone. You know he has that funny voicemail taking messages with the physics jokes or he answers, but it is never just dead, right?" she said. "There was nothing when I called him."

"That is very strange," he agreed. "But let's just get back home first and then we can snoop around. This hotel he went to in Norway…"

"Denmark," she corrected him.

"Whatever. Maybe he is just really enjoying himself. It is the man's first 'normal people' kind of holiday in - well, forever- you know, the kind where he does not have people trying to kill him and such," he shrugged.

"Something doesn't seem right. I am just going to call his pilot and get to the bottom of this," she announced.

"Fine. But we can't be late for our own flight, so get your stuff and let's go," he said, tapping her on the shoulder.

Nina had forgotten about the man who had pointed her to Purdue's disappearance in the first place over trying to think where her former lover could be. Boarding the plane, they both switched off their phones.

When Detlef tried to contact Nina again, he was met with another dead end, leaving him infuriated, immediately thinking that he was being played. If Purdue's female associate wanted to protect him by eluding the widower of the woman Purdue killed, Detlef figured, he would have to resort to what he had been trying to avoid.

From somewhere in Gabi's little office, he heard a hissing sound. At first, Detlef ignored it as an outside noise, but soon after it turned into static crackling. The widower listened to locate the origin of the sound. It sounded like someone hopping through channels on a radio and occasionally a scratchy voice would come through in unintelligible muttering, but no music. Detlef moved quietly toward the spot where the white noise was growing louder.

Finally, he looked down to the air vent just above the floor of the room. It was half concealed by the drapes, but there was no doubt that this was where the sound was coming from. Feeling the need to uncover the mystery, Detlef went to get his toolbox.

CHAPTER 12

On the flight back to Edinburgh Sam had a hard time keeping Nina calm. She was worried about Purdue, especially since she couldn't use her phone during the long flight. Unable to call his crew to confirm his whereabouts, she was extremely restless for most of the flight.

"There is nothing we can do right now, Nina," Sam said. "Just take a nap or something until we land. Time flies when you're sleeping," he winked.

She gave him one of her looks – one of that kind she tossed him when there were too many witnesses for anything more physical.

"Look, we will call the pilot as soon as we are there. Until then you may as well relax," he suggested. Nina knew he was right, but she just could not help but feel something was amiss.

"You know I will never be able to sleep. When I worry I can't function properly until I have closure," she grunted, folding her arms and leaning back and closing her eyes so she didn't have to deal with Sam. In turn, he rummaged through his carry-on bag, looking for something to do.

"Peanuts! Shh, don't tell the cabin crew," he whispered at Nina, but she ignored his attempts at humor, flashing the small packet of peanuts and shaking it. With her eyes shut, he figured it would be best to leave her be. "Yeah, maybe you should get some rest."

She said nothing. In the dark of the locked-out world, Nina wondered if her ex-lover and friend had just forgotten to contact his assistant, as Sam had suggested. If that were the case, Purdue certainly had a good talking to on the way. She did not like being worried about things that might turn out to be nothing, particularly with her tendency to overanalyze things. Occasionally, the turbulence of the flight would shake her from her light sleep. Nina did not realize how long she had been dozing on and off. It felt like minutes, but it stretched for over an hour.

Sam slammed his hand down on hers where her fingers rested on the edge of her arm rest. Instantly annoyed, Nina's eyes shot open to sneer at her companion, but he was not being silly this time. There was also no turbulence that might have startled him. But then Nina was shocked to see Sam stiffening all over, similar to the seizure she had witnessed back in the village a few days ago.

"Jesus! Sam!" she said under her breath, trying not to draw attention yet. She grabbed his wrist with her other hand, trying to pry it loose, but he was too strong. "Sam!" she ground out. "Sam, wake up!" She tried to keep her voice low, but his convulsions started to draw attention.

"What is wrong with him?" a plump lady on the other side of the isle asked.

"Please, just give us a moment," Nina snapped as amicably as she could. His eyes shot open, once again milky and absent. "Oh God no!" she moaned a little louder this time as despair gripped her, fearing what might happen. Nina remembered what had happened to the man he had touched during his last seizure.

"Excuse me, ma'am," the stewardess interrupted Nina's struggle. "Is anything wrong?" But as she asked, the flight attendant saw Sam's eerie eyes staring up to the ceiling "Oh shit," she muttered in alarm before going to the intercom to ask if there was a doctor among the passengers. Everywhere people turned to see what the commotion was about; some shrieked and others hushed their conversations.

As Nina watched, Sam's mouth opened and closed rhythmically. "Oh, Christ! Don't talk. Please don't talk," she prayed as she watched him. "Sam! You have to wake up!"

Through the clouds of his consciousness, Sam could hear her voice begging from far away. Once again she had been walking next to him toward the well, but this time, the world was red. The sky was maroon, and the ground was dark orange, like brick dust under his feet. He could not see Nina, even though he knew in his vision that she was present.

When Sam reached the well, he did not ask for a cup, yet there was an empty cup on the crumbling wall. He bent forward again to look down the well. Before him, he saw the deep cylindrical interior, but this time, the water was not deep down in the shadows. Below him was a well full of pristine water.

"Please help! He is choking!" Sam heard Nina scream from somewhere far away.

Below, in the well, Sam saw Purdue reaching up.

"Purdue?" Sam frowned. "What are you doing in the well?"

Purdue was gasping for air as his face barely broke the surface. He was coming up towards Sam as the water rose higher and higher, looking terrified. Ashen and desperate, his face contorted as his hands clawed at the sides of the well. Purdue's lips were blue, and he had dark circles under his eyes. Sam could see that his friend was naked in the churning water, but when he reached in to rescue Purdue, the water level dropped considerably.

"He cannot seem to breathe. Is he asthmatic?" another male voice came from the same place as Nina's.

Sam looked around, but he was alone in the red waste-land. In the distance, he could see a broken-down old building reminiscent of a power station. Black shadows lived beyond the four or five stories of empty window openings. No smoke rose from the towers, and the walls had sprung large weeds through cracks and crevices brought by years of neglect. From far away, deep in his being, he could hear an incessant hum ensue. It grew louder ever so slightly until he recognized it as a generator of sorts.

"We need to open his airway! Pull his head back for me!" he heard the male voice again, but Sam tried to make out the other sound, the impending hum that was still growing louder, possessing the entire wasteland until the ground began to shake.

"Purdue!" he shouted, trying one more time to save his friend. When he looked back into the well, it was empty, save for the sigil that was painted on the bottom's wet, muddy floor. He knew it all too well. The black circle with the precise rays that looked like lightning streaks lay in silence at the bottom of the cylinder like a spider in wait. Sam gasped. "The Order of the Black Sun."

"Sam! Sam, can you hear me?" Nina persisted, her voice drawing closer from the dusty air of the deserted place. The industrial hum escalated to a deafening level and then the same pulse he had seen under hypnosis clapped through the atmosphere. This time, nobody else was there who could have been burned to ashes. Sam screamed as the waves of the pulse came toward him, forcing its blistering hot air into his

83

nose and mouth. As it made contact with him, he was spirited away in the nick of time.

"There he is!" the male voice cheered as Sam woke up on the floor of the aisle where they had put him to perform emergency resuscitation. His face was cold and damp under Nina's gentle hand, and a middle-aged Indian man stood over him, smiling.

"Thank you so much, doctor!" Nina smiled up at the Indian man. She looked down at Sam. "Honey, how are you feeling?"

"Like I'm drowning," Sam managed to wheeze as he felt the heat dissipate from his eyeballs. "What happened?"

"Don't worry about that now, okay?" she soothed him, looking very relieved and happy to see him. He propped himself up to sit, annoyed about the gawking audience, but he could not lash out at them for pointing their attention to such a spectacle, could he?

"My God, I feel like I have swallowed a gallon of water in one go," he whined as Nina helped him to his seat.

"That might be my fault, Sam," Nina admitted. "I kind of... threw water in your face again. It seems to work for waking you up."

Wiping his face, Sam stared at her. "Not if it drowns me!"

"It was nowhere near your mouth," she scoffed. "I'm not stupid."

Sam took a deep breath and decided not to argue for now. Nina's big dark eyes stayed on him as if she was trying to figure out what he was thinking. And she was, in fact, wondering just that, but she allowed him a few minutes to recover from his seizure. What the other passengers had heard him mutter had been only the unintelligible gibberish of a man in the throes of a seizure for them, but Nina had understood the words all too well. It unsettled her immensely, yet she had to give Sam a moment before she started prying – *if* he even would remember what he had seen while under.

"Do you remember what you saw?" she asked inadvertently, the victim of her own impatience. Sam looked at her, looking surprised at first. After some thought, he opened his mouth to speak but remained mute until he could articulate. In truth, he recalled every detail of the revelation this time, far better than when Dr. Helberg had hypnotized him. Not wanting to cause Nina any more worry, he toned down his response a bit.

"I saw that well again. And this time the sky and ground was not yellow, but red. Oh, and this time, there were no people crowding me either " he reported in his most nonchalant tone.

"That's it?" she asked, knowing that he was omitting most of it.

"Aye, basically," he answered. After a long pause, he casually told Nina, "I think we should follow your hunch about Purdue."

"Why?" she asked. Nina knew that Sam had seen something because he had said Purdue's name when he had been unconscious, but for now, she was playing dumb.

"I just think you have a valid reason to probe into his whereabouts. The whole thing smells like trouble to me," he said.

"Good. I'm glad you finally understand the urgency. Maybe now you will stop telling me to relax," she delivered her short sermon from the Gospel of I-told-you-so. Nina shifted in her seat just as the announcement sounded through the aircraft intercom that they were about to land. It had been an unpleasant and long flight, and Sam hoped that Purdue was still alive.

Outside the airport building, they decided to get some

early dinner before returning to Sam's apartment on the Southside.

"I need to call Purdue's pilot. Just give me a minute before you get a taxi, alright?" Nina told Sam. He nodded and proceeded to place two of his cigarettes between his lips to light. Sam did a splendid job of hiding his apprehension from Nina. She was walking in circles around him while speaking to the pilot, and he casually handed her one of the fags when she passed in front of him.

While sucking on his cigarette and appearing to stare into the setting sun just above the skyline of Edinburgh, Sam went over the events in his vision in his memory, trying to find clues where Purdue could be held. In the background, he heard Nina's voice ebb and flow in emotion with every morsel of information she received over the phone. Depending on what they would get from Purdue's pilot, Sam intended to start at the very spot Purdue had last been seen.

It felt good to have a smoke again after hours of abstaining. Even the horrible sensation of drowning he had endured earlier was not enough to deter him from inhaling the therapeutic poison. Nina slipped her phone into her bag, her cigarette pursed between her lips. She looked completely flustered as she walked briskly toward him.

"Get us a taxi," she said. "We need to get to the German Consulate before they close."

CHAPTER 13

*M*uscle spasms prevented Purdue from using his arms to stay afloat, threatening to let him sink below the surface of the water. He had been swimming for several hours in the cold water of the cylindrical tank, suffering from severe sleep deprivation and slowing reflexes.

'Another sadistic Nazi torture?' he thought. 'Please God, just let me die quickly. I can't go on much longer.'

Those thoughts were not exaggerated or born from self-pity, but a rather accurate self-assessment. His body had been starved, depleted of all nutrients and forced into survival exertion. Only one thing had changed since the chamber had been illuminated two hours before. The color of the water had turned to a sickening yellow hue that was Purdue's overstrained senses perceived as urine.

"Get me out!" he had been screaming several times through intervals of absolute calm. His voice was hoarse and weak, quivering from the cold that was seeping into his bones. Although the water had stopped pouring in a while back, he was still in danger of drowning if he stopped kicking his legs. Under his blistered feet lay at least 15 feet of water-filled cylinder. He wouldn't be able to stand when his limbs grew too weary. He simply had no choice but to keep going or else he would surely die a terrible death.

Through the water, Purdue noticed a pulse every minute. It caused his body to jerk when it happened, but it did not hurt him, leading him to the conclusion that it was a low-current jolt meant to keep his synapses firing. Even in his delirious state, he found it quite peculiar. If they wanted to electrocute him, they could easily have done it already. Perhaps, he thought, they wanted to torture him with by sending an electrical current through the water but misjudged the voltage.

Warped visions entered his weary mind. His brain was barely capable of keeping his limbs moving now, exhausted from lack of sleep and nourishment.

'Don't stop swimming,' he kept urging his brain, not certain if he was speaking out loud or if the voice he was hearing was coming from inside his mind. When he looked down, he was horrified to see a nest of writhing squid-like creatures in the water below him. Screaming in fear of their appetite he tried to pull himself up the slippery glass of the basin, but without anything to hold on to, there was no escape.

One tentacle reached up to him, causing a wave of hysteria in the billionaire. He could feel the rubbery squidgy appendage curl around his leg before it pulled him down into the depth of the cylindrical tank. Water filled his lungs and his chest burned as he looked up to the surface one last time. Looking down to what was awaiting him was simply too horrifying.

'Of all the deaths I imagined for myself, I would never have thought I'd end like this! How alpha fleece going ashes,' his confused mind was struggling to think straight. Lost and scared to death, Purdue gave up on thinking, on formulating, and even on paddling. His heavy limp body sank to the bottom of the tank while his open eyes saw nothing but the yellow water when the pulse shot through him one more time.

"Now that was close," Klaus remarked amusedly. When Purdue opened his eyes, he was lying on a bed in what must have been an infirmary. Everything, from the walls to the linen was the same color as the hellish water he had just drowned in.

'But if I drowned...,' he tried to fathom the odd occurrences.

"So, do you think you are ready to fulfill your duty to the Order, Herr Purdue?" Klaus asked. He was sitting, dressed painfully neat and tidy in a lustrous tan double-breasted suit, finished off with an amber colored cravat.

'For God's sake, just play along this time! Just play along, David. No shit this time. Give him what he wants. You can be a hard ass later when you are free,' he instructed himself firmly.

"I am. I am ready for any instruction," Purdue slurred. Drooping eyelids hid his investigation of the room he was in as he combed the place with his eyes to ascertain where he was.

"You do not sound particularly convincing," Klaus remarked dryly. Between his thighs, his hands were clamped together as if he was either warming them or had the body language of a high school girl. Purdue detested him and his hideous German accent spoken with the eloquence of a debutante, but he had to do everything possible not to displease that man.

"Give me my orders and you will see just how goddamn serious I am," Purdue mumbled in labored breathing. "You want the Amber Room. I will retrieve it from its last resting place and personally bring it back here."

"You do not even know where *here* is, my friend," Klaus smiled. "But I think you are trying to figure out where we are."

"How else...?" Purdue started, but his psyche quickly reminded him that he was not to ask questions. "I have to know where to bring it."

"You will be told where to bring it once you have retrieved it. It will be your gift to the Black Sun," Klaus explained. "You do realize of course, that naturally, you can never be *Renatus* again, due to your treachery."

"That is understandable," Purdue agreed.

"But there is more to your task, my dear Herr Purdue. You are expected to eliminate your former associates Sam Cleave and this deliciously feisty Dr. Gould before you address the European Union assembly," Klaus commanded.

Purdue kept a straight face and nodded.

"Our representatives within the EU will arrange an emergency gathering of the Council of the European Union in Brussels and invite the international media, during which you will conduct a short announcement on our behalf," Klaus continued.

"I suppose that I will get the information when the time comes," Purdue said, and Klaus nodded. "Right. I will pull the necessary strings to begin the search in Königsberg right away."

"Get Gould and Cleave to join you, would you?" Klaus snarled. "Two birds, as they say."

"Child's play," Purdue smiled, still under the influence of the hallucinogenic drugs he had ingested with the water after his night in the heat. "Give me... two months."

Klaus threw his head back and cackled like an old woman, crowing in delight. He rocked forward and backward before he caught his breath. "My darling, you will do it in two weeks."

"That is impossible!" Purdue exclaimed, careful not to sound antagonistic. "Just organizing such a search takes weeks of planning."

"It does. I know. But we have a schedule – one that is considerably tighter due to all the hold-ups we had thanks to your *unpleasa*nt attitude," the German captor sighed. "And our opposition will no doubt figure out our game plan with every advance we make toward their hidden treasure."

Purdue was curious to know who was behind this opposition, but he did not dare to ask a question. He feared it might provoke his captor to another round of barbaric torture.

≈

"Now let those feet heal first and we will make arrangements for you to go home in six days. No use sending you on an errand as a...?" Klaus chuckled, "What do you English call it? A *cripple?*"

Purdue smiled submissively, genuinely distraught that he had to stay for even another hour, let alone a week. By now he had learned to just go with it, to avoid provoking Klaus to throw him in a pit of octopi again. The German stood up and left the room, crying, "Enjoy your pudding!"

Purdue looked at the delicious thick custard they served him in the confinement of his hospital bed, but it felt similar to eating brick. Several kilograms lighter from days of starving in the torture chamber, Purdue was struggling to keep any food down.

He didn't know it, but his room was one of three in their private medical wing.

After Klaus had left, Purdue looked around, trying to find anything that did not have a yellow tint or amber hue to it. It was hard for him to figure out if it was the influence of the sickening yellow water he all but drowned in that forced his eyes to see everything in amber shades. It was the only explanation he had for seeing those strange colors everywhere.

Klaus walked through the long arched hallway to where his security men waited for instructions whom to abduct next. It was his master plan, and it was going to be executed to perfection. Klaus Kemper was a third generation mason from Hesse-Kassel, who had been raised with the ideologies of the Black Sun organization. His grandfather was Hauptsturmführer Karl Kemper, commander of *Panzergruppe Kleist* during the time of the Prague Offensive in 1945.

From a young age, Klaus had been conditioned by his father to be a leader and to excel at everything he engaged in. There was no room for error in the Kemper clan and his larger than life father had often resorted to ruthless methods to enforce his doctrines. By his father's example, Klaus had learned soon enough that charisma could be as dangerous as a Molotov cocktail. Many times he had seen his father and grandfather intimidate independent and powerful men to a point of surrender by merely addressing them with certain gestures and tones of voice.

It became Klaus' desire to hold that kind of power one day since his scrawny physique would never make him a good contender in the more manly arts. Since he neither possessed athleticism nor strength, it was only natural for him to immerse himself in extensive world knowledge and verbal skill. With this seemingly meager talent, the young Klaus managed to promote his standing in the post-1946 extension of the Order of the Black Sun sporadically until he had reached the prestigious status of being the organization's premier converter. Not only did he garner a wealth of support for the organization within academic, political and financial circles, but by 2013 Klaus Kemper had established himself as one of the main facilitators of several of the Black Sun's covert offensives.

The particular project he was busy with now, and for which he had converted many high profile collaborators in past months, would be his crowning achievement. In fact, if all went according to plan Klaus would quite possibly win the highest seat in the Order – the one of the *Renatus* - for himself. From there, he would be the architect of global domination, but for that all to come to fruition he needed the baroque beauty of the treasure that once adorned the palace of Tsar Peter the Great.

Ignoring the befuddlement of his colleagues over the treasure he wished to locate, Klaus knew only the best explorer in the world could retrieve it for him. David Purdue – genius inventor, billionaire adventurer and academic philanthropist – had all the resources and knowledge Kemper needed to find the obscure artifact. It was just such a pity that he had not been able to successfully force the Scotsman into submission, even if Purdue thought Kemper could be fooled by his sudden compliance.

In the lobby, his henchmen greeted him respectfully on his way out. Klaus shook his head in disappointment as he passed them.

"I shall be back tomorrow," he told them.

"Protocol for David Purdue, sir?" the head asked.

Klaus walked out onto the barren wasteland surrounding their compound in southern Kazakhstan and answered plainly, "Kill him."

CHAPTER 14

*A*t the German Consulate, Sam and Nina were put in touch with Berlin's British Embassy. They had found out that Purdue had had an appointment with Ben Carrington and the late Gabi Holtzer a few days before, but that was all they knew.

They had to go home as it was closing time for the day, but at least they had enough to follow up on. This was Sam Cleave's strong suit. As a Pulitzer Prize-winning investigative journalist, he knew exactly how to go about obtaining the information they needed without throwing rocks in the quiet pond.

"Wonder why he had to see this Gabi woman," Nina mentioned as she stuffed her mouth with biscuits. She was going to have them with her hot chocolate, but she was starving, and the kettle just took too long.

"I am going to check just that as soon as I get my laptop on," Sam replied, slinging his bag onto the couch before taking his luggage to the laundry room. "Make me some hot chocolate too, please!"

"Sure thing," she smiled, wiping the crumbs from her

mouth. In the temporary solitude of the kitchen, Nina could not help but recall the frightening episode aboard the flight home. If she could find a way to anticipate Sam's episodes, it would be a great help, reducing the potential for disaster next time when they might not be as lucky to have a doctor around. What if it happened while they were alone?

'What if it happens while we have sex?' Nina pondered, assessing the terrifying, yet hilarious, possibilities. *'Just imagine what he could do if he channeled that energy through something other than his palm?'* She started to giggle at the funny images in her mind. *'It would justify screaming 'Oh God!' wouldn't it?'* With all manner of awkward scenarios in her head, Nina could not contain her laughter. She knew it was anything but a laughing matter, but it simply evoked some unorthodox ideas in the historian, and she found some comic relief.

"What's so funny?" Sam smiled as he entered the kitchen for his cup of ambrosia.

Nina shook her head to dismiss it, but she was shaking with laughter, snorting between giggle fits.

"Nothing," she chuckled. "Just some cartoon in my head about a lightning rod. Forget it."

"Okay," he grinned. He loved it when Nina laughed. Not only did she have a musical chortle that people found infectious, but she was usually a bit high strung and temperamental. It had sadly become rare to see her laugh this heartily.

Sam positioned his laptop so he could plug it into his landline router for faster broadband speed than through his wireless device.

"I should have let Purdue make me one of his wireless modems after all," he muttered. "Those things are precognitive."

"Do you have any more biscuits?" she called from his

kitchen while he could hear her opening and closing cupboard doors all over the place in her search.

"No, but my neighbor made me some chocolate-chip and oatmeal cookies. Check them, but I'm sure they are still good. Look in the jar on the fridge," he instructed.

"Got 'em! Ta!"

Sam opened the search for Gabi Holtzer and immediately found something that made him very suspicious.

"Nina! You won't believe this," he exclaimed as his eyes scanned the countless news reports and articles on the death of the German ministerial spokeswoman. "This woman was working for the German government, dealing with those killings a while back. Remember those assassinations in Berlin and Hamburg and a few other locations just before we went on holiday?"

"Aye, vaguely. So what about her?" Nina asked as she perched on the sofa arm rest with her cup and a cookie.

"She met Purdue at the British High Commission in Berlin, and get this: on the day she reportedly committed suicide," he stressed the last two words in his bewilderment. "It was the same day Purdue met this Carrington bloke."

"That was the last time somebody saw him," Nina remarked. "So Purdue goes missing on the same day he meets a woman who kills herself shortly after. It reeks of conspiracy, doesn't it?"

"Apparently, the only participant of the meeting who is not dead or missing is Ben Carrington," Sam added up. He looked at a picture of the Brit on the screen to memorize his face. "I would like a word with you, son."

"I take it we are going south tomorrow," Nina assumed.

"Aye, once we have paid Wrichtishousis a visit, that is," Sam said. "It won't hurt to make sure that he has not returned home yet."

"I've called his cell over and over. It's turned off, no voice box, no nothing," she reiterated.

"What was this deceased woman's involvement with Purdue?" Sam asked.

"The pilot said that Purdue wanted to know why his flight to Copenhagen was denied entry. Since she was a German government rep, she was invited to the British Embassy to discuss why it happened," Nina conveyed. "But that was all the captain knew. That was the last contact they had, so the flight crew is still in Berlin."

"Jesus. I must admit that I am beginning to get a very bad feeling about this," Sam conceded.

"Finally, you admit it," she answered. "You mentioned something while you had that seizure, Sam. And that something spells definite shit storm material."

"What?" he asked.

She took a bite of another cookie. "Black Sun."

A dark scowl fell on Sam's face as his eyes stared floorwards. "Fucking hell, I forgot that part," he said softly. "I remember now."

"Where did you see it?" she asked bluntly, aware of the horrible nature of the sigil and its power to turn conversations into ugly reminiscences.

"At the bottom of the well," he revealed. "I was thinking. Maybe I should see Dr. Helberg about this vision. He will know how to interpret it."

"While you are at it, ask him for his clinical opinion on the cataracts induced by the visions. I bet that is a new development he won't be able to explain," she said firmly.

"You have no faith in psychology, do you?" Sam sighed.

"No, Sam, I don't. There is no way that a defined set of behavioral patterns can suffice to uniformly diagnose different people," she argued. "He knows less about psychology than you do. His *knowledge* comes from studies and some other old farts' theories, and you keep trusting in his not-so-successful attempts at formulating his own theories."

"How could I possibly know more than he does?" he snapped back at her.

"Because you are *living* it, you idiot! You are experiencing these phenomena while he can only speculate. Until he has felt and heard and seen it the way you do, there is no fucking way that he could even begin to comprehend what we are dealing with!" Nina barked. She was so frustrated with him and his naive trust in Dr. Helberg.

"And what is it, in your qualified opinion, that we are dealing with, sweetheart?" he asked sarcastically. "Is it something from one of your ancient history books? Oh yes, a god. Now I remember! That, you could believe."

"Helberg is a shrink! All he knows is what a bunch of psychotic fuckwits exhibited in some study based on circumstances nowhere near the level of bizarre that you have experienced, my darling! Wake the hell up! Whatever is wrong with you is not just psychosomatic. There is something external controlling your visions. Something intelligent is manipulating your cerebral cortex," she presented her point.

"Because it talks through me?" he smiled sardonically. "Note that everything it says represents things I already know, things that are already in my subconscious."

"Then explain the thermal anomaly," she retorted rapidly, leaving Sam momentarily stumped.

"My brain apparently controls my body temperature too. Same thing," he countered without showing his uncertainty.

Nina laughed mockingly. "Your body temperature – I don't care how hot you might think you are, Playboy – cannot reach the thermal properties of a lightning bolt. And that is precisely what the doctor in Bali picked up, remember? Your eyes conducted so much concentrated electricity that 'your head should have exploded', remember?"

Sam had no comeback.

"And another thing," she continued her verbal victory, "Hypnosis is said to induce increased levels of fluctuating electrical activity within certain neurons of the brain, genius! Whatever is hypnotizing you is pushing an impossible amount of electrical power through you, Sam. Do you not see that what is happening to you is categorically outside the boundaries of mere psychology?"

"What do you suggest, then?" he shouted. "A shaman? Electroshock therapy? Paintball? A colonoscopy?"

"Oh Jesus!" she rolled her eyes. "There is no talking to you. You know what? Deal with this shit yourself. Go and see that quack and let him probe your brain a little more until you are as clueless as he is. It shouldn't be a long trip for you!"

With that, she stormed out of the room and slammed the door. Had she had her car there she would have driven straight home to Oban, but she was stranded for the night. Sam knew better than to mess with Nina when she was pissed off, so he spent the night on the couch.

The annoying ringtone of her phone woke Nina the next morning. She was coming out of a deep, dreamless sleep that had been way too short and sat up in bed. Somewhere in her purse, her phone was ringing, but she could not find it on time to answer.

"Alright, alright, dammit," she mumbled through the cotton wool of her waking mind. Fumbling madly through make-up and keys and deodorant she finally got a grip on her cellphone, but the call had already ended.

Nina frowned when she checked the clock. It was already 11.30 a.m., and Sam had let her sleep in.

"Great. Vexing me already today," she cussed Sam out in

his absence. "You better overslept yourself." When she exited the room, she realized that Sam was gone. Heading for the kettle, she checked the screen of her phone. Her eyes could barely focus yet, but still, she was sure she did not know the number. She hit redial.

"Dr. Helberg's office," the receptionist answered.

'Oh my God,' Nina thought. *'He went there.'* But she kept her cool just in case she was mistaken. "Hello, this is Dr. Gould. I just received a call from this number?"

"Dr. Gould?" the lady repeated excitedly. "Yes! Yes, we were trying to contact you. It's about Mr. Cleave. Is it possible...?"

"Is he alright?" Nina exclaimed.

"Could you come into our offices...?"

"I asked you a question!" Nina snapped. "Please just tell me if he is alright first!"

"We...we d-don't know, Dr. Gould," the lady replied hesitantly.

"What the bloody hell does that mean?" Nina fumed, her rage fueled by worry for Sam's condition. She heard a commotion in the background.

"Well, ma'am, he appears to be... um... levitating."

etlef took apart the floorboards where the air vent was, but when he inserted the screwdriver head into the second screw slit, the whole thing sank into the wall where it was mounted. A loud crack startled him, and he fell backward, kicking himself away from the wall. As he sat watching, the wall started to move sideways like a sliding door.

"What the...?" he gawked, propped up on his hands where he still cowered on the floor. The doorway led to what he thought was their neighboring apartment, but instead the dark room was a concealed space off Gabi's office for a purpose he was soon to discover. He rose to his feet, dusting off his pants and shirt. As the obscured doorway waited, he was reluctant just to walk inside because his training had taught him not to storm recklessly into unknown places – at least not without a weapon.

Detlef went to get his Glock and a flashlight, just in case the unknown room was rigged or had an alarm system. This was what he knew best – security breaches and counter-assassination protocol. With absolute precision he aimed the barrel into the darkness, steadying his heart rate to enable a clean shot if needed. But a steady pulse did not tame the thrill or the rush of adrenaline. It felt like the old days again as Detlef stepped inside the room, assessing the perimeter and scrutinizing the interior for any alarm or trigger devices.

But almost to his disappointment, it was just a room, although what was inside was far from uninteresting.

"Idiot," he cursed himself when he saw the standard light switch next to the door frame on the inside. He flicked it on to reveal the full view of the room. A single bulb hanging from the ceiling lit Gabi's radio room. He knew it was hers because her blackcurrant lipstick stood at attention next to one of her cigarette cases. One of her cardigans was still draped over the small office chair's backrest, and Detlef had to fight the sorrow again at the sight of his wife's belongings.

He took the soft cashmere cardigan and inhaled her scent deeply before replacing it to examine the equipment. Four tables furnished the place. One where her chair was, two others on either side of it, and another by the door where she kept stacks of documents in what looked like folders – he could not tell off-hand. In the timid light of the bulb, Detlef felt as if he had stepped back in time. A musty odor reminding him of a museum filled the room with the unpainted cement walls.

"Wow, honey, I would have thought you of all people would put up some wallpaper and a mirror or two," he told his wife as he looked around the radio room. "That's what you always did; beautified everything."

The place reminded him of a dungeon or an interrogation room in an old spy movie. On her table was a contraption similar to a CB radio, but it something was different. Being a complete layman at radio communication of this outdated sort, Detlef looked for an on-switch. A protruding steel switch was fixed to the bottom right corner, so he tried it. Suddenly the two small gauges lit up, their needles rising and falling as static hissed through the speaker.

Detlef looked at the other devices. "They look far too complicated to suss out without a being a rocket scientist," he remarked. "What is all this, Gabi?" he asked, as he noticed a big corkboard mounted above the table where the paper stacks were. Pinned to the board, he saw several articles on the killings Gabi had been investigating without her superiors' knowledge. On the side, she had scribbled 'MILLA' in red felt pen.

"Who is Milla, baby?" he whispered. He recalled her diary noting someone called Milla on the same time slot as the two men present during her death. "I have to know. It's important."

But all he could hear was the swishing whispers of the frequencies that came through the radio in swells. His eyes wandered further along the board where something vivid and brilliant caught his attention. Two photographs in full color depicted a palace room in gilded splendor. "Whoah," Detlef mumbled, stunned by the detail and intricate work adorning the walls of the lavish room. Amber and gold stucco formed beautiful emblems and shapes framed at the corners by small effigies of cherubs and goddesses.

"Estimated at $143 million? Geez, Gabi, do you know what this is?" he muttered as he read through the details of the lost work of art known as the *Amber Room*. "What did you have to do with this room? You must have had something to do with it; otherwise, all this would not be here, right?"

There were notes all over the articles of the murders that hinted at the possibility that the Amber Room had something to do with it. Below the word 'MILLA' Detlef found a map of Russia and its borders to Belarus, Ukraine, Kazakhstan, and Lithuania. Over the area of the Kazakh Steppe and Kharkiv, Ukraine there were numbers written in red pen, but they had no familiar pattern such as phone number or coordinates. Seemingly randomly Gabi had written these double-digit numbers on the maps she had pinned to the wall.

WHAT CAUGHT his eye was an apparently valuable relic hanging from the corner of the corkboard. The purple ribbon with a dark blue stripe down the middle held a medal inscribed with Russian lettering. Detlef removed it carefully and pinned it to his vest under his shirt.

"What the hell were you into, sweetheart?" he whispered to his wife. He took several pictures with his cell phone camera and made a short video clip of the room and its contents. "I will find out what this all had to do with you and that Purdue you were meeting, Gabi," he vowed. "And then I will find his friends to tell me where he is or else they will die."

Suddenly, a static cacophony screamed from the direction of the makeshift radio on Gabi's desk, scaring Detlef half to death. He fell back against the stacked paper desk, shoving it so hard that some of the folders slid off and fell in a mess all over the floor.

"Christ! My fucking heart!" he shouted, gripping his chest. The red needles of the gauges were dancing left and right rapidly. It reminded Detlef of old hi-fi systems that used to display loudness or clarity of the media played on it that way. From the static, he heard a voice fade in and out. On closer inspection, he realized it was not a broadcast, but a summoning. Detlef sat down on his late wife's chair and listened intently. It was a female voice speaking one word at a time. Frowning, he leaned in. His eyes widened at once. There was a distinct word he recognized.

'Gabi!'

He sat up in alert, having no idea what to do. The woman

kept calling for his wife in Russian; he could tell, but he did not speak the language. Adamant to talk to her, Detlef hastened to get his phone browser open to look up old design radios and how they were operated. In his frenzy his big fingers kept mistyping the search, frustrating him beyond words.

"Fuck! Not *'cockmunication'!*" he complained as several pornographic results appeared on his phone screen. His face glistened with sweat as he hurried to get some form of help to operate the old communication device. "Wait! Wait!" he shouted at the radio as the woman's voice called for Gabi to respond. "Wait for me! Argh, fuck!"

Furious with the unsatisfactory results of his Google search, Detlef grabbed a thick dusty book and threw it at the radio. The iron casing came loose slightly, and the receiver fell off the table, dangling by its cord. "Fuck you!" he shrieked, filled with despair at being unable to operate the device.

A crackle sounded on the radio, and a man's voice came over the speaker in a heavy Russian accent. "Fuck you too, bro."

Detlef was astonished. He jumped up and went over to where he had shoved the device. He grabbed the swinging microphone he had just assaulted with the book and clumsily picked it up. The device had no button to press to broadcast, so Detlef just began to speak.

"Hello? Hey! Hello?" he called, his eyes flitting in desperate hopes that somebody would answer him. His other hand rested gently on the transmitter. Only static noise prevailed for a while. Then the squeak of switching channels over different modulation shifts filled the small creepy room while its only occupant waited in anticipation.

Eventually, Detlef had to admit defeat. Distraught, he shook his head. "Please talk?" he moaned in English, realizing that the Russian at the other end probably couldn't speak German. "Please? I don't know how to work this thing. I need to let you know that Gabi is my wife."

The female voice grated from the speaker. Detlef perked up. "Is that Milla? Are you Milla?"

With slow reluctance, the woman answered, "Where is Gabi?"

"She is dead," he replied, then wondered out loud about the protocol. "Do I say over?"

"No, this is covert transmission via L-band using Amplitude Modulation as carrier wave," she assured him in broken English, yet she was fluent in the terminology of her trade.

"What?" Detlef shrieked in utter confusion of a subject he was completely inept at.

She sighed. "This talk is like telephone. You talk. I talk. No saying 'over.'"

Detlef was relieved to hear that. "Sehr gut!"

"Speak up. I can barely hear you. Where is Gabi?" she repeated, having not heard his previous answer clearly.

It was hard for Detlef to repeat the news. "My wife... Gabi is dead."

There was no answer for a long while, only the distant crunch of static noises. Then the man came on again. "You lie."

"No, no. Nyet! I am not lying. My wife was killed four days ago," he defended apprehensively. "Check Internet! Check CNN!"

"Your name," the man said. "Not your real name. Something to identify you. Just between Milla and you."

Detlef did not even think about it. "Widower."

Crackle.

Sweesh.

Detlef hated the hollow sound of white noise and dead

air. It felt so desolate, so lonely, and wasted by the void of information - to a measure it defined him.

"Widower. Switch to 1549MHz on the transmitter. Wait for Metallica. Get the numbers. Use your GPS and go Thursday," the man instructed.

Click

The click sound echoed like a gunshot in Detlef's ears, leaving him devastated and bewildered. Pausing in disbelief, he sat frozen with his hands outstretched. "What the fuck?"

Suddenly he was spurred on by the instructions he was about to forget.

"Come back! Hello?" he shouted on the speaker, but the Russians were gone. He threw his arms up in the air, roaring in frustration. "Fifteen forty-nine," he said. "Fifteen forty-nine. Remember that!" Frantically he searched for the approximation of the number on the dial indicator. Turning the knob slowly, he found the designated station.

"Now what?" he whined. He kept a pen and paper ready for the numbers, but he had no idea what waiting for Metallica meant. 'What if it is a code I cannot decipher? What if I don't understand the message?' he panicked.

Suddenly the station started broadcasting music. He recognized Metallica, but he did not know the song. It gradually faded off as the female voice started reading number codes and Detlef jotted them down. When the music started again, he concluded the broadcast was over. Sinking back in the chair, he breathed out a long sigh of relief. He was intrigued, but his training also warned him that he could not trust anyone he did not know.

If his wife was killed by people she had been involved with, it might well have been Milla and her associate. Until he knew for sure, he could not just follow their orders.

He had to find a scapegoat.

CHAPTER 16

*N*ina stormed into Dr. Helberg's office. The waiting room was empty save for the receptionist who looked ashen. As if she knew Nina she immediately pointed toward the closed doors. Behind them, she could hear a man's voice speaking very deliberately and very calmly.

"Please. Just go in," the receptionist motioned to Nina, standing up against the wall in terror.

"Where is the security guard?" Nina asked softly.

"He took off when Mr. Cleave started to levitate," she said. "Everyone ran out of here. On the upside, with all the trauma it caused, we will have a lot of future business," she shrugged.

Nina walked into the room where she heard only the doctor speaking. She was grateful that she did not hear "the *other* Sam" talking as she pressed down on the door handle. Carefully she stepped across the threshold into the room that was only lit by the sparse light of the midday sun that filtered through the closed blinds. The psychologist saw her but kept talking as his patient was hovering upright, inches from the ground. It was a frightening sight, but Nina had to remain calm and assess the problem logically.

Dr. Helberg was talking Sam back from his session, but as he clicked his fingers to wake Sam, nothing happened. He shook his head at Nina, indicating his befuddlement. She looked at Sam, whose head was tilted back and his milky eyes wide open.

"I have been trying to bring him out for almost half an hour," he whispered to Nina. "He told me you witnessed him in this state twice before. Do you know what is going on?"

She shook her head slowly, but she thought to make use of the opportunity. Nina drew her cell phone from her jacket pocket and pressed the record button to take a video of what was going on. Gently she lifted it to get Sam's whole body into the frame before she spoke.

Gathering her courage, Nina took a deep breath and said, "Kalihasa."

Dr. Helberg frowned at her, shrugging. "What is that?" he mouthed to her.

She held out one hand to request his silence before she said it louder. "Kalihasa!"

Sam's mouth opened, accommodating the voice that Nina feared so much. The words came out of Sam, but it was not his voice or his lips forming them. In terror, the psychologist and the historian stared at the frightful episode.

"Kalihasa!" the voice said in a choir of undefined gender. "The vessel is primitive. The vessel is few in existence."

Neither Nina nor Dr. Helberg knew what the statement was about apart from its reference to Sam, but the psychologist urged her to carry on for the sake of learning about Sam's condition. She shrugged at the doctor, having no idea what to say. There was a slim chance that this thing could be conversed or reasoned with.

"Kalihasa," Nina stammered timidly. "What are you?"

"Conscious," it replied.

"What kind of being are you?" she asked, rephrasing what she thought was a miscomprehension on the part of the voice.

"Conscious-ness," it answered. "Your mind is wrong."

Dr. Helberg gasped excitedly at the discovery of the entity's ability to converse. Nina tried not to take it personally.

"What do you want?" Nina asked somewhat more boldly.

"To exist," it said.

To her left, the endearing podgy shrink was bursting with amazement, absolutely fascinated by what was happening.

"With humans?" she asked.

"To enslave," it added while she was still talking.

"To enslave the vessel?" Nina asked, getting the hang of formulating her questions.

"The vessel is primitive."

"Are you a god?" she uttered without thinking.

"Are you a god?" it repeated.

Nina sighed irritably. The doctor motioned for her to carry on, but she was frustrated. Frowning and pursing her lips she told the doctor, "It is just repeating what I say."

"It is not answering. It is asking," the voice replied to her surprise.

"I am not a god," she answered modestly.

"That is why I am," it replied quickly.

Suddenly Dr. Helberg fell to the floor and began to convulse just like the native man at the village. Nina panicked, but she kept recording both men.

"No!" she shouted. "Stop! Stop it now!"

"Are you God?" it asked.

"No!" she shouted. "Stop killing him! Right now!"

"Are you God?" it asked her again while the poor psychologist was writhing in agony.

She shouted sternly as a last resort before she would start looking for a pitcher of water again. "Yes! I am God!"

Within a blink, Sam fell to the ground, and Dr. Helberg stopped screaming. Nina rushed to check on them both.

"Excuse me!" she called the receptionist. "Can you come in here and help me, please?"

Nobody came. Assuming that the woman left like the others, Nina opened the door to the waiting room. The receptionist sat on the waiting room sofa with the security guard's gun in her hand. At her feet lay the slain security officer, shot in the back of the head. Nina retreated slightly, not willing to risk the same fate. She swiftly helped Dr. Helberg to sit up after his painful spasms, whispering to him not to make a sound. When he was conscious, she moved to Sam to assess his condition.

"Sam, can you hear me?" she whispered.

"Aye," he groaned, "but I feel weird. Was that another fit of madness? I was half aware of it, this time, you know?"

"What do you mean?" she asked.

"I was conscious through it all, and it was as if I was gaining control over the current that went through me. That argument with you just then. Nina, that was me. It was my thoughts that came out a bit skewed and sounded like taken from the script of a horror film! And you know what?" he whispered with immense urgency.

"What?"

"I can still feel it running through me," he admitted, clutching at her upper arms. "Doc?" Sam blurted out when he saw what his haywire powers had done to the doctor.

"Shh," Nina hushed him and pointed toward the door. "Listen, Sam. I need you to try something for me. Can you try to use that… other side… to manipulate someone's intentions?"

"No, I don't think so," he reckoned. "Why?"

"Look, you just controlled Dr. Helberg's brain patterns to induce a seizure, Sam," she pressed. "You did that to him. You did it by manipulating the electrical activity in his brain, so you have to be able to do it with the receptionist. If you don't," Nina warned, "she is going to kill us all in a minute."

"I have no idea what you're talking about, but alright, I'll try," Sam agreed and stumbled to his feet. He peeked around the corner and saw the woman sitting on the sofa, smoking a cigarette with the security officer's gun in the other hand. Sam glanced back to Dr. Helberg, "What is her name?"

"Elma," the doctor answered.

"Elma?" As Sam called from behind the corner, something happened that he had not apperceived before. When she heard her name, her brain activity increased, establishing Sam's connection with her instantly. The mild electrical current shot through him like a wave, but it was not painful. Mentally it felt as if Sam had latched onto her with some invisible tether. He was not sure if he should speak to her out loud, and order her to toss aside the gun or if she should just to think it.

Sam elected to employ the same method he recalled using while under the influence of the strange force before. Just thinking of Elma, he sent her a command, feeling it slide along the perceived tether towards her mind. As it connected with her Sam could feel the merging of his thoughts with her consciousness.

"What is happening?" Dr. Helberg asked Nina, but she held him away from Sam and whispered for him to keep still and wait. They both watched from a safe distance while Sam's eyes rolled back again.

"Oh dear Lord, no! Not again!" Dr. Helberg moaned under his breath.

"Quiet! I think Sam is in control of it this time," she speculated, hoping to her lucky stars that she was correct in her assumption.

"Maybe that was why I could not snap him out of it," Dr. Helberg told her. "It was not a hypnotic state after all. It was his own mind, just expanded!"

Nina had to agree that it was a fascinating and logical deduction on the part of the shrink she had not had much professional respect for before.

Elma stood up and flung the weapon toward the middle of the waiting room. Then she walked into the doctor's office with her cigarette in her hand. Nina and Dr. Helberg ducked down at the sight of her, but all she did was smile at Sam and gave him her cigarette.

"Can I get you one too, Dr. Gould?" she smiled. "I have two more left in the pack."

"Uh, no thanks," Nina answered.

Nina was astonished. Was the woman who just murdered a man in cold blood actually offering her a fag? Sam looked at Nina with a boastful smile, to which she just shook her head and sighed. Elma went to the reception desk and called the police.

"Hello, I want to report a murder at the office of Dr. Helberg in the Old Town…" she reported her deed.

"Holy shit, Sam!" Nina gasped.

"I know, right?" he smiled, yet he looked a bit nervous at the discovery. "Doc, you are going to have to make up some sort of story to make sense to the police. I did not control any of that shit she did in the waiting room."

"I know, Sam," Dr. Helberg nodded. "You were still under hypnosis when that happened. But we both know that she was not in control of her own mind, and that bothers me. How can I let her spend the rest of her life in prison for a crime she technically did not commit?"

"I am sure you can testify as to her mental stability and

maybe find an explanation that will prove that she was in a trance or something," Nina suggested. Her phone rang, and she went to the window to take the call while Sam and Dr. Helberg watched Elma's moves to make sure she did not flee.

"In truth, whatever controlled you, Sam, wanted to kill, whether it was my assistant or me," Dr. Helberg warned. "Now that it's safe to assume that this force is your own *consciousness*, I implore you to be very mindful of your intentions or attitude, or you may end up killing someone you love."

Nina suddenly caught her breath so fiercely that both men looked at her. She looked staggered. "It's Purdue!"

CHAPTER 17

*S*am and Nina had left Dr. Helberg's office before the police showed up. They had no idea what the psychologist was going to tell the authorities, but they had more important things to think about now.

"Did he say where he was?" Sam asked as they headed for Sam's car.

"He was being held in a compound run by... guess who?" she sneered.

"The Black Sun, by chance?" Sam played along.

"Bingo! And he gave me a sequence of numbers to punch into one of his gadgets at Wrichtishousis. Some contraption that looks like an Enigma machine," she informed him.

"Do you know what that looks like?" he asked as they drove to Purdue's estate.

"Aye. It was extensively used by the Nazis during World War II to communicate. It's basically an electro-mechanical rotor cipher machine," Nina explained.

"And do you know how to work this thing?" Sam wanted to know because they knew he'd be out of his depth at trying to mess with complex codes. He once attempted coding for a software course and ended up inventing a program that did nothing but creating umlauts and stationary bubbles.

"Purdue gave me some numbers to enter into the machine, He said it would give us his location," she replied, looking over the seemingly senseless sequence she jotted down.

"I wonder how he got to a phone," Sam said as they neared the hill where Purdue's massive manor lurched over the winding road. "I hope he does not get discovered while waiting for us to get to him."

"No, he is safe for now. He told me that the guards were ordered to kill him, but that he managed to escape the room they had kept him in. Now he is apparently hiding in the computer room, and hacked into their communication lines to be able to call us," she explained.

"Ha! Old school! Well done, old cock!" Sam grinned at Purdue's resourcefulness.

They pulled into the drive at Purdue's home. Security knew their boss' closest friends and cordially waved at them when they opened the huge black gates. Purdue's assistant met them at the door.

"You found Mr. Purdue?" she asked. "Oh thank God!"

"Aye, we have to get to his electronics rooms, please. It is very urgent," Sam requested, and they rushed to the basement room Purdue had modified into one of his holy chapels of inventions galore. On one side, he kept everything he was still working on, and on the other side was everything he had completed but hadn't patented yet. To anyone who did not live and breathe for engineering or was less technically inclined, it was an impenetrable maze of wires and hardware, monitors, and tools.

"Shit, look at all this stuff! How are we supposed to find that thing in here?" Sam worried. His hands ran along the sides of his head as he scanned the place for what Nina had described as a sort of typewriter. "I see nothing like that here."

"Me neither," she sighed. "Just help me look through the cabinets as well, please Sam."

"I hope you know how to work that thing, or else Purdue is history," he told her as he opened the doors of the first cupboard, ignoring all the jokes he could crack about the pun of his statement.

"Given all my research for one of my final study papers back in 2004 I should be able to figure it out, don't fret," Nina said as she rummaged through some cabinets that stood lines up against the east wall.

"I think I found it," he said casually. From an old green army locker, Sam lifted a beat-up looking typewriter and held it up like a trophy. "Is this it?"

"That's it, yes!" she exclaimed. "Right, set it down over here."

Nina cleared a small desk and moved a chair from another table to sit down in front of it. She retrieved the paper with numbers Purdue had given her and got to work. While Nina focused on the process, Sam was thinking about the most recent events, trying to make sense of it. If he could truly make people obey his orders, it would change his life completely, but something about his convenient new talent set off a whole bunch of red lights in his head.

"Excuse me, Dr. Gould," one of Purdue's house staff called from the door. "There is a gentleman here to see you. He says he spoke to you on the phone a few days ago about Mr. Purdue."

"Oh shit!" Nina cried. "I completely forgot about that guy! Sam, the man who alerted us that Purdue was missing? That must be him. Shit, he is going to be upset."

"For what it's worth, he seems very nice," the staff member chipped in.

"I'll go talk to him. What is his name?" Sam asked her.

"Holtzer," she answered. "Detlef Holtzer."

"Nina, *Holtzer* is the surname of the woman who died at the Consulate, isn't it?" he asked. She nodded, and suddenly remembered the man's first name from the phone call now that Sam mentioned it.

Sam left Nina to her task and went up to speak to the stranger. When he entered the lobby, he was surprised to see the powerfully built man sipping tea with such refinement.

"Mr. Holtzer?" Sam smiled, reaching out a hand. "Sam Cleave. I'm a friend of Dr. Gould and Mr. Purdue. How can I help you?"

Detlef smiled cordially and shook Sam's hand. "Good to meet you, Mr. Cleave. Um, where is Dr. Gould? It seems that everyone I try to speak to disappears and I get someone else in their place."

"She is just caught up in a project right now, but she is here. Oh, and she apologizes that she has not yet gotten back to you, but it seems you were able to find Mr. Purdue's estate quite easily," Sam noted as he sat down.

"Have you managed to find him yet? I really need to speak to him regarding my wife," Detlef said, playing open cards with Sam. Sam looked at him, intrigued.

"What, may I ask, did Mr. Purdue have to do with your wife? Were they business associates?" Sam knew full well that they met at Carrington's office to talk about the landing ban, but he wanted to get a feel for the stranger first.

"No, in fact, I wanted to ask him some questions about the circumstances of my wife's death. You see, Mr. Cleave, I know she did not commit suicide. Mr. Purdue was there when she was killed. You understand where I am going with this?" he asked Sam with a sterner demeanor.

"You think Purdue killed your wife," Sam affirmed.

"I do," Detlef answered.

"And you are here to seek revenge?" Sam asked.

"Would that be so far-fetched?" the German giant retorted. "He was the last person to see Gabi alive. What else would I be here for?"

The atmosphere between them quickly grew tense, but Sam tried to apply reason and keep things civil.

"Mr. Holtzer, I know Dave Purdue. He is not a killer by any measure. The man is an inventor and explorer who is only interested in historical relics. How do you think would he benefit from your wife's death?" Sam inquired in his journalistic prowess.

"I know that she was trying to expose the people behind those assassinations in Germany and that it has something to do with the elusive Amber Room that was lost in the Second World War. Then she went to meet David Purdue and died. Do you not think that just a tad suspicious?" he asked Sam confrontationally.

"I can understand how you would come to this conclusion Mr. Holtzer, but right after Gabi's death Purdue went missing…"

"Which is precisely the point. Would a killer not try to disappear to avoid getting caught?" Detlef interrupted him. Sam had to admit that the man had a valid reason to suspect Purdue of his wife's murder.

"Alright, I tell you what," Sam proposed diplomatically, "as soon as we locate…"

"Sam! I cannot get this goddamn thing to give me all the words. Purdue's last two sentences say something about the Amber Room and the Red Army!" Nina shouted as she ran up the steps up to the Bel Etage.

"That's Dr. Gould, right?" Detlef asked Sam. "I recognize her voice from the phone. Tell me, Mr. Cleave, what is her involvement with David Purdue?"

"I am a colleague and friend. I advise him on historical

matters during his expeditions, Mr. Holtzer," she replied firmly to his query.

"Good to meet you face to face, Dr. Gould," Detlef smiled coolly. "Now tell me, Mr. Cleave, how is it that my wife was investigating something that sounds very much like the same subjects Dr. Gould was just talking about? And they both happen to know David Purdue, so why don't you tell me what I should be thinking?"

Nina and Sam exchanged frowns. It seemed like their visitor had missing pieces to their own puzzle.

"Mr. Holtzer, what subjects are you referring to?" Sam asked. "If you could help us figure this out, we are probably going to be able to find Purdue, and then I promise you can ask him anything you want."

"Without killing him, of course," Nina added as she joined the two men on the velvet seats in the drawing room.

"My wife was investigating the killings of the financiers and politicians in Berlin. But after her death, I found a room – a radio room, I think – and there I found articles about the assassinations and many documents on the Amber Room that was once given to Tsar Peter the Great by King Frederick Wilhelm I of Prussia," Detlef relayed. "Gabi knew there was a connection between the two, but I need to speak to David Purdue to find out what it is."

"Well, there is a way you *can* talk to him, Mr. Holtzer," Nina shrugged. "I think the information you need might be in his recent communication with us."

"So you do know where he is!" he snapped.

"No, we only got this message, and we need to decipher all the words before we can go and rescue him from the people that abducted him," Nina explained to the high-strung visitor. "If we can't decipher his message, I have no idea how to look for him."

"By the way, what was the rest of the message you did manage to decode?" Sam asked her inquisitively.

She sighed, still baffled by the nonsensical wording. "It mentions 'Army' and 'Steppe', probably a mountain region? Then it says 'search for Amber Room or die' and the only other thing I got was a bunch of punctuation marks and asterisks. I'm not sure if his machine is quite on point."

Detlef thought about the information. "Look at this," he said suddenly, reaching into his jacket pocket. Sam assumed a defensive position, but the stranger only pulled out his cell phone. He flicked through the pictures and showed them the contents of the secret room. "One of my sources gave me coordinates to follow to find the people Gabi was threatening to expose. See those numbers? Put them in your machine and see what it does."

They went back in the room in the basement of the old mansion where Nina had been working with the Enigma machine. Detlef's pictures were clear and close enough for them to discern each combination. For the next two hours, Nina entered the numbers one by one. Finally, she had a print-out of the words coinciding with the ciphers.

"Now this is not Purdue's message; this one is based on the numbers from Gabi's maps," Nina clarified before she read out the result. "First, it says 'Black vs. Red in Kazakh Steppe', then 'radiation cage' and the last two combinations 'Mind control' and 'ancient orgasm'."

Sam raised an eyebrow. "Ancient orgasm?"

"Ugh! I misspoke. It's 'ancient organism'," she stammered, much to Detlef and Sam's amusement. "So the '*Steppe*' is mentioned by both Gabi and Purdue, and it is the only clue that happens to be a location."

Sam looked at Detlef. "So, you came all the way from Germany to find Gabi's murderer. How about a trip to the Kazakh Steppe?"

CHAPTER 18

*P*urdue's feet still stung like hell. Every step he took felt like walking on nails, shooting up to his ankles. It made it virtually impossible for him to wear shoes, yet he knew he had to if he wanted to escape his prison. After Klaus had left the infirmary, Purdue had immediately pulled the IV out of his arm and started checked whether his legs were strong enough to carry his weight. At no point in time, he believed that they intended to nurse him for the next few days. He was expecting more torture to cripple his body and mind.

With his affinity for technology, Purdue knew he could fiddle with their communication devices as well as whatever access control and security they employed. The Order of the Black Sun was a sovereign organization, utilizing only the best of everything to shield their interests, but Dave Purdue was a genius they could only fear. He was capable of perfecting any invention of their engineers without much effort.

He sat up on the bed and then carefully slipped off the

side to slowly put pressure on his sore soles. Wincing, Purdue tried to ignore the excruciating pain of the second-degree burns. He did not want to be discovered while he still couldn't walk or run, or he would be done for.

While Klaus was instructing his men before leaving, their captive had already been limping through the vast maze of hallways and corridors, making a mental map to plan his escape. On the third floor, where he had been confined, he stalked along the north wall to find the end of the corridor, since he assumed there had to be a flight of stairs there. He was not at too surprised to see that the entire fortress was in fact round and that the external walls consisted of iron beams and truss members reinforced by enormous sheets of bolted-together steel.

'It looks like a goddamn space ship,' he thought to himself as he examined the architecture of the Kazakh Black Sun citadel. In the center, the building was empty, a huge space where mammoth machines or aircraft could be stored or constructed. All around it, the steel structure provided ten stories of offices, server stations, interrogation chambers, dining halls and accommodations, boardrooms, and laboratories. Purdue was in awe of the efficiency of the power supply and scientific infrastructure of the building, but he had to keep moving.

He crept through the dark crawlspaces of out-of-commission furnaces and dusty workshops in search of an exit or at least any working communication apparatus he could use to call help. To his relief, he discovered an old air traffic control room that appeared to have been unused for decades.

'Probably part of some Cold War launch stations,' he frowned as he surveyed the equipment in the rectangular room. Keeping his eye on the tinged old piece of mirror he had

taken from an empty laboratory, he proceeded to hot-wire the only device he recognized. *'Looks like an electronic version of a Morse Code transmitter,'* he guessed as he sank to his haunches to find the cable to connect to the socket in the wall. The machine was only for broadcasting number sequences, so he had to try and remember the training he had received long before his stint to Wolfenstein years ago.

After getting the machine to work and directing its antennae toward what he reckoned was north, Purdue found a transmission device that worked like a telegraph machine, but could link up to geostationary telecommunications satellites with the correct codes. With this machine, he could convert phrases into their numerical equivalents and employ an Atbash cipher in conjunction with a mathematical coding system. *'Binary would have been so much quicker,'* he seethed as the antiquated device kept losing his results due to short sporadic power outages from voltage fluctuations in the power lines.

When Purdue finally produced adequate clues for Nina to solve on his Enigma machine at home, he hacked into the old system to establish a link to the telecommunication feed. It was a stretch to attempt contacting a phone number this way, but he had to try. This was the only way he could get the number sequences to Nina with a transmission window of twenty seconds to her service provider, but surprisingly he succeeded.

It did not take long before he heard Kemper's men running through the steel and concrete stronghold looking for him. His nerves were frayed, even though he had managed to make his emergency call. He knew it would realistically take days until they found him, so there were harrowing hours ahead for him. If they found him, Purdue feared his punishment would be of the kind he would never recover from.

With his body still aching, he had nestled himself into a deserted sub-basement water basin behind locked iron doors covered with cobwebs and eaten by rust. It was plain to see that nobody had entered there in years, making it the perfect hideout for the injured fugitive.

Purdue was hidden so well while waiting for his rescue, that he did not even notice that the citadel was under attack two days later. Nina had contacted Haim and Todd, Purdue's computer experts, to shut down the power grid in the surrounding area. She had given them with the coordinates Detlef had received from Milla after he had tuned into the numbers station. With this information, the two Scots wreaked havoc on the compound's electricity supply and main communication system and caused interferences on all devices such as laptops and cell phones within a radius of two miles around the Black Sun stronghold.

Sam and Detlef breached the main entrance stealthily with a strategy they had prepared before flying into the Kazakh Steppe's desolate countryside by helicopter. They had secured the assistance of Purdue's Polish affiliate, *Pole-Tech Air & Transit Services.* While the men invaded the compound, Nina waited in the craft with the military-trained pilot, checking the vicinity with infrared imaging on the lookout for hostile movements.

Detlef was armed with his Glock, two hunting knives, and one of his two expandable batons. The other one he had given to Sam. The journalist, in turn, had brought his own Makarov and four smoke grenades. They charged through the main entrance, expecting a hail of bullets in the dark, but instead tripped over several bodies scattered on the floor in the entryway.

"What the hell is going on?" Sam whispered. "These people work here. Who would have killed them?"

"From what I hear these Germans kill their own for the

sake of promotion," Detlef replied under his breath, aiming his torch at the dead men on the floor. "There are about twenty of them. Listen!"

Sam stopped and listened. They could hear the chaos the blackout had caused on the other floors of the building. Carefully they stalked up the first flight of stairs. It was too dangerous to split up in a compound as big as this without knowledge of weaponry or numbers of its occupants. They carefully walked in single-file, guns at the ready, using their torches to light the way.

"Let's hope they don't recognize us as intruders right away," Sam remarked.

Detlef smiled. "True. Let's just keep moving."

"Aye," Sam said. They watched the bobbing lights of some occupants move race toward the generator room. "Oh shit! Detlef, they are going to power up the generator!"

"Move! Move!" Detlef ordered his associate and grabbed him by the shirt. He dragged Sam with him to intercept the security men before they could reach the generator room. Following the flashlight orbs, Sam and Detlef cocked their weapons for the inevitable. As they ran, Detlef asked Sam, "Have you ever killed anyone?"

"Aye, but never deliberately," Sam answered.

"Good, now you are going to have to – with extreme prejudice!" the big German declared. "No mercy. Or we will never make it out alive."

"Roger that!" Sam promised as they came face to face with the first four men not more than three feet from the door. The men didn't know that the two figures coming from the other direction were intruders until the first slug split open the first man's skull.

Sam grimaced as he felt the hot splatter of brain matter and blood graze his face, but aimed at the second man in line and he squeezed the trigger without flinching, hitting him dead on. The slain man fell limply at Sam's feet, as he crouched to retrieve his sidearm. He aimed it at the oncoming men who had started firing at them, hitting two more. Detlef took down six men with perfect center-mass shots before following up on Sam's two targets with a slug to the skull each.

"Nicely done, Sam," the German smiled. "You smoke, right?"

"I do, why?" Sam asked as he wiped the bloody mess from his face and ear. "Give me your lighter," said his partner from the doorway. He tossed Detlef his Zippo before they entered the generator room and set the fuel tanks on fire. On their way out they disabled the engines with a few well-placed bullets.

Purdue had heard the madness from his small shelter and made for the main entrance, but only because it was the only exit he knew of. Limping heavily with his hand braced against the wall to guide him in the darkness, Purdue slowly climbed the emergency stairs to the foyer of the ground floor.

The doors were wide open, and in the sparse light that fell into the room, he carefully stepped over the bodies until he reached the welcoming breath of the warm, dry air of the desert landscape outside. Weeping with gratefulness and fear, Purdue ran toward the helicopter with his arms waving, hoping to God that it didn't belong to the enemy.

Nina jumped out and came running toward him. "Purdue! Purdue! Are you okay? Come this way!" she cried as she approached him. Purdue looked up at the beautiful historian. She was shouting into her transmitter, telling Sam and Detlef that she had Purdue. When Purdue fell into her arms, he collapsed, dragging her down with him onto the sand.

"I couldn't wait to feel your touch again, Nina," he panted. "You came through."

"I always do," she smiled and held her emaciated friend in her arms until the others arrived. They boarded the helicopter and took off in a westward direction where they had secured accommodation on the edge of the Aral Sea.

CHAPTER 19

"We have to find the Amber Room, or else the Order will. It is of utmost importance that we find it before they do because this time they will topple the world's governments and instigate violence of genocidal proportions," Purdue insisted.

They were huddled around a fire in the backyard of a house that Sam had rented in the settlement of Aral. It was semi-furnished three-bedroom shack and did not possess half the amenities the group was used to in First World Countries. But it was inconspicuous and quaint, and they could rest there until Purdue felt better, at least. In the meantime, Sam had to keep a close eye on Detlef to make sure the widower did not lash out and kill the billionaire before sorting out the matter of Gabi's death first.

"We will get on that as soon as you feel better, Purdue," Sam said. "For now, we just lay low and rest."

Nina's hair hung in a braid from under her knitted beanie as she lit up another smoke. Purdue's warning, intended to be foreboding, did not strike her as much of a problem with the way she felt about the world lately. It was not so much the verbal exchange with the godlike entity in Sam's psyche that spurred her indifferent thoughts. She was just more aware of the repeating mistakes of mankind and the ever-present failure to maintain balance all over the world.

Aral used to be a fishing port and harbor city before the mighty Aral Sea virtually dried up completely, leaving only a bare desert basin as legacy. It saddened Nina that so many beautiful bodies of water had dried up and vanished because of human infestation. Sometimes, when she felt particularly apathetic, she wondered if the world would not be better off without the human race killing everything in it, not excluding itself.

Humans reminded her of toddlers left in charge of an anthill. They simply did not possess the wisdom or humility to realize that they were *part* of the world, not *in charge* of it. In arrogance and irresponsibility they bred like cockroaches without considering that instead of killing the planet to accommodate their numbers and needs, they should have curbed their own population growth. Nina felt vexed that, as a collective, humans refused to see that producing smaller populations with higher intellectual faculty would yield a far more efficient world without destroying all beauty for their greed and reckless existence.

Deep in thought Nina smoked her cigarette next to the fire. Thoughts and ideologies that she was not supposed to be entertaining entered her mind, where it was safe to harbor taboo subjects. She thought about the Nazi objectives and found that some of those superficially atrocious ideas were, in fact, feasible solutions to a lot of problems that had brought the world to its knees in the present age.

Naturally, she abhorred genocide, cruelty, and oppression. But ultimately she agreed that to a degree eradicating weak genetic make-up and implementing birth control by sterilization after two children per family was not altogether monstrous. It would keep human numbers down, therefore preserve forest and agricultural land instead of constant deforestation for the construction of more human habitat.

When she had looked at the land below during their flight to Aral, Nina had lamented all these things in her mind. The glorious landscapes, once full of life had shriveled and withered under the foot of man.

No, she did not condone the acts of the Third Reich, but its proficiency and order were undeniable. *'If only today there were people with such rigid discipline and singular aspiration wanting to change the world for the better,'* she sighed as she finished the last of her butt. *'Imagine a world in which someone like that didn't oppress people but stopped ruthless corporations. In which, instead of exterminating cultures, they would destroy media brainwashing, and we would all be better off. And there would be fucking lake to feed the people here now.'*

She flicked her cigarette butt into the fire. Her eyes caught Purdue's staring at her, but she pretended not to be fazed by his attention. Perhaps it was the dancing shadows of the fire that gave his gaunt face such a menacing look, but she did not like it.

"How will you know where to start looking?" Detlef asked. "I read that the Amber Room was destroyed during the war. Do these people expect you to magically make something re-appear that does not exist anymore?"

Purdue seemed agitated, but the others assumed it was due to his traumatic experience at the hands of Klaus Kemper. "It still exists, they say. And if we don't beat them to it they will undoubtedly get the upper hand for good."

"Why?" Nina asked. "What's so powerful about the Amber Room – if it even still exists?"

"I don't know, Nina. They did not go into the specifics, but they made it clear that it had undeniable power," Purdue rambled. "What it has or does, I have no idea. I just know that it is very dangerous – as things of perfect beauty usually are."

Sam could see that the phrase was directed at Nina, but Purdue's tone was not lovelorn or soppy. If he was not mistaken, it almost sounded antagonistic. Sam was wondering how Purdue really felt about Nina spending so much time with him, and it appeared to be a sore matter for the usually buoyant billionaire.

"Where was its last location?" Detlef asked Nina. "You are a historian. Do you know where the Nazis could have taken it if it was not destroyed?"

"I only know what's written in the history books, Detlef," she admitted, "but sometimes there are facts hidden in the details that give us clues."

"And what do your history books say?" he asked amicably, appearing to be quite interested in Nina's vocation.

She sighed and shrugged as she recalled the legend of the Amber Room as dictated by her textbooks. "The Amber Room was made in Prussia in the early 1700's, Detlef. It was fashioned from amber panels and gold inlays of leaves and carvings with mirrors behind them to make it look even more splendid when the light fell on it."

"Who did it belong to?" he asked, biting into a dry crust of home-baked bread.

"The then king, Frederick Wilhelm I, but he gave the Amber Room to the Russian Tsar Peter the Great as a gift. But here is the cool thing," she said. "While it belonged to the Tsar it was actually expanded several times! Imagine the value, even then!"

"By the Tsar?" Sam asked her.

"Aye. They say when he was done expanding the chamber it contained six tons of amber. So as always the Russians earned their reputation for their affinity for size." she laughed. "But then it was looted a Nazi unit during World War II."

"Of course," Detlef lamented.

"And where did they keep it?" Sam wanted to know. Nina shook her head.

"What was left was taken to then Königsberg to be restored, and it was subsequently put on display there. But… that is not the end of it," Nina continued, taking a glass of red wine from Sam. "There it was reputedly destroyed once and for all by Allied air attacks when the castle was bombed in 1944. Some records indicate that when the Third Reich fell in 1945, and the Red Army occupied Königsberg, the Nazis had already taken the remnants of the Amber Room and smuggled them onto a passenger liner in Gdynia to get it out of Königsberg."

"And where did it go?" Purdue asked with intense interest. He knew much of what Nina had relayed already, but only up to the part where the Amber Room had been razed by the Allied air strikes.

Nina shrugged. "Nobody knows. Some accounts tell that the ship was torpedoed by a Soviet submarine, and the Amber Room was lost at sea. But in truth nobody really knows."

"If you had to guess," Sam challenged her cordially, "according to what you know about the situation as a whole during the war. What do you think happened?"

Nina had her own theory of what she did and did not believe from the records. "I really don't know, Sam. I just don't believe the torpedo story. It sounds too much like a cover story to stop everyone from looking for it. But then again," she sighed, "I don't have any idea what could have happened. I'll be honest; I believe the Russians intercepted the Nazis, but not like that." She chuckled awkwardly and shrugged again.

Purdue's light blue eyes stared at the fire in front of him. He was considering the possible consequences of Nina's tale, along with what he learned about what had happened in the Bay of Gdansk at the same time. He snapped out of his frozen state.

"I think we should take that account on faith," he announced. "I suggest we start where the ship has supposedly sunk, just to have a starting point. Who knows, we might even find some clues there."

"You mean diving?" Detlef exclaimed.

"Correct," Purdue affirmed.

Detlef shook his head, "I don't dive. No, thank you!"

"Come now, old boy!" Sam smiled, lightly slapping Detlef on the back. "You can run into live fire, but you cannot take a swim with us?"

"I hate water," the German admitted. "I can swim. I just don't. Water makes me very uncomfortable."

"Why? Did you have a bad experience?" Nina asked.

"Not that I know of, but perhaps I made myself forget whatever made me despise swimming," he revealed.

"That doesn't matter," Purdue weighed in. "You can keep watch for us since there is no way we can get the necessary permits to dive there. Can we count on you for that?"

Detlef gave Purdue a long hard look that had Sam and Nina alarmed and ready to intervene, but he simply answered, "That, I can do."

It was shortly before midnight. They waited for their meat and fish on the grill to be done, and the soothing crackle of the fire lulled them into a sense of reprieve from their troubles.

"David, tell me about the business you had with Gabi Holtzer," Detlef insisted suddenly, finally bringing forth the inevitable.

Purdue frowned, perplexed by the strange request from

the stranger he had assumed to be a private security consultant. "What do you mean?" he asked the German.

"Detlef," Sam warned gently, advising the widower to keep his cool. "You remember the deal, right?"

Nina's heart jumped. She had been anxiously anticipating this all night. Detlef kept his cool as far as they could tell, but he repeated his question in a cold voice.

"I want you to tell me about your business with Gabi Holtzer at the British Consulate in Berlin the day she died," he said in a calm tone that was deeply unsettling.

"Why?" Purdue asked, infuriating Detlef with his apparent sidestepping.

"Dave, this is Detlef *Holtzer*," Sam said, hoping that the introduction would explain the German man's urging. "He is - no was - Gabi Holtzer's husband and he has been looking for you so you could tell him what happened that day." Sam deliberately formulated his words this way to remind Detlef that Purdue was entitled to the benefit of the doubt.

"I am so sorry for your loss!" Purdue replied almost instantly. "My God, it was awful!" It was evident that Purdue was not putting on a fake face. His eyes filled with tears as he relived those last moments before he had been abducted.

"The media says that she committed suicide," Detlef said. "I know my Gabi. She would never…"

Purdue stared at the widower with wide eyes. "She did not commit suicide, Detlef. She was killed right in front of me!"

"Who did it?" Detlef roared. He was emotional and unstable, being so close to the revelation he had been seeking all this time. "Who killed her?"

Purdue gave it some thought and looked at the distraught man. "I—I cannot remember."

CHAPTER 20

*A*fter two days of recuperation at the small house, the group took off toward the Polish coast. The matter between Purdue and Detlef felt unresolved, but they got along relatively well. Purdue owed Detlef more than just the revelation that Gabi's death had not been her own doing, especially since Detlef was still suspicious at Purdue's memory loss. Even Sam and Nina wondered if perhaps Purdue was unknowingly responsible for the diplomat's death, but they could not pass judgment on something they didn't know anything about.

Sam, for one, tried to get a better peek with his new ability to latch onto the minds of others, but he was unsuccessful. He secretly hoped that he had lost the unwelcome gift that had been bestowed on him.

They decided to follow their plan. The discovery of the Amber Room would not only thwart the efforts of the sinister Black Sun, but it would be quite beneficial financially. Still, the urgency of finding the magnificent chamber was a mystery to them all. There had to be more to the

Amber Room than riches or reputation. Of that, the Black Sun had enough of their own.

Nina had an old university colleague who was now married to a wealthy businessman residing in Warsaw.

"From one phone call, people," she bragged to the three men. "One! I have gotten us a free four-day stay in Gdynia and with it comes a reasonable fishing boat for our little not-so-legal investigation."

Sam playfully ruffled her hair. "You are a magnificent animal, Dr. Gould! Do they have whiskey?"

"I could kill for some Bourbon right now, I admit," Purdue smiled. "What is your poison, Mr. Holtzer?"

Detlef shrugged, "Anything that can be used in surgery."

"Good man! Sam, we have to get some of that, mate. Can you make that happen?" Purdue asked eagerly. "I will have my assistant transfer some money in a few minutes so we can get what we need. The boat – is it your friend's?" he asked Nina.

"It belongs to the old man we are staying with," she replied.

"Won't he be suspicious of what we are going to do there?" Sam worried.

"No. She says he is an old diver, fisherman, and marksman that moved to Gdynia right after the Second World War from Novosibirsk. Apparently, he never got any gold stars for good behavior," Nina laughed.

"Good! He will fit right in then," Purdue chuckled.

After buying some food and plenty of alcohol to present to their gracious host, the group drove to the location Nina had gotten from her former colleague. Detlef paid a visit to the local hardware store, and also purchased a small radio and some batteries for it. Such basic little radios were hard to get in more modern cities, but he found one next to the fish bait shop on the last street before they arrived at their temporary lodging.

The yard was carelessly fenced with barbed wire tied to rickety posts. Inside the fence, the yard consisted mostly of tall weeds and big neglected plants. From the creaky iron gate to the deck steps, the small walkway to the eerie little wooden cabin was overgrown with vines. The old man was awaiting them on the porch, looking almost exactly as Nina had imagined him. Big dark eyes contrasted with wild gray hair and a beard. He had a pot belly and a face riddled by scars that made him look scary, but he was friendly.

"Zdravstvuyte!" he called as they came through the gate.

"God, I hope he speaks English," Purdue muttered.

"Or German," Detlef concurred.

"Hello! We brought something for you" Nina smiled, holding out the bottle of vodka to him and the old man clapped his hands in glee.

"I see we will get along very well!" he shouted cheerfully.

"Are you Mr. Marinesko?" she asked.

"Kiril! Call me Kiril, please. And please, come in. I don't have big house or best food, but it is warm and comfortable," he apologized. After they had introduced themselves, he dished up some vegetable soup he had been preparing all afternoon.

"After the meal, I take you to see the boat, yes?" Kiril offered.

"Splendid!" Purdue replied. "I would love to see what you have in that boat house."

He served the soup with freshly baked bread that quickly became Sam's favorite. He helped himself to slice after slice. "Did your wife bake this?" he asked.

"No, I did. I am good baker, right?" Kiril laughed. "My wife taught me. She is dead now."

"So is mine," Detlef murmured. "Happened just recently."

"I'm sorry to hear that," Kiril sympathized. "I don't think our wives ever leave us. They stay to give us a hard time when we screw up."

Nina was relieved to see Detlef smile at Kiril, "I think so too!"

"You will need my boat to dive?" their host asked, changing the subject for his guest's sake. He knew the pain that could eat away a person when such a tragedy strikes, and it was not something he could talk about at length either.

"Yes, we want to do some diving, but it shouldn't take more than a day or two," Purdue informed him.

"In the Bay of Gdansk? Which area?" Kiril pried. It was his boat, and he was putting them up, so they couldn't deny him the details.

"In the area where the *Wilhelm Gustloff* sank in 1945," Purdue said.

Nina and Sam exchanged glances, hoping that the old man would not get suspicious. Detlef did not care who knew. All he wanted was to find out what role the Amber Room had played in his wife's death and what was so important to those strange Nazi people. Around the dinner table, a brief, tense silence ensued.

Kiril looked at them all, one after the other. His eyes pierced through their defenses and intentions as he scrutinized them with a smirk that could have meant anything. He cleared his throat.

"Why?"

The single word question unsettled them all. They had expected an elaborate attempt at dissuasion or some locally flavored reprimand, but the simplicity was almost impossible to fathom. Nina looked at Purdue and shrugged, "Tell him."

"We are looking for remnants of an artifact that was on board the ship," Purdue told Kiril, using as wide a description as possible.

"The Amber Room?" he laughed, spoon erect in his waving hand. "You too?"

"What do you mean?" Sam asked.

"Oh, my boy! So many people have been looking for that damned thing over the years, but they all back up disappointed!" he chuckled.

"So you are saying it doesn't exist?" Sam asked.

"Tell me, Mr. Purdue, Mr. Cleave and my other friends here," Kiril smiled, "what do you want with the Amber Room, huh? Money? Fame? Go home. Some beautiful things are just not worth the curse."

Purdue and Nina glanced at each other at the similarity of the phrasing between the old man's warning and Purdue's sentiment.

"Curse?" Nina queried.

"Why are you looking for it?" he asked again. "What is it you are after?"

"My wife was killed because of it," Detlef suddenly chipped in. "If whoever was after that treasure was ready to kill her for it, I want to see it myself." His eyes pinned Purdue.

Kiril frowned. "What did your wife have to do with it?"

"She was investigating the Berlin assassinations because she had reason to believe that the murders were committed by a secret organization looking for the Amber Room. But she was killed before she could complete her investigation," the widower filled Kiril in.

Wringing his hands, their host took a deep breath. "So you don't want it for money or fame, then. Good. Then I will tell you where the *Wilhelm Gustloff* went down, and you can look for yourself, but I hope you stop this nonsense then."

Without another word or explanation, he stood up and left the room.

"What the hell was that?" Sam probed. "He knows more than he wants to admit. He is hiding something."

"How do you know that?" Purdue asked.

Sam looked a little uncomfortable. "I just have a gut feeling." He shot Nina a glance before he rose from his seat to take his soup bowl to the kitchen. She knew what his glance meant. He must have found something in the old man's thoughts.

"Excuse me," she told Purdue and Detlef and followed Sam. He was standing in the doorway to the garden, watching Kiril venture out to the boat house to check the fuel. Nina placed her hand on his shoulder. "Sam?"

"Aye."

"What did you see?" she fished curiously.

"Nothing. He knows something very important, but that's just journalistic instinct. I swear, it has nothing to do with the new thing," he told her quietly. "I feel like just asking outright, but I don't want to push him, you know?"

"I know. That's why I am going to ask him," she said confidently.

"No! Nina! Get back here," he cried, but she was adamant. Knowing Nina, Sam was perfectly aware that he couldn't stop her now. Instead, he elected to go back inside to keep Detlef from killing Purdue. As he approached the dinner table, he could feel the tension, but Sam found Purdue looking at the pictures on Detlef's phone.

"Those were the number codes," Detlef explained. "Now look at this."

Both men squinted as Detlef zoomed in on the photo he had taken of the diary page where he found Purdue's name. "My God!" Purdue uttered in astonishment. "Sam, come see this."

Under Purdue and Carrington's meeting, a notation was made referring to a 'Kiril'.

"Am I just finding ghosts everywhere or could it all be one big web of conspiracy?" Detlef asked Sam.

"I could not tell you for sure, Detlef, but I also have a feeling he knows about the Amber Room," Sam shared his suspicions with them as well. "Things we are not supposed to know."

"Where is Nina?" Purdue asked.

"Chatting to the old boy. Just making friends, in case we need to know more," Sam put him at ease. "If he is the name on Gabi's diary we need to know why."

"I agree," Detlef concurred.

Nina and Kiril entered the kitchen, laughing about something silly he was telling her. Her three associates perked up to see if she got any more information, but to their disappointment, Nina shook her head furtively.

"That's it," Sam declared. "I am getting him drunk. We'll see how much he hides when he is off his tits."

"Feeding a Russian vodka won't make him drunk, Sam," Detlef smiled. "It will only make him happy and loud. What is the time now?"

"Almost 9 pm. Why, do you have a date?" Sam teased.

"Actually, I do," he replied proudly. "Her name is Milla."

Intrigued by Detlef's answer, Sam asked, "Want to make it a threesome?"

"Milla?" Kiril suddenly hollered, looking ashen. "How do you know Milla?"

CHAPTER 21

"You know Milla too?" Detlef gasped. "My wife was in contact with her almost daily, and after my wife had died, I found her radio room. That is where Milla spoke to me and told me how to find her with a shortwave radio."

Nina, Purdue, and Sam sat listening to all this, having no idea what was going on between Kiril and Detlef. While they listened, they poured some wine and vodka and waited.

"Who was your wife?" Kiril asked eagerly.

"Gabi Holtzer," Detlef replied, his voice still cracking when he said her name.

"Gabi! Gabi was my friend from Berlin!" the old man exclaimed. "She had been involved with us since her great grandfather left behind documents about Operation Hannibal! Oh God, how terrible! How sad, so wrong." The Russian lifted his bottle and shouted, "To Gabi! Daughter of Germany and defender of freedom!"

They all joined in and drank to the fallen heroine, but Detlef could hardly get the words out. His eyes welled up, and his chest ached with grief for his wife. Words could not describe how much he missed her, but his wet cheeks said it all. Even Kiril had bloodshot eyes at the tribute to a fallen ally. After a few consecutive shots of vodka and some of Purdue's Bourbon, the Russian was feeling nostalgic, telling Gabi's widower how his wife and the old Russian had become acquainted.

Nina felt a warm compassion for both men as she watched them share fond stories of a special woman they both knew and adored. It made her wonder if Purdue and Sam would sit celebrating her memory so fondly once she was gone.

"My friends," Kiril roared in sadness and inebriation, kicking out his chair as he stood up and slammed his hands down hard on the table, spilling Detlef's leftover soup, "I will tell you what you must know. You are," he slurred and stammered, "allies in the fires of liberation. We cannot let them use that bug to oppress our children or us!" He concluded this strange statement with a swirl of unintelligible Russian war cries that sounded positively wicked.

"Tell us," Purdue egged Kiril on with his glass raised. "Tell us how the Amber Room is a threat to our freedom. Should we destroy it or should we just eradicate those who want it for nefarious causes?"

"Leave it where it is!" Kiril shouted. "It cannot be reached by mere men! Those panels – we knew how evil they were. Our fathers told us! Oh yes! They told us early on how that evil beauty made them kill their brothers, their friends. They told us how Mother Russia almost bent to the will of the Nazi dogs, and we vowed never to let it be found!"

Sam was getting concerned for the Russian's mind as he seemed to mash up several stories into one. He concentrated on the tingling force that coursed through his brain, summoning it carefully, hoping that it would not take over as fiercely as it had before. With intent, he linked onto the old man's mind and formed the mental tether while the others were watching.

Suddenly Sam said: "Kiril, tell us about *Operation Hannibal.*"

Nina, Purdue, and Detlef turned to look at Sam in amazement. Sam's request instantly silenced the Russian. Not a moment after he had gone quiet he sat down and folded his hands. "Operation Hannibal was the evacuation of the German troops by sea to get away from the Red Army that would soon be there to kick their Nazi asses," the old man chuckled. "They got on the Wilhelm Gustloff right here in Gdynia and made for Kiel. They were told to load that goddamn Amber Room's panels, too. Well, what was left of it. But!" he shouted, his torso swaying slightly as he continued "But, they secretly loaded it onto the Gustloff's escort vessel, torpedo boat *Löwe*. Do you know why?"

The group sat spellbound, reacting only when asked to. "No, why?"

Kiril laughed jovially. "Because some of the 'Germans' at Gdynia harbor were Russians, as well as the crew of the torpedo escort boat! They dressed as Nazi soldiers and intercepted the Amber Room. But it gets even better!" He looked thrilled with every detail he spilled, while Sam held him on that cerebral leash for as long as he could. "Did you know that the Wilhelm Gustloff received a radio message while their idiot captain sailed them into open waters?"

"What did it say?" Nina asked.

"It told them that there was another German convoy approaching, so the Gustloff's captain switched on the ship's navigation lights to avoid any collisions," he recounted.

"And that would have made them visible to enemy vessels," Detlef deduced.

The old man pointed at the German and smiled. "Correct!

Soviet submarine *S-13* torpedoed the ship and sank it – without the Amber Room."

"How do you know this? You are not old enough to have been there, Kiril. Could it be you read some sensational story someone wrote," Purdue refuted. Nina scowled as she gave Purdue an unspoken reprimand for second-guessing the old man.

"I know all this, Mr. Purdue, because the captain of the S-13 was Captain Alexander Marinesko," Kiril boasted. "My father!"

Nina's jaw dropped.

A smile spread over her face for being in the presence of somebody who knew the secrets of the Amber Room's whereabouts first hand. It was a special moment for her, being in the physical company of history. But Kiril was far from done. "He would not have seen the ship so easily had it not been for that unexplained radio message telling the captain about an approaching German convoy, would he?"

"But who sent that message? Did they ever find out?" Detlef asked.

"No-one ever found out. The only people who knew were the men involved with the confidential plan," Kiril said. "Men like my father. That radio message came from friends of his, Mr. Holtzer, and friends of ours. That radio message was sent by Milla."

"That is impossible!" Detlef dismissed the revelation that had them all dumbstruck. "I spoke to Milla via radio the night I found my wife's radio room. There is no way someone that operated in the Second World War would still be alive, let alone broadcast this numbers radio station."

"You are right, Detlef, if Milla was a person," Kiril insisted. Now he kept spilling his secrets, much to the delight of Nina and her associates. But Sam was losing his hold on the Russian, growing fatigued from the enormous psychic effort.

"Then what is Milla?" Nina asked quickly, aware that Sam was about to lose his command over the old man, but Kiril passed out before he could reveal more, and without Sam keeping his brain under his spell, there was nothing keeping the drunk old man talking. Nina sighed in frustration, but Detlef was not perturbed by the old man's words. He was planning to listen to the broadcast later and hoped that it would shed some light on what danger was lurking in the Amber Room.

Sam took a few deep breaths to regain his focus and his energy, but Purdue locked eyes with him from across the table. It was a look of sheer mistrust, one that made Sam very uncomfortable. He did not want Purdue to know that he could manipulate people's minds. It would make him even more suspicious, and he didn't want that.

"Are you tired, Sam?" Purdue asked without hostility or suspicion.

"Fucking exhausted," he answered. "And the vodka doesn't help either."

"I am going to turn in, too," Detlef announced. "I suppose there will be no diving after all then? That would be great!"

"If we could wake our host, we could figure out what happened to the escort boat," Purdue chuckled. "But I think he is done for, at least for the rest of the night."

Detlef locked himself in his room at the far end of the hallway. It was the smallest of them all, adjacent to Nina's designated bedroom. Purdue and Sam were to share the other bedroom next to the living room, so Detlef was not going to disturb them.

He switched on the transistor radio and started slowly turning the dial, minding the frequency number under the moving needle. It was capable of FM, AM, and shortwave, but Detlef knew where to set it. Since the discovery of his wife's secret communication room, he had developed a fondness for the sound of the cracking swish of the empty airwaves. Somehow the sheer possibilities it presented soothed him. Subconsciously, it reassured him that he was not alone; that there were lots of life and many allies hidden in the vast ether of the upper atmosphere. It presented the potential for anything imaginable to exist if one was only inclined to reach out to it.

A knock on his door startled him. "Scheisse!" Reluctantly he put down the radio to answer the door. It was Nina.

"Sam and Purdue are drinking, and I cannot sleep," she whispered. "Can I listen to Milla's broadcast with you? I brought a pen and paper."

Detlef was elated. "Sure, come in. I was just trying to find the right station. There are so many that sound almost the same, but I'll recognize the music."

"There is music?" she asked. "They play songs?"

He nodded. "Just one, in the beginning. It must be some sort of a marker," he speculated. "I think the channel is used for different things, and when she broadcasts to people like Gabi, there is a specific song that notifies us that the numbers are for us."

"Jesus! A whole science," Nina marveled. "There is so much going on out there that the world is not even aware of! It is like a whole sub-universe full of clandestine operations and ulterior motives."

He looked at her with dark eyes, but his voice was tender. "Frightening, isn't it?"

"Aye," she agreed. "And lonely."

"Lonely, yes," Detlef repeated, sharing her sentiment. He looked at the pretty historian with longing and admiration. She was quite unlike Gabi. She looked nothing like Gabi, yet in her own way she felt familiar to him. Perhaps it was because they were of the same mind about the world or maybe just because their souls were alone together. Nina got a bit uncomfortable at his forlorn stare, but she was saved by the sudden crackling over the speaker that made him jump.

"Listen, Nina!" he whispered. "It is starting."

The music began to play, tucked far away into the nothingness out there, smothered by static and whistling modulation fluctuations. Nina scoffed in amusement at the melody she recognized.

"Metallica? Really?" she shook her head.

Detlef was happy to hear that she knew it. "Yes! What does it have to do with the numbers, though? I have been racking my brain to figure out why they chose this song."

Nina smiled. "The song is called 'Sweet Amber', Detlef."

"Ah!" he exclaimed. "Now it makes sense!"

While they were still chuckling about the song, Milla's broadcast began.

'Median 85-45-98-12-74-55-68-16...'

Nina jotted everything down.

'Geneva 48-66-27-99-67-39...'

'Jehovah 30-59-69-21-23...'

'Widower...'

"Widower! That's me! That's for me!" he whispered loudly in excitement.

Nina took down the numbers that followed. *'87-46-88-37-68...'*

When the first 20-minute broadcast was done, and the music ended the segment, Nina gave Detlef the numbers she had written down. "Do you have any idea what to make of these?"

"I don't know what they are or how they work. I just write them down and keep them. We used them to find the location of the compound where Purdue was held, remember? But I still have no idea what it all means" he complained.

"We have to use Purdue's machine. I brought it. It's in my suitcase," Nina said. "If this message is specifically for you, we have to decipher it right away."

"his is fucking unbelievable!" Nina raved in awe at what she had discovered. The men had gone out on the boat with Kiril, and she had stayed at the house to do some research, as she had told them. In truth, Nina was busy deciphering the numbers Detlef had received from Milla the night before. There was some concern in the historian's gut that Milla knew where Detlef was well enough to present him with valuable and pertinent information, but so far it had served them well.

It had been half a day before the men returned with some cock-and-bull fishing stories, but they all felt the urge to carry on with their journey as soon as they had something to go on. Sam had been unable make another connection to the old man's mind, but he didn't tell Nina that the strange ability had begun escaping him lately.

"What did you discover?" Sam asked, taking off his spray-soaked sweater and hat. Detlef and Purdue entered behind him, looking exhausted. Kiril had made them earn their keep today by helping him with the nets and engine work, but they had had fun listening to his entertaining stories. Unfortunately though, none of those stories involved historical secrets. He had told them to head home while he delivered his catch to a local market a few miles from the docks.

"You are not going to believe this!" she smiled, hovering over her laptop. "The numbers station broadcast Detlef and I have been listening to has given us with something unique. I don't know how they do it, and I don't care," she continued as they gathered around her, "but they have managed to turn a soundtrack into numerical codes!"

"What do you mean?" Purdue asked, impressed that she brought his Enigma machine with her in case they needed it. "It is a simple conversion. Like encryption? Like data from an mp3 file, Nina," he smiled. "It is nothing new to use data to convert coding into sound."

"But numbers? Proper numbers, nothing else. No codes and gibberish like what you do when you write software," she contested. "Look, I'm a complete layman when it comes to technology, but I have never heard of sequential double-digit numbers making up a sound clip."

"Me neither," Sam admitted. "But then again I am also not exactly a geek."

"That is all great, but I think the most important part here is what the sound clip says," Detlef suggested.

"It is a radio broadcast that was sent out over Russian airwaves; I'm guessing. On the clip, you will hear a broadcaster interview a man, but I don't speak Russ…" she frowned. "Where is Kiril?"

"On his way," Purdue said reassuringly. "I suppose we're going to need him to translate."

"Aye, the interview carries on for almost 15 minutes before it is interrupted by this squeak that almost burst my eardrums," she said. "Detlef, Milla wanted you to hear this for some reason. We have to keep that in mind. This might be pivotal to the location of the Amber Room."

"That loud squeak," Kiril suddenly muttered as he entered the front door with two bags and a bottle of liquor clutched under his arm, "is military interference."

"Just the man we want to see," Purdue smiled, coming to help the old Russian with the bags. "Nina has a radio broadcast in Russian. Will you be so kind to translate it for us?"

"Of course! Of course," Kiril chuckled. "Let me have a listen. Oh, and pour me a drink there, please."

While Purdue obliged, Nina played the audio clip on her laptop. By the bad quality in recording, it sounded much like an old broadcast. She could discern two male voices. One asked questions, and the other gave lengthy answers. Crackling interference persisted over the recording and the voices of the two men faded now and then, only to come back louder than before.

"This is not an interview, my friends," Kiril told the group within the first minute of listening. "It is an interrogation."

Nina's heart skipped a beat. "Is it authentic?"

Sam motioned from behind Kiril for Nina not to speak, to wait. Intently the old man listened to every word, his face falling into a dark scowl. Occasionally he would shake his head very slowly, looking somber at what he had heard. Purdue, Nina, and Sam were dying to know what the men were saying.

Waiting for Kiril to finish listening had them all on tenterhooks, but they had to keep quiet so he could hear over the hissing of the recording.

"Watch out for the squeal, guys," Nina warned when she saw the timer nearing the end of the clip. They all braced themselves for it, and rightly so. It split the atmosphere with a high pitched wail that persisted for several seconds. Kiril's body jerked from the sound. He turned to look at the group.

"There is a gunshot in there. Did you hear it?" he said casually.

"No. When?" Nina asked.

"In that god awful noise, there is a man's name and a gunshot. I have no idea if the squeal was supposed to mask the shot or if it was just a coincidence, but there is definitely a gun shot," he revealed.

"Wow, good ears," Purdue said. "None of us even heard that."

"Not good ears, Mr. Purdue. Trained ears. My ears have been trained to listen to hidden sounds and messages, thanks to years of radio work," Kiril bragged, smiling and pointing at his ear.

"But a gunshot should have been loud enough to detect under that, even for untrained ears," Purdue supposed. "Then again, it depends on what the conversation is about. That should tell us if it's even relevant."

"Aye, please tell us what they said, Kiril," Sam implored.

Kiril emptied his glass and cleared his throat. "It is an interrogation between a Red Army official and a *Gulag* inmate, so that must have been recorded just after the fall of the Third Reich. I hear a man's name shouted outside before the shot."

"Gulag?" Detlef asked.

"Prisoners of war. Soviets captured by Wehrmacht were ordered by Stalin to commit suicide when captured. Those who did not kill themselves - like the man interrogated in your clip - were considered traitors by the Red Army," he explained.

"So kill yourself or your own army will?" Sam clarified. "Can't catch a bloody break, these lads."

"Exactly," Kiril agreed. "No surrender. This man, the interrogator, he is a commander, and the Gulag is from 4th Ukrainian Front they say. Now, in this conversation the

Ukrainian soldier is one of three men who survived...," Kiril did not know the word, but he gestured with his hands, "...*unexplained* drowning at coast of Latvia. He says they intercepted the treasure that was supposed to be taken by the Nazi Kriegsmarine."

"The treasure. The Amber Room panels, I presume," Purdue added.

"Must be. He says that the plates, the panels, were crumbling?" Kiril struggled with his English.

"Brittle," Nina smiled. "I remember they said that the original panels had become brittle from age by 1944 when they had to be removed by Heeresgruppe Nord."

"Da," Kiril winked. "He is telling about how they cheated the *crew of the Wilhelm Gustloff* and made away with the amber panels to make sure the Germans would not take those panels with them. But he says during the trip to Latvia, where their mobile units waited to pick them up, something went very wrong. The crumbling amber set free something that went into their heads – no, captain's head."

"Excuse me?" Purdue perked up. "What went into his head? Does he say?"

"It may not make sense to you, but he says something was in the amber, trapped there for centuries and more centuries. An insect, I think, is what he says. It went into the captain's ear. None of them could see it again, because it was very, very small, like a gnat bug," Kiril relayed the soldier's account.

"Jesus," Sam mumbled.

"The man says when the captain made his eyes white all the men did terrible things?"

Kiril frowned, thinking over his words. Then he nodded, satisfied his account of the soldier's bizarre statements was correct. Nina looked at Sam. He looked stunned, but he said nothing.

"Does he say what they did?" Nina asked.

"They all started to think like one man. They had one brain, he says. When the captain told them to drown themselves, they all walked onto the ship's deck, and without looking worried about it, they jumped into the water and drowned just off the coast," the old Russian declared.

"Mind control," Sam affirmed. "That is why Hitler wanted the Amber Room to be taken back to Germany during Operation Hannibal. With that kind of mind control, he would have been able to subjugate the world without much effort!"

"How did he know that, though?" Detlef wanted to know.

"How do you think the Third Reich managed to turn tens of thousands of normal, morally sound German men and women into uniformly thinking Nazi soldiers?" Nina challenged. "Haven't you ever wondered how those soldiers were so innately evil and irrefutably cruel when they wore those uniforms?" Her words echoed in the silent contemplation of her companions. "Think about the atrocities committed on even small children, Detlef. Thousands upon thousands of Nazis were of the same mind, the same level of cruelty, unquestioning of their despicable orders like brainwashed zombies. I bet Hitler and Himmler discovered this ancient organism during one of Himmler's experiments."

The men agreed, looking shocked at the new development.

"That makes a lot of sense," Detlef said, rubbing his chin, thinking about the moral corruption of Nazi soldiers.

"We always thought they were brainwashed through propaganda," Kiril told his guests, "but there was too much discipline. That level of unity is not natural. Why do you think I called the Amber Room a curse last night?"

"Wait," Nina scowled, "you *knew* about this?"

Kiril returned her reproachful look with a glare. "Da! What

do you think we have been doing all these years with our numbers stations? We are all over the world, sending out codes to warn our allies, to share intelligence on anyone who might try to use them on people. We know about the bugs that were trapped in the amber because another Nazi bastard used it on my father and his company a year after the Gustloff disaster."

"That is why you wanted to dissuade us from looking for it," Purdue stated. "Now I understand."

"So, is that all the soldier told the interrogator?" Sam asked the old man.

"He is asked how come he survived the captain's order and then he replies that the captain could not come near him, so he never heard the command," Kiril explained.

"Why couldn't he come near him?" Purdue inquired, taking notes of the facts on a small notepad.

"He does not say. Just that the captain could not be in the same room as him. Maybe this is why he gets shot before the session is over, perhaps by the man's name they shout. They think he is hiding information, so they kill him," Kiril shrugged. "I think maybe it was the radiation."

"The radiation of what? As far as I know there was no nuclear activity in Russia back then," Nina said as she poured Kiril another vodka and herself some wine. "Can I smoke in here?"

"Of course," he smiled. Then he answered her question. "*First Lightning*. You see, the first atomic bomb was detonated in the Kazakh Steppe in 1949, but what nobody will tell you is that nuclear experiments have been going on since the late 1930's. I imagine this Ukrainian soldier lived in Kazakhstan before he was drafted into the Red Army, but," he shrugged indifferently, "I can be mistaken."

"What name do they shout in the background before the soldier is killed?" Purdue asked out of the blue. It had just occurred to him that the identity of the shooter was still a mystery.

"Oh!" Kiril chuckled. "Yes, you can hear someone shout as if they try to stop him." He softly imitated the shout. "*Kemper!*"

CHAPTER 23

*P*urdue felt a twinge of terror claw at his insides at the sound of the name. He could not help it. "Excuse me," he apologized and darted for the toilet. Falling to his knees, Purdue disgorged the content of his stomach. It perplexed him. He had by no means been nauseous before Kiril had mentioned the familiar name, but now his entire body was shaking from the menacing sound.

While the others jested about Purdue's ability for holding his drink, he was suffering from a dreadful sickness in his stomach to a point where he fell into a new depression. Perspiring and plagued by fever, he clutched the toilet for the next imminent purge.

"Kiril, can you tell me about this?" Detlef asked. "I found it in Gabi's communications room with all her intel on the Amber Room." He stood up and unbuttoned his shirt, revealing the medal pinned to his vest. He removed it and passed it to Kiril, who looked impressed.

"Bloody hell, what is that?" Nina smiled.

"This is a special medal that was given to soldiers who took part in the liberation of Prague, my friend," Kiril said nostalgically. "You got this from Gabi's things? Looks like she knew a lot about the Amber Room and the Prague Offensive. It is a remarkable coincidence, hey?"

"What is?"

"The soldier who gets shot in this audio clip was part of the Prague Offensive, where this medal comes from," he explained excitedly. "Because the unit he was with, the 4th Ukrainian Front was involved in the operation to liberate Prague from the Nazi occupation."

"For all we know it could come from that very soldier," Sam speculated.

"That would be unnerving and awesome at the same time," Detlef admitted with an accomplished grin. "It has no name on it, or does it?"

"No, sorry," their host said. "It would have been interesting though if Gabi got the medal from this soldier's descendent while she was investigating the disappearance of the Amber Room." He smiled sadly, remembering her fondly.

"You called her a freedom fighter," Nina remarked absentmindedly, propping her head up on her fist. "That's a good description of someone trying to expose an organization attempting to subjugate the whole world."

"Exactly, Nina," he replied.

Sam went to see what was ailing Purdue.

"Hey, old cock. Are you alright?" he asked, looking down at Purdue's kneeling frame. There was no answer and no sound of sickness coming from the man hunched over the toilet bowl. "Purdue?" Sam stepped forward and pulled Purdue back by his shoulder only to find him limp and unresponsive. At first, Sam figured that his friend had knocked himself out when he passed out, but when Sam checked his vitals, he found that Purdue was in severe shock.

Trying to wake him, Sam kept calling his name, but Purdue was unresponsive in his arms. "Purdue," Sam beckoned firm and loud and felt the tingling in the back of his mind. Suddenly energy flowed, and he felt recharged. "Purdue, wake up," Sam commanded, forming a tether with Purdue's mind but he failed to rouse him. He attempted it three times, each time increasing concentration and intent, but to no avail. "I don't understand it. It should work when it feels like this!"

"Detlef!" Sam called. "Can you help me here, please?"

The tall German came racing down the hallway to where he heard Sam yelling.

"Help me get him to bed," Sam groaned as he tried to lift Purdue to his feet. With Detlef's help, they got Purdue into bed and gathered to figure out what was wrong with him.

"This is strange," Nina said. "He wasn't drunk. He didn't look sick or anything. What happened?"

"Just puked his guts out," Sam shrugged. "But I could not wake him up at all," he told Nina, indicating that he even employed his new ability, "no matter what I tried."

"That is reason for concern," she acknowledged his message.

"He is burning up. Looks like food poisoning," Detlef hypothesized only to be dealt a nasty look from their host. "I'm sorry, Kiril. I don't mean to insult your cooking. But his symptoms look like that."

Checking on Purdue every hour and trying to wake him yielded no results. They were baffled by this sudden onset of fever and nausea that he suffered.

"I think it might be late complications resulting from something that happened to him at that snake pit where they tortured him," Nina whispered to Sam while they sat on Purdue's bed. "We don't know what they have done to him. What if they injected him with some toxin or God forbid – a deadly virus?"

"They did not know he was going to escape," Sam replied.

"Why would they have kept him in the infirmary if they meant to make him sick?"

"Maybe to infect us when we rescue him?" she whispered urgently, her big brown eyes fraught with panic. "They are an insidious bunch of tools, Sam. Would you be surprised?"

Sam agreed. There was nothing he would have put past those people. The Black Sun had near unlimited capacity to cause damage and the necessary malevolent intellect to initiate it.

Detlef was in his room, gathering information from Milla's numbers station. The female voice read the numbers monotonously, muffled by the bad reception behind Detlef's bedroom door down the hall from Sam and Nina. Kiril had to close up his shed and pull in his car before starting dinner. Tomorrow his guests would leave, but he was yet to convince them not to continue their search for the Amber Room. Ultimately he could do nothing if they, like so many others, insisted on seeking out the remnants of the deadly marvel.

After wiping Purdue's forehead with a wet washcloth to alleviate his still rising temperature, Nina went to see Detlef while Sam took a shower. She knocked softly.

"Come in, Nina," Detlef answered.

"How did you know it was me?" she asked with an amused smile.

"Nobody finds this as interesting as you do, besides me, of course," he said. "Tonight I got a message from the man on the station. He told me that we would die if we keep looking for the Amber Room, Nina."

"Are you sure you got the numbers right?" she asked.

"No, not numbers. Look." He showed her his cell phone. An untraceable number sent a text with a station reference. "I tuned the radio to that station, and he told me to quit - in plain English."

"He threatened you?" she frowned. "Are you sure it is not someone else fucking with you?"

"How would he send me a text with the frequency of the station and then talk to me there?" he countered.

"No, that is not what I mean. How do you know it is from Milla? There are many of these stations scattered all over the world, Detlef. Be careful who you communicate with," she warned.

"You are right. I did not even think about that," he admitted. "I have been so desperate to hold on to things Gabi loved, the things she was passionate about, you know? It has made me blind to danger and sometimes…I don't care."

"Well, you have to care, Widower. The world depends on you," Nina winked with a reassuring pat on his arm.

Detlef felt a renewed sense of purpose at her words. "I like that," he grinned.

"What?" Nina asked.

"That name – *Widower*. It sounds like a superhero, don't you think?" he boasted.

"I think it is pretty cool, actually, even though it is a word that denotes a sad state. It refers to something heartbreaking," she said.

"That is true," he nodded, "but that's who I am now, you know? Widower means that I am still Gabi's husband, you see?"

Nina loved the way Detlef saw things. Through all the hell of his loss, he still managed to take his sad moniker and turn it into an ode. "That is very cool, Widower."

"Oh, by the way, these are the numbers from the actual station, from Milla today," he pointed out, giving Nina the sheet of paper. "You decipher it. I am terrible at anything without a trigger or a pull pin."

"Alright, but I think you should get rid of your phone," Nina advised. "If they have your number they can track us, and I get a very foreboding vibe from that text you received. Let's not lead them to us, okay? I don't want to wake up dead."

"You know people like these can find us without tracking our phones, right?" he retorted, getting a firm look from the pretty historian. "Alright. I'll dump it."

"So we have someone threatening us via text messages now?" Purdue said, leaning casually against the doorway.

"Purdue!" Nina cried and lunged forward to throw her arms around him with delight. "I'm so glad you're awake. What happened?"

"You really should get rid of your phone, Detlef. The people who killed your wife might be the ones who contacted you," he told the widower. Nina felt a little neglected by his seriousness. She promptly withdrew. *'Suit yourself.'*

"Who are *those people*, by the way?" Detlef sneered. Purdue was not his friend. He did not like being dictated to by someone he suspected of murdering his wife. He still did not have a real answer to the question who killed his wife, so as far as he was concerned, they were only getting along for Nina and Sam's sake – for now.

"Where is Sam?" Nina asked, breaking up the looming cock fight.

"In the shower," Purdue said indifferently. Nina didn't like his attitude, but she was used to being in the middle of testosterone-driven pissing contests, even though that didn't mean she liked it. "Must be his longest shower ever," she scoffed, pushing past Purdue to get into the corridor. She went into the kitchen to make coffee to defuse the brooding atmosphere. "Are you clean yet, Sam?" she teased as she passed the bathroom where she heard the water clattering on the tiles. "Going to cost the old man all his hot water." Nina intended to decipher the latest codes while savoring the coffee she had been craving for over an hour.

"Jesus Christ!" she screamed suddenly. She stumbled back against the wall and covered her mouth at the sight. Her knees buckled as she collapsed slowly. Her eyes were frozen, just staring at the old Russian who sat in his favorite chair. Before him on the table sat his full tumbler of vodka waiting while next to it rested his blood stained hand, still gripping the shard of a broken mirror he had slit his own throat with.

Purdue and Detlef came rushing out, ready to fight. They faced the horrific scene and stood stunned until Sam joined them from the bathroom.

As the shock set in, Nina started to shake profusely, sobbing at the heinous incident that must have taken place while she had been in Detlef's room. Sam, only wearing a towel, approached the old man curiously. He scrutinized the position of Kiril's hand and the direction of the gash across his upper throat. The circumstances were consistent with suicide; he had to accept that. He looked at the other two men. There was no suspicion in his gaze, but there was a dark warning there that provoked Nina to distract him.

"Sam, once you are dressed, would you help me clean him up?" she asked, sniffing as she got to her feet.

"Aye."

CHAPTER 24

*A*fter they had taken care of Kiril's body and wrapped it in sheets on his bed, the atmosphere in the house was thick with tension and grief. Nina sat at the table, still sporadically shedding tears over the death of the sweet old Russian. In front of her, she had Purdue's machine and her laptop, deciphering Detlef's number sequences slowly and without enthusiasm. Her coffee was cold, and even her pack of smokes was untouched.

Purdue joined her und gently pulled her in a sympathetic embrace. "I'm so sorry, love. I know you adored the old man." Nina said nothing. Purdue affectionately pressed his cheek against hers, and all she could think of was how quickly his temperature had returned to normal. Under the shelter of her hair, he whispered, "Be wary of that German, please, love. He seems to be a damn good actor, but he is German. Catch my drift?"

Nina gasped. Her eyes found Purdue's as he frown silently demanded an explanation. He sighed and looked around to make sure they were alone.

"He is adamant to keep his cell phone. You know nothing about him, other than his involvement with the Berlin assassinations investigation. For all we know he could be the kingpin. He could have been the one who killed his wife when he realized that she was playing for the opposing side," he stated his case softly.

"Did you see him killing her? At the embassy? Are you even listening to yourself?" she asked in a tone full of resentment. "He helped save you, Purdue. If it weren't for him, Sam and I would never have known you were missing. If it weren't for Detlef, we would never have known where to find the Black Sun's Kazakh shit hole to rescue you."

Purdue smiled. His expression conveyed his victory. "Exactly my point, my dearest. This is a trap. Don't just follow his every direction. How do you know he was not leading you and Sam to me? Maybe you were supposed to find me; supposed to get me out. All part of the grand plan?"

Nina did not want to believe it. Here she was preaching for Detlef not to be blind to danger out of nostalgia, but she was doing precisely the same thing! There was no doubt that Purdue had a valid point, but she could not process the possible betrayal just yet.

"The Black Sun is predominantly German," Purdue continued to whisper while checking the hallway. "They have people everywhere. And who do they want to wipe off the planet most of all? Me, you and Sam. What better way to get us all together to chase an elusive treasure than to insert a double agent, a Black Sun operative, to play the victim? A victim with all the answers is more like… a villain."

"Have you managed to decode the information, Nina?" Detlef asked as he came in from outside, dusting off his shirt.

Purdue gave her an intense look as he stroked her hair one last time before going into the kitchen to get a drink.

Nina had to keep her cool and play along until she could somehow figure out if Detlef was playing for the wrong team. "Almost done," she told him, hiding any doubt she was harboring. "I just hope we get enough information to find anything useful. What if this message is not about the location of the Amber Room?"

"Don't worry. If that is the case, we will attack the Order head-on. To hell with the Amber Room," he said. He made a point of staying away from Purdue, at least avoiding being alone with him. The two did not get along anymore. Sam was distant and spent most of the time alone in his room, leaving Nina feeling utterly alone.

"We will have to leave soon," Nina suggested loudly for everyone to hear. "I am going to decipher this broadcast and then we have to be on our way before somebody finds us. We will call the local authorities regarding Kiril's body as soon as we are far enough from here."

"I agree," Purdue tossed in his vote from the door where he was watching the sun die. "The sooner we get to the Amber Room the better."

"Provided we get the right information," Nina added as she wrote down the next line.

"Where is Sam?" Purdue asked.

"He went to his room after we cleaned up Kiril's mess," Detlef answered.

Purdue wanted to talk to Sam about his suspicions. As long as Nina could keep Detlef occupied, he could warn Sam as well. He knocked on the door, but there was no answer. Purdue knocked louder to wake Sam in case he was sleeping. "Master Cleave! This is no time to snooze. We have to pack up soon!"

"Got it," Nina exclaimed. Detlef came to join her at the table, eager to know what Milla had to say.

"What does she say?" he asked, falling into the chair next to Nina.

"This looks like coordinates, maybe? See?" she suggested, shifting the paper to him. While he looked at it, Nina wondered what he would if he noticed that she had written down a fake message just to see if he already knew every move. She had fabricated the message, waiting for him to doubt her work. Then she would know if he was steering the group with his number sequences.

"Sam is gone!" Purdue shouted.

"Can't be!" Nina shouted back, waiting for Detlef's response.

"No, he is really gone," Purdue wheezed after searching the entire house. "I have looked everywhere. I even checked outside. Sam is gone."

Detlef's cell phone rang.

"Put it on speaker, champ," Purdue insisted. With a vindictive leer, Detlef obliged.

"Holtzer," he answered.

They could hear the phone being passed on to someone while men were talking in the background. Nina was disappointed that she could not finish her little test for the German.

The true message from Milla she had deciphered did not yield just numbers or coordinates. It was far more disturbing. While she was listening to the phone call, she was hiding the paper with the original message in her slender fingers. It read, 'Teufel ist gekommen' first, followed by 'shelter object' and 'contact compulsory'. The last part simply said 'Pripyat, 1955'.

Through the speaker of the phone they heard a familiar voice, confirming their worst fears.

"Nina, ignore what they say! I can survive this!"

"Sam!" she shrieked.

They heard scuffling, as his captors physically disciplined Sam for his audacity. In the background, a man told Sam to say what he had been told.

"The Amber Room is in the Sarcophagus," Sam stammered, spitting out the blood of the blow he had just received. "You have 48 hours to retrieve it or they kill the German Chancellor. And…and," he panted "take control of the EU."

"Who? Sam, who?" Detlef asked quickly.

"It is no mystery *who*, my friend," Nina told him outright.

"Who do we deliver it to?" Purdue jumped in. "Where and when?"

"You will receive instructions at a later time," a man said. "The German knows where to listen for it."

The call ended abruptly. "Oh my God," Nina moaned through her hands as she buried her face in her palms. "You were right, Purdue. Milla is behind it all."

They looked at Detlef.

"You think *I* am responsible for this?" he defended. "Are you out of your minds?"

"You are the one who has given us all the directions so far, Mr. Holtzer - from Milla's broadcasts no less. The Black Sun is going to send our instructions through the same channel. Do the fucking math!" Nina shouted, restrained by Purdue not to attack the large German.

"I knew nothing about this! I swear! I was looking for Purdue to get an explanation how my wife died, for Christ's sake! My mission was just to find my wife's killer, not this! And he is standing right there, Liebchen, right there with you. You are covering for him, still, after all this time, and all along you *knew* he killed Gabi," Detlef shouted furiously. His face had turned red, and his lips quivered in rage as he drew his Glock on them, opening fire.

Purdue grabbed Nina and pulled her to the floor with him. "To the bathroom, Nina! Go! Go!"

"If you say I told you so I swear I'll kill you!" she yelled at him as he pushed her forward, barely dodging the well-placed slugs.

"I won't, I promise. Just move! He is right on us!" Purdue pleaded as they slithered over the threshold of the bathroom. Detlef shadow, massive against the corridor wall, swiftly moved closer to them. They slammed the bathroom door shut and locked it just as another shot rang out, chiming against the steel door frame.

"Jesus, he is going to kill us," Nina wheezed as she checked the medicine cabinet for anything sharp she could use when Detlef would inevitably crash through the door. She found a pair of steel scissors and slipped them into her back pocket.

"Try the window," Purdue suggested, wiping his brow.

"What is wrong?" she asked. Purdue looked sick again, sweating profusely and clutching at the handle of the bath tub. "Oh God, not again."

"That voice, Nina. The man on the phone. I think I recognized him. His name is Kemper. When they said the name on your recording, I felt the same way I do now. And when I heard that man's voice on Sam's call, this horrible nausea hit me again," he confessed through ragged breaths.

"You think these spells are caused by someone's voice?" she asked hurriedly as she pressed her cheek flat on the floor to see under the door.

"I'm not sure, but I think so," Purdue answered, fighting the overwhelming embrace of oblivion.

"There is someone in front of the door," she whispered. "Purdue, you have to stay awake. He is at the door. We have to go through the window. Do you think you can manage?"

He shook his head. "I'm too exhausted," he huffed. "You have to g-get...uh, out..."

Purdue spoke incoherently as he stumbled toward the toilet with outstretched hands.

"I am not leaving you here!" she protested. Purdue vomited until he was too weak to sit up. It was suspiciously quiet in front of the door. Nina guessed that the psychotic German would be patiently waiting for them to exit so he could shoot them. He was still in front of the door, so she opened the taps in the bath to mask their movements. She opened the faucets all the way and then carefully opened the window. Patiently Nina unscrewed the burglar bars with the blade of the scissors, one by one, until she could remove the contraption. It was heavy. Nina groaned as she twisted her torso to put it down, but found Purdue's hands raised to help her. He put the bars down, looking like his old self again. She was absolutely taken aback by these strange spells that made him terribly sick only to release him shortly after.

"Feeling better?" she asked. He nodded with relief, but Nina could see that the constant attacks of fever and vomiting were rapidly dehydrating him. His eyes looked weary, and his face was pallid, but he acted and spoke as he always did. Purdue helped Nina through the window, and she jumped onto the grass outside. His tall body arched awkwardly through the rather narrow opening before he leaped down beside her.

Suddenly, Detlef's shadow fell over them.

When Nina looked up at the giant threat, her heart nearly stopped. Without a thought, she jumped up and stabbed him in the groin with the scissors. Purdue knocked the Glock from his hand and claimed it, but the slide was locked back, indicating an empty magazine. The big man had Nina in his grip, laughing at Purdue's failed attempt to shoot him. Nina pulled the scissors out and stabbed him again. Detlef's eye burst as she shoved the closed blades into his eye socket.

"Come Nina!" Purdue shouted, discarding the useless weapon. "Before he gets up. He is still moving!"

"Yeah?" she sneered. "I can change that!"

But Purdue pulled her away, and they fled in the direction of town, leaving behind their belongings.

CHAPTER 25

Sam stumbled behind the tyrant with the scrawny frame. From a laceration right below his right eyebrow, blood was trickling down his face and stained his shirt. The thugs were holding him by his arms, dragging him along to the large boat that was bobbing on the Gdynia bay water.

"Mr. Cleave, I expect you to comply with our every command or else your friends will be blamed for the death of the German Chancellor," his captor informed him.

"You've got nothing to pin on them!" Sam contested. "Besides, if they play into your hand we are all going to end up dead anyway. We know how sick the Order's objectives are."

"And here I thought you knew the extent of the Order's genius and capabilities. How silly of me. Please, don't force me to make an example of your associates to show you how serious we are," Klaus snapped snidely. He turned to his men. "Get him on board. We have to go."

Sam decided to bide his time before trying to summon his new skills. He wanted to get some rest first to make sure it would not fail him again. They roughly dragged him over the jetty and pushed him onto the unsteady vessel.

"Bring him!" one of the men ordered.

"I shall see you when we reach the destination, Mr. Cleave," Klaus said genially.

'Oh God, here I am on a fucking Nazi ship again!' Sam bemoaned his fate, but his mood was hardly docile. *'This time, I am going to rip their brains apart and make them kill each other.'* Oddly he felt stronger in his ability when his emotions were negative. The darker his thoughts became the more powerful the tingling in his brain felt. *'It is still there,'* he smiled.

He had grown used to the sensation of the parasite. Knowing that it was nothing but an insect from the youthful days of earth made no difference to Sam. It gave him an immense power of mind, probably hotwiring some abilities long forgotten or yet to be developed in a distant future. Perhaps, he thought, it was an organism specifically conditioned to kill, much like the instincts of a predator. Maybe it diverted energy from certain lobes of the modern brain, rerouting it to primal psychic instincts; and since those instincts served survival, they were not out to torment but to subdue and kill.

Before shoving the battered journalist into the cabin, they had reserved for their captive, the two men who handled Sam stripped him naked. Unlike Dave Purdue, Sam did not struggle. Instead, he spent the time inside his mind, locking out everything they did. The two German gorillas stripping him was odd, and from what little German he understood, they were taking bets on how long it would take the Scottish runt to break.

"The silence is usually the denial portion of the descent," the bald one smiled as he pulled Sam's briefs down to his ankles.

"My girlfriend does that just before she throws a fit," the

scrawny one remarked. "100 euros that he'll cry like a bitch by tomorrow."

The bald thug gave Sam a stare of intense scrutiny, standing uncomfortably close to him. "You're on. I say he tries to escape before we make it to Latvia."

The two men chuckled as they left their prisoner naked, tattered, and seething behind the mask of his straight face. When they closed the door, Sam remained motionless for a while longer. He did not know why. He simply did not feel like moving, although his mindset was not at all in chaos. Inside he felt strong, capable and powerful, but he stood still right there to just take in the situation. The first movement was that of his eyes alone, studying the room where they had left him.

Around him, the cabin was far from accommodating, as he would have expected from cold and calculating masters. Cream colored steel walls met in four bolted corners with the floor cold and bare under his feet. There was no bed, no toilet facilities, and no window. Only the door, bolted around its edges in a similar fashion as the walls. There was but one lonely bulb weakly illuminating the miserable room, leaving him with little sensory stimulus.

Sam did not mind the deliberate lack of distraction, because what was intended to be a torture method courtesy of Kemper was a welcome blankness for his hostage to engage into fully focusing on his mental abilities. The steel was frigid, lending Sam the choice of standing all night of getting his buttocks frozen. He sat down without much consideration for his quandary, hardly impressed by the sudden coldness.

"Fuck it," he said to himself. "I'm Scottish, you imbeciles. What do you think we endure under our kilts on an average day?" The chill under his genitals was certainly not pleasant but it was bearable, and that was what was needed here. Sam wished there was a switch to turn off the light above him. The light was disturbing his meditation. As the boat rocked under him, he closed his eyes, trying to lock out the throbbing headache and the burn of his knuckles where the skin had ruptured during his fight against his kidnappers.

Gradually, one by one, Sam locked out small inconveniences such as pain and cold, slowly sinking into more hefty cycles of thought until he could feel the current in his skull escalate like a restless worm waking in the core of his skull. The familiar surge coursed through his brain, and some of it oozed into his spinal cord like trickles of adrenaline. He felt his eyeballs heat up as the mysterious lightning filled his head. Sam smiled.

The tether formed in his mind's eye as he tried to lock on to Klaus Kemper. He did not have to locate him on the ship as long as he spoke his name. After what seemed like an hour he still had not been able to latch his control onto the tyrant in his vicinity, leaving Sam weak and sweating profusely. Frustration threatened his control as well as his hope at the attempt, but he kept trying. Finally, he had exerted his mind so much that he lost consciousness.

When Sam came to it was dark in the room, leaving him uncertain of his state of being. No matter how he stretched his eyes, he could not see anything in the pitch dark. Eventually, Sam started to question his psyche.

'Am I dreaming?' he wondered as he reached out in front of him, his fingertips left unsatisfied. 'Am I under the influence of that monstrous thing right now?' But he could not be. After all, when the *other* took control, Sam usually witnessed what was happening through what felt like a thin veil. Resuming his previous endeavor, he extended his mind like a seeking tentacle into the darkness to find Klaus. Manipulation was an elusive pursuit, it appeared. Nothing came of it, apart from distant voices in a heated discussion and others in clamorous laughter.

Suddenly, like a lightning strike, his perception of his surroundings disappeared, making way for a vivid memory he had not been aware of before now. Sam frowned as he recalled lying on a table under dirty lamps shedding pitiful light in a workshop. He remembered the extreme heat he was subjected to in the small workplace filled with tools and containers. Before he could see more, his memory yielded another sensation his mind had chosen to forget.

Excruciating pain filled his inner ear while he was lying in the dusky hot place. Above him, a dripping mess of tree sap spilled from a barrel, barely missing his face. Under the barrel, a large fire crackled in the wavering visions of his reminiscence. It was the source of the intense heat. Deep in his ear, a sharp sting provoked him to scream out in agony as the yellow syrup dribbled onto the table next to his head.

Sam caught his breath as the realization hammered itself into his mind. 'The amber! The organism was caught in the amber that old bastard was melting! Of course! When it melted, the bloody thing was free to escape. It should be dead after all that time, though. I mean, ancient tree sap is hardly cryogenics!' Sam bickered with his logic. It had happened while he had been half conscious under the blanket in the work room – the possession of Kalihasa – while he had still been waking from his ordeal on the cursed vessel *DKM Geheimnis* after it had spewed him out.

From there, with all the confusion and pain, things grew murky. But Sam did remember the old man rushing in to stop the spilling yellow goo. He also recalled the old man asking him if he had been expelled from hell and who he belonged to. Sam had instantly answered *'Purdue'* at the old man's inquiry, more of a subconscious reflex than actual coherence, and two days later found himself en route to some distant, covert facility.

It was there that Sam had made his gradual and difficult recovery under the supervision and medical science of Purdue's handpicked team of physicians until he was ready to join Purdue at Wrichtishousis. To his delight, it was also there that he was reunited with Nina, his inamorata and object of his ongoing joust with Purdue over the years.

The whole vision lasted only twenty seconds, yet it felt as if Sam had relived every detail in real time - if the concept of time even still existed in this distorted sense of existence. From the fading recollection, Sam's reasoning returned to an almost normal range. Between the two worlds of psychic wandering and physical reality his senses switched like levers adjusting to alternating currents.

Once more he was in the room, his sensitive and feverish eyes assaulted by the meager effort of the bare light bulb. Sam was lying on his back, shivering from the cold floor underneath. From his shoulders to his calves the skin had gone numb from the unyielding temperature of the steel. Footsteps approached the chamber he was in, but Sam elected to play possum, again disappointed by his ineptitude to elicit the furious *entomo-god*, as he named it.

"Mr. Cleave, I have enough training to know when someone is faking. You are no more incapacitated than I am," Klaus rambled indifferently. "However, I also know what you have been trying to do, and I must say, I admire your boldness."

Sam was curious. Without moving, he asked, "Oh, do tell, old boy." Klaus was not amused by the snide imitation Sam Cleave used to mock his refined, almost feminine, eloquence. His fists almost balled up at the journalist's impudence, but he was an expert at composure and held his form. "You tried to steer my thoughts. Either that or you were just adamant to be on my mind like the unpleasant memory of an ex-girlfriend."

"Like you know what a girlfriend is," Sam mumbled amusedly. He expected a blow to the ribs or a kick to the head, but nothing happened.

Dismissing Sam's efforts to rile up his vengeance, Klaus clarified, "I know you have *Kalihasa*, Mr. Cleave. I am flattered you deem me a prominent enough threat to use it on me, but I have to implore you to resort to more restful practices." Just before leaving Klaus smiled at Sam, "Please save your special gift for... *the hive.*"

CHAPTER 26

"*Y*ou do realize that it is an approximate drive of fourteen hours to Pripyat, right?" Nina informed Purdue as he stalked Kiril's garage. "Not to mention the fact that Detlef could still be here, as you might surmise by the fact that his corpse is not occupying the very space where I stabbed him last, right?"

"Nina, my dear," Purdue hushed her in a low voice, "where is your faith? Better yet, where is that daring enchantress you normally turn into when things get rough? Trust me. I know how to do this. How else are we going to rescue Sam?"

"This is about Sam? Are you sure it is not about the Amber Room?" she called him out. Purdue did not merit her accusation with an answer.

"I don't like this," she grunted as she sank down on her haunches next to Purdue, surveying the perimeter of the house and yard where they had barely escaped from less than two hours before. "I have a bad feeling he is still there."

Purdue crept closer to Kiril's garage door, two decrepit old iron sheets barely held in place with wire and hinges. The doors were joined by a locked padlock on a thick rusty chain, with a few inches between them from the slightly askew position of the right door. Behind the gap, the interior of the shed was dark. Purdue tried to see if he could break the padlock, but an awful creak prompted him to abandon the effort to avoid alarming a certain killer widower.

"This is a bad idea," Nina insisted, growing steadily impatient with Purdue.

"Noted," he said absent-mindedly. Deep in thought, he placed his hand on her thigh to attract her attention. "Nina, you are quite a small woman."

"Thanks for noticing," she mumbled.

"Do you reckon you might be able to wedge your body through between the doors?" he asked sincerely. With one eyebrow raised, she stared at him, saying nothing. In truth, she was contemplating it, what with time running out and a considerable distance to travel to get to their next destination. Finally, she exhaled, closing her eyes and carrying a proper look of preconceived regret for what she was about to endeavor.

"I knew I could count on you," he smiled.

"Shut it!" she snapped at him, pursing her lips in annoyance and utmost concentration. Nina stole forward through the tall weeds and thorny bushes thorns that poked through the thick denim of her jeans. She winced, cursed and muttered her way to the double door conundrum until she reached the bottom of the obstacle that stood between her and Kiril's beat-up Volvo. With her eyes, Nina measured the width of the dark slit between the doors, shaking her head at Purdue.

"Go! You'll fit," he mouthed at her, peeking over the weeds to keep watch for Detlef. The house and especially the bathroom window area were clearly visible from his vantage point. However, the advantage was also a curse as it meant than anybody could have been watching them from the house. Detlef would be able to see them as easily as they could see him and that was cause for urgency.

"Oh God," Nina whispered as she slipped her arms and shoulders between the doors, cringing at the crude edge of the slanting door that was chafing her back as she worked her way through. "Christ, it's a good thing I didn't go the other way around," she murmured quietly. "This tuna can would have skinned me tits something awful, goddammit!" Her frown deepened as her hip dragged over tiny pointy stones following her equally afflicted palms.

Purdue's keen eyes stayed on the house, but he heard and saw nothing to arouse alert – yet. His heart pounded at the prospect of the deadly gunman emerging from the back door of the shack, but he trusted Nina to get them out of the bind they were in. On the other hand, he was dreading the possibility that Kiril's car keys would *not* be in the ignition. When he heard the rattling clang of the chain, he saw Nina's thighs and knees enter the gap, followed by her boots disappearing into the darkness. Unfortunately, he was not the only one who heard the noise.

"Well done, love," he whispered, smiling.

Inside, Nina was relieved that the car door she tried was unlocked, but she was soon devastated to find that the keys were in none of the places suggested by the numerous action films she had seen.

"Fuck," she hissed as she rummaged through fishing gear, beer cans, and a few other items the purpose of which she did not even want to consider. "Where the fuck are your keys, Kiril? Where do crazy old Russian soldiers keep their damn car keys – *other* than in their pocket?"

Outside, Purdue heard the kitchen door close with a click. As he had feared, Detlef appeared from behind the corner. Purdue dropped flat into the grass, hoping that

Detlef had come outside for something trivial. But the German giant kept walking toward the garage where Nina was obviously having trouble finding the car keys. His head was wrapped in some blood stained cloth, covering the eye Nina had impaled with her scissors. Knowing that Detlef was hostile toward him, Purdue decided to distract him from Nina.

"Hope he doesn't have that bloody gun on him," Purdue mumbled as he jumped up into plain sight and made for the boathouse quite a distance away. He heard shots shortly after, feeling a hot nudge at his upper arm and another whistling past his ear. "Shit!" he yelped, when he stumbled, but jumped up and kept going.

Nina had heard the shots. Doing her best not to panic, she grabbed the small gutting knife on the floor behind the passenger seat where the fishing gear was piled.

"I hope none of those shots just killed my ex-boyfriend, Detlef, or I'm going to flay your ass with this tiny little pick stick," she sneered as she switched on the car's roof light and keeled over to get to the wiring under the steering wheel. She did not intend on rekindling her past romance with Dave Purdue, but he was one of her two best friends, and she adored him, even though he always dragged her into life-threatening situations.

Just short of the boathouse Purdue realized that his arm was burning. A warm streak of blood ran down his elbow and hand as he raced for the shelter of the building, but another lousy surprise awaited him when he finally got to look back. Detlef was not pursuing him at all. Not considering him a risk any more, Detlef had holstered his Glock and made for the rickety garage.

"Oh no!" Purdue gasped. He knew, though, that it would be impossible for Detlef to get to Nina through the narrow gap between the chained doors. His impressive size did have its downsides, and that was a saving grace for the petite and feisty Nina, who was inside, hotwiring the car with sweaty hands and barely any light.

Distressed and wounded, Purdue watched helplessly as Detlef checked the lock and the chain to ascertain if anyone could have breached it. *'He probably thinks I am here alone. God, I hope so,'* Purdue thought. While the German was occupied with the garage doors, Purdue slipped into the house to retrieve as many of their belongings as he could carry. Nina's laptop bag contained her passport as well, and Sam's he found in the journalist's room on the chair beside the bed. From the German's wallet, Purdue appropriated cash and a gold AMEX credit card.

If Detlef believed that Purdue had left Nina in town and would get back to finish the battle with him, that would have been great; the billionaire hoped as he watched the German mull the situation over from the kitchen window. Purdue felt his arm numbing all the way into his fingers already, and the loss of blood was making him light-headed, so he utilized the strength he had left to sneak back to the boat house.

"Hurry Nina," he whispered, taking off his glasses to clean them and wipe the sweat from his face with his shirt. To Purdue's relief, the German decided not to pursue the futile venture of trying to get into the garage, mostly because he did not have the padlock key. As he replaced his glasses, he saw Detlef heading his way. *'He is coming to make sure I am dead!'*

From behind the large widower, the sound of an ignition firing echoed through the evening. Detlef swung around and hurried back to the garage, drawing his gun. Purdue was determined to keep Detlef away from Nina, even if it cost him his life. Again he emerged from the grass and shouted, but Detlef ignored him as the car attempted to start again.

"Don't flood it, Nina!" was all Purdue could cry as Detlef's massive hands locked onto the chain and started prying apart the doors. The chain would not give. It was sturdy and thick, much more secure than the flimsy iron doors. Behind the doors, the engine revved again but died a moment later. Just the sound of the clattering doors under the furious strength of the German rung through the afternoon air now. A metallic tear shrieked as Detlef disassembled the entire set-up by ripping the doors from their flimsy hinges.

"Oh my God!" Purdue groaned, desperate to save his beloved Nina, but lacking the strength to run. He watched the doors fly off like leaves shed from a tree as the engine roared once more. Gaining in revolutions, the Volvo screamed under Nina's foot and rocketed forward as Detlef tossed aside the second door.

"Thanks, mate!" Nina said as she floored the accelerator and released the clutch.

Purdue only saw Detlef's frame collapse as the old car struck him full on, flinging his body a few feet away under the force of its velocity. The boxy, ugly brown sedan slid over the muddy grass lawn, careening toward where Purdue was flagging her down. Nina opened the passenger door as she ground the vehicle to a near halt, just long enough for Purdue to throw himself into the seat before she took off for the street.

"Are you alright? Purdue! Are you okay? Where did he hit you?" she kept shouting over the laboring engine.

"I'll be fine, my dear," Purdue smiled timidly as he gripped his arm. "It is a bloody stroke of luck that the second round missed my skull."

"It is a stroke of luck that I learned to hotwire a car to impress a shit hot Glasgow hooligan when I was seventeen!" she added proudly. "Purdue!"

"Just keep driving, Nina," he replied. "Just get us over the border to Ukraine as fast as you can."

"Provided Kiril's old clunker can handle the trip," she sighed, checking the fuel gauge threatening to hit the *Reserve* line. Purdue flashed Detlef's credit card and grinned through the pain as Nina let out a roar of victorious laughter.

"Give me that!" she smiled. "And get some rest. I will get you some bandage as soon as we hit the next town. From there we don't stop until we get within distance of the Devil's Cooking Pot and get Sam back."

Purdue did not get that last bit. He had already fallen asleep.

CHAPTER 27

*I*n Riga, Latvia, Klaus, and his small crew moored for the next leg of their journey. There was little time to get everything ready for the acquisition and transport of the Amber Room panels. There was not much time to waste, and Kemper was a very impatient man. He barked orders out on the deck while Sam listened from his steel prison. Kemper's choice of words hounded Sam immensely – *hive* – the thought made him shudder, but more so because he did not know what Kemper was up to and that was enough reason for emotional turmoil.

Sam had to concede; he was afraid. Plain and simple, image and self-respect aside, he was terrified of what was coming. Based on the little information he had been given, it already felt like he was doomed beyond salvation this time. Many times before he had escaped what he had feared to be certain death, but this time felt different.

'*You can't give up, Cleave,*' he scolded himself from the pit of depression and hopelessness. '*This defeatist shit is not for the likes of you. What harm could possibly trump the hell on board of that teleporting ship you were trapped on? Do they even have the* slightest idea of the things you endured while it made its hellish voyage over and over through the same traps of physics?' But when Sam gave his own coaching some thought, he soon realized that he could not remember what happened on the *DKM Geheimnis* during his detention there. What he did recall was the deep despair it cultivated deep in his soul, the only remnant of the whole affair he could still consciously feel.

Above him, he could hear the men unload heavy equipment onto what must have been some large heavy-duty vehicle. Had he not known better, Sam would have guessed it was a tank. Rapid footsteps approached the door of his room.

'Now or never,' he told himself, gathering his courage to make an escape attempt. If he could manipulate those coming to get him, he could make his way off the boat stealthily. The locks clicked from the outside. His heart pounded wildly as he got ready to pounce. When the door opened, Klaus Kemper himself stood in it, smiling. Sam lunged forward to tackle the loathsome captor. Klaus uttered, "24-58-68-91."

Sam's attack instantly ended, and he fell to the floor at the feet of his target. A deep scowl painted Sam's brow with confusion and fury, but as much as he tried, he could not move a muscle. All he could hear above his bare and bruised frame was the triumphant snickering of a very dangerous man who harbored deadly information.

"I tell you what, Mr. Cleave," Kemper said in that tone of annoying tranquility. "Because you have shown so much determination I will fill you in on what just happened to you. But!" he patronized like a forthcoming teacher bestowing mercy on a transgressing student. "But…you have to agree to give me no more reasons to have to worry about your relentless and ridiculous efforts at fleeing my company. Let's just call it… professional courtesy. You cease your childish behavior and in turn, I will grant you the interview of the ages."

"I am sorry. I don't interview swines," Sam retorted. "Your kind will never get any publicity from me, so go fuck yourself."

"And again, here is where I will give you one more chance to rethink your counterproductive behavior," Klaus repeated with a sigh. "In plain language – I will trade your compliance for information only I hold. Do you journalists not crave the… how do you say? *Scoop?*"

Sam held his tongue; not because he was obstinate, but because he was giving the proposition some thought. *'What harm could it do to make this prick believe you are playing nice? He is planning to kill you anyway. You might as well learn more about the riddle you have been dying to solve thus far,'* he reckoned. *'Besides, it is better than parading around with your bagpipe for all to see while you get pummeled by the enemy. Take it. Just take it for now.'*

"If I get my clothes back you have a deal. Although I believe you deserve the punishment of looking on something you apparently don't have much of, I really prefer to wear pants in this cold," Sam mocked him.

Klaus had become used to the journalist's incessant insults, so he was not easily offended anymore. Once he noticed that verbal piss-taking was Sam Cleave's defense system, it was easy to let it roll off, if not to return the favor. "Sure. I'll let you blame the cold for that," he retorted, pointing at Sam's obviously shy genitals.

Without relishing the effect of his counter-slur, Kemper turned and called for Sam's clothing to be returned to him. He was allowed to clean up, dress, and join Kemper in his SUV. From Riga they would be leading the way over two borders toward Ukraine, followed by a mammoth military tactical vehicle carrying a container specially designed for transporting the valuable remaining panels of the Amber Room to be recovered by Sam's associates.

"Impressive," Sam told Kemper as he joined the Black Sun commander outside the local boat yard. Kemper was overseeing the transfer of the large Perspex container, maneuvered by two hydraulic arms from the lean deck of the Polish ocean vessel onto the huge cargo truck. "What kind of vehicle is this?" he asked, examining the enormity of the hybrid truck as he strolled along its side.

"It is a prototype by Enrick Hubsch, a gifted engineer from our ranks," Kemper bragged as he accompanied Sam. "We modeled it on the American made Ford XM656 cargo vehicle from the late 1960's. However, in true German fashion, we improved it vastly by extending the original design with 10 meters more flatbed space and reinforced tensile steel welded along the axles, see?"

Proudly Kemper pointed out the construction above the powerful tires paired along the stretch of the vehicle. "The spacing of the wheels is expertly calculated to bear the exact weight of the container with structural leniency to permit the inevitable rocking brought on by a rocking water tank, so stabilizing the truck while driving."

"And what is the giant aquarium for, exactly?" Sam asked as they watched the enormous box of water being hoisted onto the back of the military grade cargo monster. Thick bulletproof exterior Perspex was joined at each of the four corners by angled copper plates. The water flowed freely through twelve narrow compartments which were framed in copper as well.

Running along the width of the cube, the slots were prepared for one single amber panel to be inserted in each of them and kept separate from the next. As Kemper explained the contraption and its purpose, Sam could not help but wonder obsessively about the incident in the door of his holding quarters on the boat an hour before. He was eager to remind Kemper to disclose what he had promised, but for now, he tempered their tumultuous relationship by playing along.

"Is there some chemical compound in the water?" he asked Kemper.

"No, just water," the German commander answered plainly.

Sam shrugged, "So what is this plain water for? What does it do to the Amber Room's panels?"

Kemper smiled. "Think of it as a containment measure."

Sam locked eyes with him and asked nonchalantly, "To contain, say, a *swarm* from a *hive* of sorts?"

"How melodramatic," Kemper replied, his arms folded confidently across his chest as the men secured the container with cable and cloth. "But you are not altogether wrong, Mr. Cleave. It is just a precaution. I do not dabble in risk unless I have considerable alternatives."

"Noted," Sam nodded affably.

Together they watched Kemper's men complete the loading process, neither engaging in conversation. Inside his mind, Sam wished he could tap into Kemper's thoughts, but not only could he not read minds, but the Nazi spin doctor already knew Sam's secret – and evidently more to boot. It would be superfluous to pry covertly. Something peculiar struck Sam about the way in which the small crew was laboring. There was no specific foreman, yet each man moved as if governed by particular commands to assure that their respective tasks were executed fluently and concluded at the same time. It was uncanny how they moved swiftly, efficiently and without any verbal exchange.

"Come, Mr. Cleave," Kemper urged. "It is time to go. We have two countries to cross and very little time. With a cargo this delicate we cannot traverse the Latvian and Belarusian landscape in less than 16 hours."

"Holy crap! How bored are we going to be?" Sam exclaimed, already fatigued by the prospect. "I don't even have a magazine. Better yet, with a trip this long I could probably read through the entire Bible!"

Kemper laughed, clapping his hands in amusement as they climbed into the beige SUV. "Now reading that would be a colossal waste of time. It would be like reading contemporary fiction to determine the history of the Mayan civilization!"

They shifted into the back of the vehicle, which waited ahead of the cargo truck to lead it along a secondary route to the Latvia/ Belarus border. Once they started moving at a snail's pace, the luxurious interior of the car started filling with cool air to alleviate the midday heat, accompanied by soft classical music.

"I hope you don't mind Mozart," Kemper said purely out of propriety.

"Not at all," Sam accepted the formality. "Although I am more of an ABBA man myself."

Once again Kemper was highly amused at Sam's entertaining indifference. "Really? You play!"

"I do not," Sam insisted. "There is something irresistible to Swedish retro pop with one's impending death on the menu, you know."

"If you say so," Kemper shrugged. He got the hint, but he was not in a hurry to entertain Sam Cleave's curiosity on the subject at hand. He knew full well that the journalist was shocked by the inadvertent reaction his body exhibited when he attacked. Another fact he kept from Sam was the information pertinent to Kalihasa and the fate that awaited him.

While traveling through the remainder of Latvia, the two men hardly spoke. Kemper had his laptop computer open, mapping strategic locations for unknown purposes Sam could not spy from his seat. But he knew it had to be nefarious – and it had to involve his part in the insidious agenda of the sinister commander. For his own part, Sam refrained from prying about the pressing matters on his mind, electing to spend the time relaxing. After all, he was almost certain he would not get the chance to do it again anytime soon.

After crossing the border into Belarus, things changed. Kemper offered Sam a drink for the first time since they had left Riga, having tested the endurance of body and will of the investigative journalist who was so highly regarded in the United Kingdom. Sam accepted readily, receiving a sealed can of Coca-Cola. Kemper took one as well, putting Sam at ease about being duped into drinking a laced beverage.

"Prost!" Sam said before emptying a quarter of the can in one big gulp, relishing the bubbly burn of the drink. Of course, Kemper drank his steadily, retaining his refined composure at all times. "Klaus," Sam unexpectedly addressed his captor. Now that his thirst was quenched, he had summoned his courage. "The numbers trick if you please."

Kemper knew he owed Sam an explanation. After all, the Scottish journalist was not going to survive past the next day anyway, and he was rather tolerable. A pity that he was going to meet his end by suicide.

CHAPTER 28

On their way to Pripyat, Nina drove several hours after she had filled the Volvo's tank in Wloclawek. With Detlef's credit card she had purchased Purdue a first aid kit to treat the flesh wound on his arm. Searching the unfamiliar town for a pharmacy had been a detour, but a necessary one.

Even though Sam's captors had directed her and Purdue to the Sarcophagus in Chernobyl - the tomb of the ill-fated Reactor 4 - she recalled the radio message from Milla. It mentioned *Pripyat 1955*, a term that simply would not relent since she jotted it down. Somehow it stood out among the other phrases, almost as if it glowed with promise. It had to be resolved and so Nina had spent the last few hours trying to discover the meaning of it.

She did not know of anything of significance related to 1955 about the ghost town that was in the *Exclusion Zone* that had been evacuated after the reactor disaster. In fact, she doubted that Pripyat had ever been involved in anything important before its infamous evacuation in 1986. The words kept the historian's mind busy until she looked at the

195

watch to determine how long she had been driving for and realized that 1955 could refer to time, not a date.

At first, she thought it might be a reach, but it was all she had. For her to make it to Pripyat by 8 pm there would hardly be enough time for a good sleep, a very dangerous prospect given the fatigue she was already experiencing.

It was dreadful and lonely on the dark road through Belarus while Purdue was snoring through his Antidol-induced sleep in the passenger seat next to her. What kept her going was her hope that she could still save Sam if she did not falter now. The small digital clock on the dashboard of Kiril's old car announced the time in eerie green.

02:14

Her body ached, and she was exhausted, but she popped a fag in her mouth, lit it, and took a few deep breaths to fill her lungs with slow death. It was one of her most favorite sensations. Rolling down the window was a good idea. The furious whip of the cold night air revitalized her somewhat, although she wished she had a flask of strong caffeine to keep her wired.

From the surrounding land hidden beyond darkness on both sides of the lonely road, she could smell the soil. On the pale concrete meandering towards the border between Poland and the Ukraine, the car hummed a melancholic dirge with its worn rubber tires.

"God, this is like Purgatory," she complained as she flicked her spent butt out into the beckoning oblivion outside. "I hope your radio works, Kiril."

With a click, the knob turned at the command of Nina's twisting grip and a frail light proclaimed that there was life in the radio. "Hell yeah!" she smiled, keeping her weary eyes on the road as her hand turned the other dial for a suitable station to listen to. There was an FM station that came through on the car's only speaker, one fitted in her car door.

But Nina was not picky tonight. She direly needed company, any company, to soothe her rapidly growing moroseness.

With Purdue out cold most of the time, she had to make the decisions. They would head for the Chelm, a city 25km shy of the Ukraine border and get some sleep at a lodge. As long as they reached the border by 2 pm, Nina was confident they would be in Pripyat by the designated time. Her only concern was how to get into the ghost town with guarded check points everywhere in the Exclusion Zone surrounding Chernobyl, but little did she know that Milla had friends even in the harshest camps of the forgotten.

AFTER A FEW HOURS' sleep at a quaint family-owned motel in Chelm, a fresh Nina and a wide awake Purdue had taken on the road across the border from Poland, Ukraine-bound. It was just past 1 pm when they reached Kovel, an approximate 5-hour drive away from their destination.

"Look, I am aware that I was under the weather for just about the entire trip, but are you sure we should not just proceed to this Sarcophagus rather than to chase our tails in Pripyat?" Purdue asked Nina.

"I understand your concern, but I have a thick hunch that that message was important. Don't ask me to explain it or make sense of it," she replied, "but we have to see why Milla mentioned it."

Purdue looked stunned. "You do realize that Milla's broadcasts come straight from the Order, right?" He could not believe that Nina would choose to play right into the hands of the enemy. As much as he trusted her, he could not fathom her logic on this endeavor.

She looked at him sharply. "I told you that I cannot explain it. Just…" she hesitated, doubting her own hunch, "… trust me. If we run into trouble, I will be the first to admit I fucked up, but something about the timing of that broadcast feels different."

"Women's intuition, right?" he scoffed. "May as well have let Detlef shoot me in the head back in Gdynia."

"Jesus, Purdue, can you be a bit more supportive?" she glowered. "Do not forget how we got into this in the first place. Sam and I had to, once again, come to your aid when you got into a scrap with these bastards for the umpteenth time!"

"I had nothing to do with this, my darling!" he sneered at her. "I was ambushed by that bitch and her hackers while I was minding my own business, trying to vacation in Copenhagen, for God's sake!"

Nina could not believe her ears. Purdue was beside himself, acting like a high-strung stranger she had never met before. Granted, he had been pulled into the Amber Room affair by the doing of agents beyond his control, but he had never exploded like this before. With an aversion for tense silences, Nina turned on the radio and kept the volume low to serve as a third, more cheerful presence in the car. She did not say anything after that, leaving Purdue to fume while she was trying to make sense of her own ludicrous decision.

They had just passed the small city of Sarny when the music on the radio began to fade and swell in turn. Purdue ignored the sudden change, staring out the window at the unremarkable scenery. Normally such interference irritated Nina, but she dared not switch off the radio and plummet into Purdue's silent treatment. As it persisted, it grew steadily louder until it got impossible to ignore. The familiar tune last heard on the Gdynia shortwave broadcast floated forth from the battered speaker by her side, identifying the emerging broadcast.

"Milla?" Nina muttered, half afraid and half excited.

Even Purdue's stone face became animated as he listened

to the slowly waning melody in astonished apprehension. They exchanged suspicious glances as the static scratches violated the airwaves. Nina checked the frequency. "It is not in its usual frequency," she declared.

"How do you mean?" he asked, sounding much more like his old self. "Is this not the place you usually tuned it to?" he asked, pointing to the needle sitting well away from where Detlef used to set it to tune into the numbers station. Nina shook her head, intriguing Purdue even more.

"Why would they be on a diff…?" she wanted to ask, but the explanation came to her as Purdue answered, "Because they are hiding."

"Aye, that's what I'm thinking. But why?" she wondered.

"Listen," he rasped excitedly, perking up to hear.

The female voice sounded insistent, but even. "Widower."

"That's Detlef!" Nina told Purdue. "They are transmitting to Detlef."

After a brief pause, the fuzzy voice continued, "Wood-pecker, eight-thirty." A loud click popped on the speaker, and only white noise and static was left in place of the concluded transmission. Dumbstruck, Nina and Purdue considered what had just happened by apparent happenstance while the radio waves hissed into the current broadcast of a local station.

"What the hell is Woodpecker? I assume eight-thirty is the time they wish us to be there," Purdue speculated.

"Aye, the message to go to Pripyat was for seven fifty-five, so they have moved location and adjusted the time frame to reach it. It is not much later than before, so I take it Wood-pecker is close to Pripyat," Nina ventured to guess.

"God, I wish I had a phone! Do you have your phone?" he asked.

"I might - if it is still in my laptop bag you snuck it out of Kiril's house," she replied, glancing back to the zipped-up case on the backseat. Purdue reached back and rummaged through the front pocket of the bag, digging between her notebook, pens, and shades.

"Got it!" he smiled. "Now I hope it is charged."

"It should be," she said, peeking over to see. "That should do for the next two hours at least. Go ahead. Find our Woodpecker, old boy."

"On it," he replied, browsing the Internet for something with a nickname of the sort in the vicinity. They were rapidly approaching Pripyat as the late afternoon sun lit up the pale brown and gray of the flat landscape, making eerie black giants of sentinel pylons.

"It feels so foreboding," Nina remarked as her eyes recorded the scenery. "Look, Purdue, this is the graveyard of Soviet science. You can almost feel the lost brilliance in the atmosphere."

"That would be the radiation talking, Nina," he jested, evoking a giggle from the historian who was happy to have the old Purdue back. "I got it."

"Where do we go?" she asked.

"South of Pripyat, towards Chernobyl," he directed casually. Nina gave him the raised eyebrow, showing her reluctance to visit such a devastating and hazardous patch of Ukrainian soil. But in the end, she knew they had to go. After all, they were already there – contaminated by the remnants of the radioactive material left there after 1986. Purdue checked the map on her phone. "Carry on straight from Pripyat. The so-called 'Russian Woodpecker' is located in the surrounding forest," he reported, leaning forward in his seat to look upward. "Night is coming soon, love. It is going to be a cold one too."

"What is the Russian Woodpecker? Will I be looking for a large bird plugging holes in the local roads or something?" she chuckled.

"It is actually a relic of the Cold War. The nickname comes from… you're going to appreciate this… a mysterious radio interference that plagued broadcasts all over Europe in the 80's," he shared.

"More radio phantoms," she remarked, shaking her head. "It makes me wonder if we are not being programmed daily by hidden frequencies fraught with ideologies and propaganda, you know? Without a clue that our opinions might be formed by subliminal messages…"

"There!" he exclaimed suddenly. "The secret military base where the Soviet military broadcasted from about 30 years ago. It was called *Duga-3*, a state-of-the-art radar signal they used to detect potential ballistic missile attacks."

Vividly visible from Pripyat's region stood a terrible vision, captivating and grotesque. Looming silently over the tree tops of the irradiated forests ablaze with the touch of the setting sun, the assembly of identical steel towers lined the deserted military base. "You might have a point, Nina. Look at the sheer size of it. Transmitters here could easily manipulate the airwaves to alter thought patterns," he hypothesized in awe of the creepy wall of steel grids.

Nina looked at the digital clock. "It's almost time."

CHAPTER 29

*T*hroughout the Red Forest predominantly pine trees populated the area, born from the very soil that covered the graves of the former forest. Contaminated by the Chernobyl disaster, the previous vegetation had been bulldozed and buried. The ginger red pine skeletons beneath the thick layer of earth had given birth to a new generation planted by authorities. The Volvo's only headlight, the high beam on the right, haunted the grave rustling tree trunks of the Red Forest as Nina drove toward the dilapidated steel gates at the entrance of the forlorn compound. Painted green and mounted with Soviet stars, the two gates fell askew, barely held up by the collapsing wooden perimeter fence.

"Good God, this is depressing!" Nina remarked, leaning on the steering wheel to get a good look at the hardly visible surroundings.

"Where are we supposed to go, I wonder," Purdue said, looking for signs of life. The only signs of life, though, came in the form of surprisingly abounding wildlife such as the deer and beavers Purdue had seen on the way to the entrance.

"Let's just go in and wait. I give them 30 minutes tops, then we get the hell out of this death trap," Nina asserted. The car advanced very slowly, creeping along the decrepit walls where the fading Soviet era propaganda peeled from the crumbling masonry. Only the scrunching of the tires sounded in the lifeless night at the Duga-3 military base.

"Nina," Purdue said softly.

"Yeah?" she replied, fascinated by an abandoned Willys Jeep.

"Nina!" he said louder with eyes frozen ahead. She slammed on the brakes.

"Holy shit!" she shrieked as the grill of the car stopped inches short of a tall, thin Balkan beauty dressed in boots and a white dress. "What is she doing in the middle of the road?" The woman's light blue eyes pierced through the beam of the car's light into Nina's dark stare. With a subtle wave of her hand, she beckoned them, turning to show them the way.

"I don't trust her," Nina whispered.

"Nina, we are here. We are expected. We are in deep already. Let's not keep the lady waiting," he smiled at the pretty historian's pout. "Come. This was your idea." He gave her a reassuring wink and got out of the car. Nina shouldered her laptop bag and followed along with Purdue. The young blonde woman said nothing while they trailed her, occasionally glancing at one another for encouragement. Finally, Nina gave in and asked, "Are you Milla?"

"No," the woman said casually without turning around. They ascended two flights of stairs up to what resembled a cafeteria of the bygone era, where glaring white light fell through the doorway. She opened the door and held it for Nina and Purdue who reluctantly entered, keeping their eye on her.

"This is Milla," she informed the Scottish guests, stepping aside to reveal five men and two women sitting in a circle with laptops. "It stands for *'Militum Indicina Leonid Leopoldt Alpha'*.

Each had their own style and purpose, taking turns to occupy the only control desk for their respective broadcasts. "I am Elena. This is my partners," she explained in a thick Serbian accent. "Are you Widower?"

"Aye, he is," Nina answered before Purdue could. "I am his associate, Dr. Gould. You can call me Nina, and this is Dave."

"We have been hoping you will come. There is much to warn you about," one of the men said from over at the circle.

"About what?" Nina said under her breath.

One of the ladies was seated in the isolation booth behind the control desk, unable to hear their conversation. "No, we will not disturb her transmission. No worry," Elena smiled. "That is Yuri. He is from Kiev."

Yuri raised a hand in greeting but carried on with his work. They were all under 35 years of age, but they all shared the same tattoo – the star Nina and Purdue had seen outside on the gates, with writing underneath in Russian.

"Cool ink," Nina said approvingly, pointing at the one Elena sported on her neck. "What does that say?"

"Oh, it says *Krasnaya Armiya 1985*...um, 'Red Army' and the date of birth. We all have our year of birthday next to our stars," she smiled coyly. Her voice was like satin over the articulation of her words which only made her more appealing than her physical beauty alone.

"That name in Milla's abbreviation," Nina asked, "who is Leonid...?"

Elena quickly responded. "Leonid Leopoldt was German-born Ukrainian operative in World War II who survived the mass suicide drowning off the coast of Latvia. Leonid killed the captain and radioed to submarine commander Alexander Marinesko."

Purdue nudged Nina, "Marinesko was Kiril's father, remember?"

Nina nodded, eager to hear more from Elena.

"Marinesko's men removed the Amber Room pieces and hid them while Leonid was sent to a Gulag. While he was in Red Army interrogation room, he was shot dead by SS swine Karl Kemper. That Nazi scum was not supposed to be in Red Army facility!" Elena fumed in her genteel way, looking distraught.

"Oh my God, Purdue!" Nina whispered. "Leonid was the soldier on the recording! Detlef has his medal pinned to his chest."

"You are *not* affiliated with the Order of the Black Sun then?" Purdue asked sincerely. With great hostile looks, the entire group reprimanded and cursed him. He did not speak the languages, but it was clear that their response was not favorable.

"Widower means no offense," Nina interjected. "Um, he was told by an unknown agent that your broadcasts came from the Black Sun High Command. But we have been lied to by many people, so we don't really know what is going on. We don't know *who* serves *what*, you see."

Nina's words were met by appreciative nods from the Milla group. Instantly they accepted her explanation, so she dared ask a pressing question. "Did the Red Army not disband in the early Nineties, though? Or is it just to show your devotion?"

A striking man in his mid-thirties answered Nina's question. "Did the Order of the Black Sun not disband after that *zasranees* Hitler killed himself?"

"No, the next generations of followers are still active," Purdue answered.

"There you go," the man said. "The Red Army is still

fighting the Nazis; only this is new generation operatives fighting old war. Red vs. Black."

"That is Misha," Elena chimed in out of courtesy to the strangers.

"We are all military-trained personnel, like our fathers and their fathers, but we fight with new world's most dangerous weapon - *information technology*," Misha preached. He was clearly the leader. "Milla is the new Tsar Bomba, baby!"

Cries of victory erupted among the group. Amused and perplexed, Purdue looked at a smiling Nina and whispered, "What is 'Tsar Bomba', may I ask?"

"Only the most powerful nuclear weapon ever detonated in the entire history of the human race," she winked. "A hydrogen bomb; I believe it was a tested somewhere in the Sixties."

"And these are the *good* guys," Purdue remarked playfully, making sure he kept his voice down. Nina chuckled and nodded. "I'm just relieved we are not behind enemy lines here."

After the group had quieted down, Elena offered Purdue and Nina some black coffee which both gratefully accepted. It had been an exceptionally long drive, not to mention the emotional strain for what they still had to deal with.

"Elena, we have some questions about Milla and its involvement with the Amber Room relic," Purdue inquired respectfully. "We have to find the artwork, or what is left of it before tomorrow night."

"Nyet! Oh no, no!" Misha protested blatantly. He ordered Elena to move aside on the couch and sat down opposite the misinformed visitors. "Nobody takes the Amber Room out of its tomb! Never! If you want to do this, we will have to resort to severe measures with you."

Elena tried to calm him as the others stood up and encircled the small space where Misha and the strangers were sitting. Nina took Purdue's hand as they all drew their firearms. The terrifying clicks of hammers being pulled back proved how serious Milla was.

"Alright, relax. Let us discuss an alternative, by all means," Purdue proposed.

Elena's soft voice was the first to respond. "Look, last time someone stole a piece of that masterpiece, the Third Reich almost destroyed the freedom of all people."

"How?" Purdue asked. Of course, he had an idea, but was as yet unable to realize the true threat within. All Nina wanted was for the bulky hand guns to be holstered so she could relax, but the members of Milla didn't budge.

Before Misha went on another tirade, Elena implored him to wait with one of those enthralling waves of her hand. She sighed and proceeded, "The amber used to produce original Amber Room was from the Balkan region."

"We know about the ancient organism – Kalihasa – that was inside the amber," Nina interrupted gently.

"And you know what it does?" Misha snapped.

"Aye," Nina affirmed.

"Then why the fuck do you want to let them have it? Are you crazy? You are crazy people! You West and your greed! Money whores, all of you!" Misha barked at Nina and Purdue in an uncontrollable rage. "Shoot them," he told his group.

Nina threw up her hands in horror. "No! Please listen! We want to destroy the amber panels once and for all, but we just don't know how. Listen, Misha," she pleaded for his attention, "our colleague… our *friend*… is being held by the Order and they will kill him unless we deliver the Amber Room by tomorrow. So Widower and I are in deep, very deep shit! Do you understand?"

Purdue cringed at Nina's trademark ferocity toward the trigger-happy Misha.

"Nina, may I remind you that the guy you are yelling at pretty much has our proverbial balls in his grip," Purdue said as he tugged gently at Nina's shirt.

"No, Purdue!" she fought, slapping his hand aside. "We are in the middle here. We are neither Red Army, nor Black Sun, yet we are being threatened by both sides and forced to be their bitches, doing the dirty work and trying not to get killed!"

Elena sat silently nodding in agreement, waiting for Misha to let the predicament of the strangers sink in. The woman who had been broadcasting all this time exited the booth and stared at strangers seated in the cafeteria and the rest of her group, guns at the ready. At over six foot three, the dark-haired Ukrainian looked beyond intimidating. Her dreadlocks swung about her shoulders as she strode elegantly to meet them. Nonchalantly Elena introduced her to Nina and Purdue, "This is our explosives expert, Natasha. She is former Spetsnaz and direct descendent of Leonid Leopoldt."

"Who is this?" Natasha asked firmly.

"Widower," Misha answered, pacing as he considered Nina's recent assertion.

"Ah, Widower. Gabi was our friend," she replied as she shook her head. "Her death was a great loss to world freedom."

"Yes, it was," Purdue agreed, unable to peel his eyes from the newcomer. Elena filled Natasha in on the sticky situation the visitors found themselves in, upon which the Amazon-like woman responded, "Misha, we have to help them."

"We wage war with data, with information, not with fire-power," Misha reminded her.

"Was it *information* and *data* that stopped that American

Intelligence officer who tried to help the Black Sun obtain the Amber Room during the last era of the Cold War?" she asked him. "No, Soviet firepower stopped him in West Germany."

"We are hackers, not terrorists!" he protested.

"Was it hackers who destroyed the Chernobyl Kalihasa threat in 1986? No, Misha, it was terrorists!" she argued. "Now we have that problem again, and we are going to have it as long as the Amber Room exists. What will you do when the Black Sun succeeds? Are you going to send out number sequences to de-program the minds of the few who would still listen to radio for the rest of your life while the fucking Nazis take over the world by mass hypnosis and mind control?"

"The Chernobyl disaster was not an accident?" Purdue asked inadvertently, but the sharp warning glares of the Milla members shut him right up. Even Nina could not believe his misplaced query. By the looks of it, Nina and Purdue had just stirred up the deadliest hornet's nest in history, and the Black Sun was about to learn why red was the color of blood.

CHAPTER 30

*S*am thought of Nina while he waited for Kemper to return to the vehicle. The bodyguard who drove them remained at the wheel, leaving the engine running. Even if Sam could escape the gorilla with the black suit, there was really nowhere to flee to. To all sides of them, stretching as far as the eye could see, the landscape resembled a very familiar sight. In fact, it was more of a familiar *vision*.

Unnervingly similar to Sam's hypnosis-induced hallucination during those sessions with Dr. Helberg, the flat, featureless expanse of colorless grassland disturbed him. It was good that Kemper had left him alone for a bit so that he could process the surreal occurrence until it did not frighten him anymore. But the more he observed, acknowledged, and absorbed the scenery to adjust to it, the more Sam realized that it did not terrify him any less.

Shifting uncomfortably in his seat, he involuntarily recalled the dream of the well and the barren landscape before the devastating pulse that lit up the sky and exterminated nations. The significance of what had once been no more than a subconscious manifestation of turmoil attested to have been, to Sam's dread, a prophecy.

'Prophecy? Me?' he pondered on the absurd nature of the idea. But then another memory wedged itself into his mind like another piece of the puzzle. His mind revealed the words it recorded while he had been in the grips of his seizure, back in the village on the island; words Nina's attacker had screamed at her.

"Take your evil prophet away from here!"
"Take your evil prophet away from here!"
"Take your evil prophet away from here!"
Sam was spooked.

'Holy shit! How did I not hear it at the time?' he racked his brain, neglecting to consider that this was the very nature of the mind and all its miraculous abilities. *'He called me a prophet?'* Ashen, he swallowed hard when it all came together – the vision of the exact terrain and the laying waste of an entire race under a sky of amber. But what bothered him most was the pulse he had seen in his vision, similar to that of a nuclear explosion.

Kemper startled Sam when he opened the door to get back in. That sudden thwack of the central locking system followed by the loud click of the handle came just as Sam recalled that all-consuming pulse that had rippled across the entire land.

"Entschuldigung, Herr Cleave," Kemper apologized when Sam jolted in fright, clutching his chest. It did give the tyrant a chuckle, though. "Why so jumpy?"

"Just nervous about my friends," Sam shrugged.

"I am sure they will not let you down," Klaus attempted to be cordial.

"Problem with the cargo?" Sam asked.

"Just a minor problem with a petrol gauge, but it's sorted out now," Kemper replied earnestly. "So, you wanted to know how the number sequences thwarted your attack on me, correct?"

"Aye. It was amazing, but even more impressive was the fact that it only affected me. The men with you showed no sign of manipulation," Sam marveled, stroking Klaus' ego as if he was a huge admirer. It was a tactic Sam Cleave had utilized many times before while conducting his investigations to expose criminals.

"Here is the secret," Klaus smiled smugly, wringing his hands slowly and brimming with conceit. "It is not necessarily the numbers as much as the combination of the numbers. Mathematics, as you know, is the language of Creation itself. Numbers control everything in existence, whether on a cellular level, geometrically, in physics, chemical compounds or whatever else. It is the key to converting all data - like a computer inside the task-specific part of your brain, you see?"

Sam nodded. He gave it some thought and replied, "So it is like a cipher to a biological Enigma machine."

Kemper applauded. Literally. "That is an exceptionally accurate analogy, Mr. Cleave! I could not have explained it better myself. That is precisely how it works. By applying strings of specific combinations one could quite possibly expand the field of influence, essentially short-circuiting the brain's receptors. Now, if you add an electrical current to this action," Kemper reveled in his superiority, "it enhances the effect of the thought form tenfold."

"So by using electricity you could actually increase the amount of data absorbed? Or is that to heighten the manipulator's ability to control more than one person at a time?" Sam asked.

'Keep talking, dobber,' Sam thought from behind his expertly played charade. *'And the award goes to... Samson Cleave for his role* as fascinated-journalist-enthralled-by-

smarter-man!' Not in the least less exceptional at his own game, Sam registered every detail the German narcissist spewed out.

"What do you think the first thing was Adolf Hitler did when he assumed power over the idle *Wehrmacht* personnel in 1935?" he asked Sam rhetorically. "He implemented mass discipline, martial efficacy, and unshakable loyalty to enforce SS ideologies using subliminal programming."

With great delicacy, Sam posed the question that shot to mind almost immediately after Kemper's statement. "Did Hitler have Kalihasa?"

"After the Amber Room was resident at Berlin City Palace, a German craftsman from Bavaria..." Kemper uttered a grunt as he tried to remember the name of the man. "Uh, no, I don't remember – he was summoned to join Russian craftsmen to restore the artifact after it had been gifted to Peter the Great, you see?"

"Aye," Sam replied eagerly.

"According to legend, while he worked on the new design for the Catherine Palace erection of the restored room, he 'claimed' three pieces of amber, you know, for his trouble," Kemper winked at Sam.

"Don't really blame him, actually," Sam remarked.

"No, how could anyone blame him for that? I agree. Anyway, he sold one piece. The other two were feared to have been swindled by his wife and sold as well. However, this was apparently incorrect, and the wife in question happened to be the early matriarch of a blood line that would meet an impressionable Hitler ages later."

Kemper clearly relished his own storytelling while killing time en route to kill Sam, but the journalist paid attention nonetheless as the story unfolded ever more. "She had passed down the remaining two amber pieces from the original Amber Room to her descendants, and it ended up being bestowed on none other than Johann Dietrich Eckart! How is that for chance?"

"I'm sorry, Klaus," Sam apologized sheepishly, "but my German history knowledge is embarrassing. That is what I keep Nina for."

"Ha! Just for historical information?" Klaus teased. "I doubt that. But let me clarify. Eckart, an extremely educated man, and metaphysical poet was directly responsible for Hitler's admiration for the occult. It was Eckart, we suspect, who discovered the power of Kalihasa, and then used the phenomenon when he assembled the first Black Sun members. And of course, the most prominent member who could actively apply the undeniable opportunity to alter the ideologies of men..."

"...was Adolf Hitler. I get it now," Sam filled the blanks, acting very fascinated to beguile his captor. "Kalihasa gave Hitler the ability to turn individuals into, well, drones. This explains how the masses in Nazi Germany were basically of the same mind... the synchronized movement, and this obscenely instinctive, inhumane level of cruelty."

Klaus smiled endearingly at Sam. "Obscenely instinctive...I like that."

"I thought you might," Sam sighed. "This is all positively fascinating, you know? But how did you learn about all this?"

"My father," Kemper replied matter-of-factly. He struck Sam as a would-be celebrity with his pretend coyness. "Karl Kemper."

'Kemper was the name called out on Nina's sound clip,' Sam remembered. *'He was responsible for the death of the Red Army soldier in the interrogation room. The puzzle is coming together now.'* He stared in the eyes of the small-framed monster before him. *'I cannot wait to watch you choke,'* Sam thought as he paid the Black Sun commander all the attention he craved. *'Can't believe I am drinking with a genocidal fuckwit.*

How I would dance on your ashes, Nazi scum!' The notions that materialized inside Sam's psyche felt alien and detached from his own personality, and it alarmed him. The Kalihasa in his brain was at it again, feeding negativity and primal violence into his thoughts, but he had to admit that the terrible things he was thinking were not altogether exaggerated.

"Tell me, Klaus, what was the objective behind the assassinations in Berlin?" Sam extended the so-called ad hoc interview for a glass of good whiskey. "Fear? Public alarm? I always thought it was your way of just preparing the masses for the coming implementation of a new system of order and discipline. How close I was! Should have placed a bet."

Kemper looked less starry on hearing the new route the investigative journalist was taking, but he had nothing to lose in exposing his reasons to a walking dead man.

"That is a very simple agenda, actually," he replied. "With the German Chancellor at our mercy, we have leverage. The killings of high-profile citizens, mostly responsible for the country's political and financial well-being, prove that we are aware and that we are not hesitant to enforce our threats, of course."

"So you picked them based on their elite status?" Sam inquired simply.

"That too, Mr. Cleave. But each of our targets had a deeper investment in our world than mere money and power," Kemper revealed, yet he did not appear too eager to share what exactly that investment had been. Only until Sam pretended to lose interest with a simple nod and started staring out the window at the moving terrain outside did Kemper feel compelled to tell him. "Each of those seemingly random targets was in fact Germans assisting our contemporary comrades of the Red Army in concealing the location and shrouding the existence of the Amber Room. Milla has been the single-most effective hindrance in the Black Sun's search for the original masterpiece. My father heard it first hand from Leopoldt – a Russian traitor – that the relic had been intercepted by the Red Army and had not gone down with the *Wilhelm Gustloff*, as legend dictates. Since then some Black Sun members, changing their opinions about world domination, have defected from our ranks. Can you believe that? Aryan descendants, powerful and intellectually superior, chose to break ranks with the Order. But the ultimate betrayal was helping the Soviet bastards keeping the Amber Room hidden, even funding the covert operation in 1986 to destroy six of the ten remaining slabs of amber containing Kalihasa!"

Sam perked up. "Wait, wait. What are you saying about 1986? Half of the Amber Room was destroyed?"

"Yes, thanks to our freshly deceased elite members of society who funded Milla for *Operation Motherland*, Chernobyl is now the tomb of half of the magnificent relic," Kemper sneered, clenching his fists. "But this time we are going to kill them off – make them extinct along with their countrymen and anyone who questions us."

"How?" Sam asked.

Kemper laughed, surprised that a sharp man like Sam Cleave did not realize what was really going on. "Why, we have you, Mr. Cleave. You are the Black Sun's new Hitler… with that special creature that is feeding on your brain."

"Excuse me?" Sam gasped. "How do you believe am I going to serve your purpose?"

"Your mind has the ability to manipulate the masses, my friend. Like the Führer, you will be able to subjugate Milla and all other agencies like them – even governments. They will do the rest themselves," Kemper grinned.

"What about my friends?" Sam asked, alarmed at the prospects ahead.

"It will not matter. By the time you have projected Kali-hasa's power over the world, the organism will have consumed most of your brain," Kemper revealed as Sam stared at him in raw horror. "Either that or the abnormal increase in electrical activity will have fried your brain. Either way, you will go down in history as a hero of the Order."

CHAPTER 31

"Give them the fucking gold. Gold will soon be useless unless they can find a way to convert vanity and density into feasible survival paradigms," Natasha sneered at her colleagues. Milla's visitors were seated around the large table with the group of militant hackers that Purdue now found were the people behind Gabi's mysterious air traffic control communication. It was Marko, one of Milla's more quiet members, who circumvented the Copenhagen air control and told Purdue's pilots to divert to Berlin, but Purdue was not going to blow his cover of Detlef's 'Widower' moniker to reveal who he really was – not yet.

"I have no idea what gold has to do with the plan," Nina muttered to Purdue in the midst of the Russian quarrel.

"A large part of the amber sheets still in existence still has the gold inlays and framing in place, Dr. Gould," Elena explained, leaving Nina feeling silly for bitching a bit too loudly about it.

"Da!" Misha chipped in. "That gold is worth a lot to the right people."

"You a capitalist pig now?" Yuri asked. "Money is useless. Value only information, knowledge, and practical things. We give them the gold. Who cares? We need the gold to fool them into believing that Gabi's friends are not up to something."

"Better still," Elena suggested, "we use the gold carvings to house the isotope. All we need then is the accelerant and enough electricity to heat the pot."

"Isotope? Are you a scientist, Elena?" Purdue charmed.

"Nuclear physicist, Class of 2014," Natasha boasted about her soft-spoken friend with a smile.

"Damn!" Nina raved, impressed at the intelligence hidden in the beautiful woman. She looked at Purdue and nudged him. "This place is a sapiosexual's Valhalla, hey?"

Purdue raised his eyebrows flirtatiously at Nina's accurate assumption. Suddenly the heated discussion between the Red Army hackers was interrupted by a loud crackle that had them all frozen in anticipation. Listening intently, they waited. Over the wall-mounted speakers of the broadcast center, the wail of an incoming signal announced something sinister.

"Guten Tag, meine Kameraden."

"Oh God, it is Kemper again," Natasha hissed.

Purdue felt sick to his stomach. The sound of the man's voice provoked a dizzy spell in him, but he held his own for the sake of the group.

"We will be arriving in Chernobyl in two hours," Kemper reported. "This is your first and only warning that we expect you to have the Amber Room excavated from its Sarcophagus by our ETA. Non-compliance will result in..." he chuckled to himself and elected to abandon formality, "... well, it will result in the death of the German Chancellor and Sam Cleave, after which we will release nerve gas in Moscow, London and Seoul simultaneously. David Purdue will be implicated by our vast network of political media representatives, so do not attempt to defy us. Zwei Stunden. Wiedersehen."

A click ended the interference and silence fell over the cafeteria like a blanket of defeat.

"This is why we had to change locations. They have been hacking into our broadcast frequencies for a month now. Sending number sequences different from ours, they are making people kill themselves and kill others by means of subliminal suggestion. Now we have to squat in Duga-3 ghost site," Natasha scoffed.

Purdue swallowed hard as his temperature spiked. Trying not to uproot the meeting, he placed his cold, clammy hands on the seat by his sides. Immediately Nina could see that something was wrong.

"Purdue?" she asked. "Are you sick again?'

He smiled faintly and dismissed it with a shake of his head.

"He does not look well," Misha remarked. "Contamination? How long have you been here? More than a day?"

"No," Nina replied. "Just a few hours. But he has been getting sick for two days now."

"Don't worry, people," Purdue slurred, still keeping a cheerful face. "It goes away after."

"After what?" Elena asked.

Purdue jolted up, his face drained of color as he tried to compose himself, but he propelled his lanky body towards the door in a race with the urging need to puke.

"After *that*," Nina sighed.

"The men's toilet is one floor down," Marko advised casually, watching the guest hasten down the steps. "Drinking or nerves?" he asked Nina.

"Both. The Black Sun tortured him for days before our friend Sam went to break him out. I think the trauma is affecting him still," she explained. "They kept him at their fortress in the Kazakh Steppe and tormented him without rest."

The women looked as indifferent as the men. Obviously, torture was embedded so deeply in their cultural past of war and tragedy that it was a matter of course in conversation. At once, Misha's blank expression lit up and animated his features. "Dr. Gould, do you have the coordinates of this place? This... fortress in Kazakhstan?"

"Aye," Nina replied. "That was how we found him in the first place."

The temperamental man held out his hand to her, and Nina quickly fumbled through her front zipper pouch for the paper she jotted on in Dr. Helberg's office that day. She passed Misha the scribbling of numbers and information.

'So the first messages Detlef brought us in Edinburgh were not sent by Milla. Otherwise, they would have known about the location of the compound,' Nina thought, but she kept it to herself. *'Then again, Milla dubbed him 'Widower'. They recognized the name as Gabi's husband right away too.'* Her hands rested in her dark, tousled hair as she propped up her head and elbows on the table like a bored schoolgirl. It occurred to her that Gabi - and therefore Detlef - had been deceived by the Order's interference in the broadcasts too, just like the people affected by the maleficent number sequences. *'Oh my God, I owe Detlef an apology. I'm sure he survived the little Volvo incident. I hope?'*

Purdue had been gone a long time, but it was more important to devise a plan before their time ran out. She watched the Russian geniuses discuss urgently in their tongue, but she did not mind. It sounded beautiful to her, and by their tone she guessed that Misha's idea was solid.

Just as she started to worry about Sam's fate again, Misha and Elena faced her to explain the plan. The other members followed Natasha out of the room, and Nina could hear them thundering down the iron steps like during a fire drill.

"I take it you have a plan. Please tell me you have a plan. Our time is almost up, and I don't think I can take anymore. If they kill Sam, I swear to God I will dedicate my life to wasting them all," she moaned in frustration.

"That is the Red attitude," Elena smiled.

"And yes, we have a plan. Good plan," Misha claimed. He almost seemed happy.

"Great!" Nina smiled, although she still looked tense. "What is the plan?"

Misha announced boldly, "We give them the Amber Room."

Nina's smile withered.

"Come again?" she blinked profusely, half with rage and half eager to hear his explanation. "Should I hope for more attached to your deduction? Because if that is your plan, I have lost all faith in my dwindling admiration for Soviet ingenuity."

They laughed absent-mindedly. It was clear that they did not give a rat's ass about the opinion of a Westerner; not even enough to hasten toward alleviating her doubts. Nina folded her arms. Thinking about Purdue's persistent malady and Sam's constant subjugation and absence only riled the feisty historian up more. Elena could sense her frustration and bravely took her by the arm.

"We will not get involved in the actual, um, claim of the Amber Room or collection after by Black Sun, but we will give you what you need to combat them. Okay?" she told Nina.

"You're not going to help us get Sam back?" Nina gasped. She felt like breaking down in tears. After all this she had been turned down by the only allies, she had thought they had against Kemper. Maybe the Red Army was not as potent

as their reputation stated, she thought with bitter disappointment in her heart. "What the fuck are you actually
going to help with then?" she seethed.

Misha's eyes grew dark with intolerance. "Look, we don't
have to help you. We broadcast information, not fight your
battles."

"That's obvious," she scoffed. "So what is going to
happen now?"

"You and Widower have to get the Amber Room's
remaining pieces. Yuri is getting a man with heavy truck and
pulleys for you," Elena tried to sound more proactive.
"Natasha and Marko are in the sub-level sector reactor
Medvedka right now. I am going soon to help Marko with
the poison."

"Poison?" Nina winced.

Misha pointed to Elena. "That is what they call chemical
elements they put in bombs. I think they try to be funny.
Like, poisoning a body with wine they poison objects with
chemicals or something."

Elena kissed him and excused herself to join the others at
the secret fast breeder reactor basement, a section of the
massive military base once used for equipment storage.
Duga-3 was one of three locations Milla used to migrate to
sporadically every year to evade capture or discovery, and
the group had secretly adapted each of their sites into fully
functional bases of operation.

"When the poison is ready, we will give you the materials,
but you have to prepare your own weapon down at *Shelter
Object*," Misha explained.

"Is that the Sarcophagus?" she asked.

"Da."

"But the radiation there will kill me," Nina protested.

"You will not be in the Shelter Object. In 1996, my uncle
and grandfather moved the Amber Room plates to an old

well near Shelter Object, but there is ground, much earth, where the well is. It is not connected to Reactor 4 at all, so you should be fine," he clarified.

"Jesus, it's going to peel my skin off," she muttered, seriously reconsidering abandoning the entire venture and leaving Purdue and Sam to their own devices. Misha scoffed at the paranoia of the spoiled Western woman and shook his head. "Who is going to show me how to prepare it?" Nina finally inquired, having made up her mind that she did not want the Russians to think Scots were wimps.

"Natasha is explosives expert. Elena is chemical hazard expert. They will tell you how to turn the Amber Room into a coffin," Misha smiled. "One thing, Dr. Gould," he continued in a subdued tone uncharacteristic of his dominant nature. "Please handle the metal with protective gear and try not to breathe without covering over your mouth. And after you give them the relic, stay far away. Big distance, okay?"

"Okay," Nina replied, grateful for his concern. It was a side of him she had not had the pleasure of seeing until now. He was mature and human. "Misha?"

"Da?"

In all seriousness, she begged to know. "What weapon am I making here?"

He did not answer, so she pried some more.

"How far away should I be after giving Kemper the Amber Room?" she wished to determine.

Misha blinked a few times while he looked deep into the dark eyes of the pretty woman. He cleared his throat and advised, "Leave the country."

CHAPTER 32

When Purdue awoke on the toilet floor, his shirt was a mess of bile and saliva. Embarrassed, he did his best to remove it with hand soap and cold water at the sink. After some scrubbing, he surveyed the condition of the fabric in the mirror. "Like it never happened," he smiled, satisfied with his effort.

When he entered the cafeteria, he found Nina being dressed by Elena and Misha.

"Your turn," Nina grinned. "I see you had another bout of sickness."

"This one was nothing short of violent," he said. "What is happening?"

"We are padding Dr. Gould's clothing with radioactive-resistant materials for when you two go down to get the Amber Room," Elena informed him.

"This is ridiculous, Nina," he bitched. "I refuse to wear all that. Like our task is not already impeded by a deadline, now you have to resort to absurd and time-consuming measures to hold us up even longer?"

Nina frowned. It seemed Purdue had once again become

225

the whiny bitch she had had a tiff with in the car, and she was not going to stand for his childish moods. "Would you like your balls to fall off by tomorrow?" she nipped back. "Otherwise you better get a cup; a lead one."

"Grow up, Dr. Gould," he countered.

"Radiation levels are next to lethal for this little expedition, Dave. I hope you have a large collection of baseball caps for that imminent hair loss you will suffer in a few weeks."

Silently the Soviets laughed at Nina's patronizing rant as they adjusted the last of her lead enforced gear. Elena gave her a medical mask to put over her mouth once down in the well and a climbing helmet for good measure.

After sulking for a while, Purdue allowed them to deck him out in similar fashion before accompanying Nina to where Natasha was ready to arm them for battle. Marko had assembled some delicate cutting tools the size of a pencil case for them, as well as instruction on how to plate the amber with the fine glass prototype he had created for just such an occasion.

"Are you people sure we will be able to pull off this highly specialized undertaking with such short notice?" Purdue asked.

"Dr. Gould says you are inventor," Marko replied. "Just like work with electronics. Use the tools to access and fit. Put pieces of metal on the amber sheet to hide as gold inlay and put the covers over it. Use clips on the corners and BOOM! Death-reinforced Amber Room for them to take home."

"I'm still not clear on what this all is," Nina complained. "Why are we doing this? I got the hint from Misha that we must be far away, which means this is a bomb, right?"

"Correct," Natasha affirmed.

"But this is just a collection of dirty silver metal frames and rings. It looks like something my mechanic grandfather hoarded in his junk yard," she groaned. For the first time,

Purdue showed some interest in their mission when he saw the junk that looked like tarnished steel or silver.

"Mary, Mother of God! Nina!" he gasped in awe, giving Natasha a look of chastisement and wonder. "You people are insane!"

"What? What is it?" she asked. They all returned his gaze, unperturbed by his panic-stricken judgment. Purdue's mouth remained open in disbelief as he turned to Nina with one piece in his hand. "This is weapons-grade Plutonium. They are sending us to turn the Amber Room into a nuclear bomb!"

They did not refute his statement, nor did they look intimidated. Nina was speechless.

"Is that true?" she asked. Elena looked down, and Natasha nodded proudly.

"It cannot explode while you handle it, Nina," Natasha explained calmly. "Just make it look like part of the art and seal Marko's glass over the panels. Then give it to Kemper."

"Plutonium ignites by contact with moist air or water," Purdue gulped, thinking about all the properties of the element. "If the covering were to chip or to be exposed there could be dire consequences."

"So don't fuck up," Natasha growled in amusement. "Now come, you have less than two hours to produce the find to our guests."

∼

JUST OVER TWENTY minutes later Purdue and Nina were being lowered into a concealed stone well, overgrown by decades of radioactive grass and shrubs. The masonry had crumbled just like the former Iron Curtain, evidence of a bygone time of superior technology and innovation abandoned and left to the decay of the Chernobyl aftermath.

"You are well away from the Shelter Object," Elena reminded Nina. "But breathe through your nose. Yuri and his cousin will wait here for you to hoist the relic out."

"How do we get it to the entrance of the well? Each panel weighs more than your car!" Purdue declared.

"There is rail system," Misha called down into the dark pit. "Tracks run to the chamber of the Amber Room where my grandfather and my uncle moved the pieces to the hiding place. You can just lower them with the ropes onto the mine car and roll them here where Yuri will bring them up."

Nina gave them thumbs up after checking her walkie-talkie for the frequency Misha had given her to communicate with any of them, should she have questions while beneath the dreaded Chernobyl Power Plant.

"Right! Let's get this done, Nina," Purdue impelled.

They ventured into the dank blackness with flash lights mounted to their helmets. A black mass in the dark proved to be the mine car Misha had spoken of, and they lifted Marko's sheets onto it with the tools, pushing the car as they walked.

"A bit uncooperative," Purdue remarked. "But I would be too had I been rusting in the dark for over twenty years."

Their light beams weakened only a few meters ahead of them, overcome by the thick darkness. A myriad of minute particles floated through the air and danced in front of the rays in the silent oblivion of the underground channel.

"What if we come back, and they have closed the well?" Nina said suddenly.

"We'll find a way out. We have been through worse than this before," he reassured.

"It is so eerily quiet," she persisted with her gloomy mood. "Once there was water down here. I wonder how many people have drowned in this well or perished from radiation while seeking refuge down here."

"Nina," was all he said to shake her from her folly.

"Sorry," Nina whispered. "I am fucking scared."

"That is unlike you," Purdue said in the dense atmosphere that denied his voice any echo. "You only fear contamination or the after-effects of radiation poisoning that lead to a slow death. This is why you find this place terrifying."

Nina stared at him in the misty illumination of her light. "Thank you, David."

A few steps onward his face changed. He was looking at something to the right of her, but Nina was adamant not to know what it was. When Purdue stopped all kinds of scary scenarios gripped Nina.

"Look," he smiled, taking her arm to face her toward the magnificent treasure that was hidden under years of dust and debris. "It is every bit as glorious as when the King of Prussia owned it."

As soon as Nina shone her light on the yellow slabs, the gold and amber married to become exquisite mirrors of lost beauty from centuries past. Intricate carvings adorned the frames and slivers of mirror detailed the clarity of the amber.

"To think that an evil god slumbers right in here," she whispered.

"A speck of what appears to be inclusions, Nina, look," Purdue pointed out. "A specimen so small that it was almost invisible came under the scrutiny of Purdue's glasses, magnifying it.

"Good God, aren't you a positively grotesque little bastard," he said. "It looks like a crab or a tick, but its head has a humanoid face."

"Oh, Jesus, that sound hideous,' Nina shivered at the thought.

"Come see," Purdue invited, bracing himself for her reaction. He placed the left magnifying glass of his spectacles over another dirty spot in the otherwise pristine gilded amber. Nina bent to bring her eye to it.

"What in the name of Jupiter's Gonads is that thing?" she gasped in horror with puzzlement on her face. "I swear I will shoot myself if that creepy thing nestles into my brain. Oh my God, can you imagine if Sam knew what his Kalihasa looked like?"

"Speaking of Sam, I think we should get a move on hotwiring this treasure for the Nazis to enjoy. What say you?" Purdue pressed.

"Aye."

WHEN THEY HAD FINISHED PAINSTAKINGLY REINFORCING the giant slabs with the metal and carefully sealed it in behind the sheeting as directed, Purdue and Nina wheeled the panels to the bottom of the well mouth, one by one.

"Look, see? They are all gone. Nobody up there," she lamented.

"At least they did not cover the entrance," he smiled. "We cannot very well expect them to be up there all day, can we?"

"I suppose not," she sighed. "I'm just glad we got it up to the well. Believe me, I have had enough of that bloody catacomb."

From a distance, they could hear a loud engine noise. Vehicles slowly crawling along a nearby road approached the area of the well. Yuri and his cousin started pulling the slabs up. Even with convenient ship cargo netting, it was still a time-consuming endeavor. With the two Russians and four locals helping Purdue get the netting over each of the slabs he hoped it was made for securing a lift of over 400kg a pop.

"Unbelievable," Nina murmured. She was standing at a safe distance, deeper into the tunnel. Her claustrophobia was crawling in on her, but she did not want to get in the way. While the men were shouting suggestions and count-outs, her two-way radio received a transmission.

"Nina, come in. Over," Elena said through the low crackle Nina had come to grow used to.

"This is Nina receiving. Over," she responded.

"Nina, we will be gone when the Amber Room has been lifted out, okay?" Elena warned. *"I need you not to worry or think we just ran away, but we have to leave before they get to Duga-3."*

"No!" Nina shouted. "Why?"

"It will be a bloodbath if we meet on the same soil. You know that." Misha responded to her. *"Now don't worry. We will be in touch. Be careful and Godspeed."*

Nina felt her heart sink. "Please don't leave." Never had she heard a lonelier phrase in her life.

"Over and out."

She heard the clapping sound of Purdue dusting off his clothing and swinging his palms along his pants to wipe the dirt off. He looked around for Nina and when his eyes found her he gave her a warm, satisfied smile.

"Accomplished, Dr. Gould!" he cheered.

Suddenly the sound of gunshots thundered above them, sending Purdue diving into the dark. Nina screamed for his safety, but he crawled further into the opposite side of the tunnel, leaving her relieved that he was okay.

"Yuri and his helpers have been executed!" they heard Kemper say outside the well.

"Where is Sam?" Nina screamed up at the light falling like supernal hell onto the floor of the tunnel.

"Mr. Cleave had a bit too much to drink... but... thank you kindly for your cooperation, David! Oh, and Dr. Gould, please accept my sincerest condolences on what will be your last agonizing moments on this earth. Cheerio!"

"Fuck you very much!" Nina screamed. "I'll see you soon, yeh bastard! Soon!"

As she unleashed her verbal fury on the smiling German, his men began to slide the thick concrete slab over the mouth of the well, gradually darkening the tunnel. Nina could hear Klaus Kemper calmly recite a sequence of numbers in a low tone of voice, much as he had sounded during radio broadcasts.

As the shadow gradually eclipsed, she looked over to Purdue and to her horror his frozen eyes looked up at Kemper in apparent thrall. With the last of the dying light, Nina saw Purdue's face contort in a lustful and evil sneer, staring right at her.

CHAPTER 33

*O*nce Kemper had his bedeviled treasure, he ordered his men to head for Kazakhstan. They were returning to the Black Sun compound with the first true prospect of world domination, their plan almost fully completed.

"Are all six in the water?" he asked his workmen.

"Yes, sir."

"That is ancient amber resin. It is brittle enough, so if it crumbles the specimens trapped inside will get out and then we will be in a lot of trouble. They must be contained under water until we reach the compound, gentlemen!" Kemper shouted before he retired to his luxury vehicle.

"Why the water, Commander?" one of his men asked.

"Because they hate water. In there, they cannot exert any influence, and they detest it, making it a perfect prison for them to be contained in without any concerns," he explained. With that, he got in the car, and the two vehicles pulled away slowly to leave Chernobyl even more barren than she had already been before.

SAM WAS STILL DRUGGED by the powder that had left a white residue at the bottom of his empty whiskey glass. Kemper paid him no mind. In his new exciting position as owner of not only a former Wonder of the World but also on the threshold of ruling the new world to come, he hardly noticed the journalist anymore. Nina's screams still echoed in his thoughts as sweet music for his rotten heart.

It seemed that using Purdue as bait had paid off after all. For a while, Kemper had not been sure if the brainwashing techniques had succeeded, but when Purdue had successfully utilized the communications devices Kemper had left for him to find, he knew that Cleave and Gould would soon be netted. The betrayal of not releasing Cleave to Nina after all her drudgery was positively delectable to Kemper. Now he had tied up loose ends no other Black Sun commander had ever been able to.

Dave Purdue, the traitorous Renatus, was now left to rot under the godforsaken soil of cursed Chernobyl, soon killing the annoying little bitch that had always inspired Purdue to wreck the Order. And Sam Cleave...

Kemper looked at Cleave. He was bound for a bit of water himself. And as soon as Kemper had conditioned him he would play a valuable role as the ideal media representative for the Order's public relations. After all, how could the world fault anything presented by a Pulitzer Award winning investigative journalist that single-handedly exposed arms rings and toppled crime syndicates? With Sam as his media puppet, Kemper could announce whatever he wished to the world while nurturing his own Kalihasa to wield mass control over entire continents. And when that little god's power ran out, he would have several others safely shelved to replace it.

Things were looking up for Kemper and his Order. Finally, the obstacles from the Scotland were eradicated and his path cleared to make the necessary changes that Himmler failed at. In all this Kemper could not help but wonder how things were going for the sexy little historian and her former lover.

⌇

NINA COULD HEAR her heart beating, and it was not a difficult feat by the way it was thundering in her body while her sense of hearing was in overdrive for even the slightest noise. Purdue was quiet, and she had no idea where he could be, but she moved as quickly as she could in the opposite direction, keeping her light off so he couldn't see her. He was doing the same thing.

'Oh sweet Jesus, where is he?' she thought, crouching near where the Amber Room had been. Her mouth was parched, and she ached for relief, but now was not the time to pursue comfort or sustenance. A few feet away she heard a few small rocks scrunch, and it made her gasp loudly. *'Shit!'* Nina considered talking him down, but by the look of his glazed-over eyes, she doubted that anything she said would get through. *'He is coming my way. I can hear the sounds are closer every time!'*

They had been underground in the vicinity of Reaktor-4 for over three hours already, and she was beginning to feel the effects. She was starting to feel nauseous, while a migraine practically crippled her ability to concentrate. But danger was coming in many shapes and forms for the historian lately. Now she had become a target for a brainwashed mind, programmed by an even sicker mind to kill her. To be murdered by her own friend would be so much worse than running from a deranged stranger or a mercenary on a mission. It was Dave! Dave Purdue, her long-time friend and ex-lover.

Without warning her body convulsed and she fell to her knees on the cold hard ground, throwing up. It grew more violent with every convulsion until she started to cry. There was no way for Nina to do it quietly and she was convinced Purdue would easily track her by the din she caused. She was sweating profusely, and the flash light strap around her head turned into an annoying itch, so she jerked it from her hair. In a spell of panic, she pointed the light downward a few inches from the ground and switched it on. The beam spread over the small radius on the ground, and she took stock of her surroundings.

Purdue was nowhere to be found. Suddenly a large steel rod came hurling towards her face from the darkness ahead. It struck her on the shoulder, evoking a yelp of agony from her. "Purdue! Stop! Jesus Christ! Are you going to kill me because of that Nazi prick? Wake the fuck up!"

Nina killed her light, panting like an exhausted hunting hound. Crouched forward on her knees she tried to ignore the throbbing migraine that was splitting her skull while she held down another pressing bout of regurgitation. Purdue's footsteps moved towards her in the dark, indifferent to her quiet sobbing. Nina's numb fingers fiddled with her strapped two-way radio.

'Leave it here. Switch it on for noise and then run in another direction,' she suggested to herself, but her other inner voice was not for it. 'Idiot, you cannot abandon your last chance for outside communication. Get something you can use as a weapon, over where the debris was.'

The latter was a more feasible idea. She grabbed a handful of stones and waited for a sign of his location. The dark was a solid robe wrapped around her, but what made her frantic was the dust that burned her nose when she breathed. Deep in the darkness, she heard something stir. Nina launched the handful of stones out ahead of her to throw him off before she darted to her left, running straight into a protruding rock that hit her like a truck. With a suppressed gasp, she fell limply to the floor.

As her state of consciousness jeopardized her life, she felt a boost of energy and crawled along the floor on her knees and elbows. Like a bad flu, the radiation started to plague her body. Her skin was crawling, her head was as heavy as lead. Her forehead hurt from the collision while she was struggling to regain her equilibrium.

"Hey Nina," he whispered a few inches from her shivering frame, shocking her heart into a leap of terror. Purdue's bright light momentarily blinded her as he flicked it on in her face. "I found you."

~

30 HOURS LATER - SHALKAR, *Kazakhstan*

SAM WAS LIVID, but he dared not stir up trouble before his escape plan was secure. When he had awoken to find himself still in the clutches of Kemper and the Order, the transport vehicle ahead of them had been creeping steadily along a miserable, desolate stretch of road. By then, they had already progressed past Saratov and had crossed the border into Kazakhstan. It was too late for him to get out. They had traveled almost a day from where Nina and Purdue were, making it impossible for him to simply jump out and run back to Chernobyl or Pripyat.

"Breakfast, Mr. Cleave," Kemper offered. "We have to keep your strength up."

"No thanks," Sam snapped. "I have had my quota of drugs this week."

"Oh, come on now!" Kemper replied evenly. "You are like

237

a whining teenager throwing a tantrum. And I thought PMS was a women's issue. I had to drug you or else you would have run off with your friends and gotten killed. You should be grateful that you are alive." He held out a wrapped sandwich bought at a shop in one of the towns they had passed.

"Did you kill them?" Sam asked.

"Sir, we have to fill up the truck at Shalkar soon," the chauffer announced.

"That's fine, Dirk. How long?" he asked the driver.

"Ten minutes until we get there," he informed Kemper.

"Alright." He looked at Sam, and a mean smile jumped onto his face. "You should have been there!" Kemper laughed in glee. "Oh, I know you were there, but I mean you should have *seen* it!"

Sam grew intensely upset with every word the German bastard spat out. Every muscle in Kemper's face fueled Sam's hatred, and every hand gesture pushed the journalist to a point of unadulterated wrath. *'Wait. Just wait a bit longer.'*

"Your Nina is now rotting beneath the highly radioactive Reaktor-4 ground zero." Kemper imparted with no small measure of enjoyment. "Her sexy little ass is blistered and decomposing as we speak. Who knows what kind of things Purdue has done to her! But even if they survived each other, the starvation and radiation sickness will have ended them."

'Wait! Don't. Not yet.'

Sam knew that Kemper could shield his thoughts from Sam's influence and that attempting to get a hold of him would not only waste his energy but be futile altogether. They pulled into Shalkar, a small town adjacent to a lake in the middle of a flat desert landscape. A petrol station on the side of the main road accommodated the vehicles.

'Now.'

Sam knew that although he could not manipulate Kemper's mind, the skinny commander would be easy to subdue physically. Rapidly Sam's dark eyes checked the back of the front seats, the foot well and the items lying on the seat within reach of Kemper. The only threat to Sam was a Taser device next to Kemper, but *Highland Ferry Boxing Club* taught a pre-teen Sam Cleave that surprise and speed trumped defense.

He took a deep breath and began to latch on to the chauffer's mind. The big gorilla had physical prowess, but his mind was like cotton candy to the battery Sam was packing in his skull. Not even a minute later Sam had gained complete control of Dirk's brain and decided to get nasty. The suited thug stepped out of the car.

"Where are you g…?" Kemper started, but his effeminate face was obliterated by a devastating punch from a well-trained fist bent on freedom. Before he could even think of grabbing the Taser, Klaus Kemper received another hammer – and a few more – until his face was a mess of swollen bruises and blood.

On Sam's command, the chauffer pulled his gun and started opening fire on the workmen on the giant truck. Sam took Kemper's phone and slipped out of the back seat, heading for a secluded place near the lake they had passed on their way into town. With the ensuing chaos, the local police arrived quickly to arrest the gunman. When they found the battered man in the backseat, they assumed it was Dirk's doing. As they tried to capture Dirk, he took one last shot – to the roof of his mouth.

Sam scrolled through the tyrant's contact list, adamant to make his call quickly before having to discard the cell phone to prevent getting tracked. The name he was looking for appeared on the list and he could not help but throw an air fist pump for it. He dialed and waited anxiously, lighting up when the call was answered.

"Detlef! It's Sam."

CHAPTER 34

*N*ina had not seen Purdue since she had struck him against the temple with her two-way radio the day before. However, she had no idea how much time had passed since, but by her exacerbated condition she knew it had to have been a while. Tiny blisters had formed on her skin, and her inflamed nerve endings had made it impossible to touch anything. Over the past day, she had attempted to contact Milla several times, but walloping Purdue had rattled the wiring out of place and left her with a device that could only produce white noise.

"Just one! Just give me one channel, you piece of shit," she wailed softly in despair as she pushed the talk button incessantly. Only the hiss of white noise persisted. "I'm going to run out of batteries soon," she muttered. "Milla, come in. Please. Anyone? Please, please come in!" Her throat was on fire and her tongue swollen, but she held on. "Christ, the only people I can contact with white noise are ghosts!" she shouted in frustration, aggravating her throat. But Nina did not care anymore.

The smell of ammonia and coal and death reminded her

that hell was closer than her last breath. "Come on! Dead people! Dead...fucking Ukrai...dead people of Russia! The Red Dead, come in! Over!"

Hopelessly lost inside the bowels of Chernobyl, her hysterical cackle traveled through the underground system the world had forgotten decades ago. Inside her mind everything was nonsensical. Memories flashed and melted with plans for the future, becoming lucid nightmares. Nina was losing her mind faster than losing her life, so she just laughed and laughed.

"Didn't I kill you yet?" she heard a familiar threat in the pitch darkness.

"Purdue?" she sniffed.

"Aye."

She could hear him lunge, but she had lost all feeling in her legs. Moving or fleeing was not an option anymore, so Nina closed her eyes and welcomed the end of her pain. A steel pipe came down on her head, but her migraine had numbed her skull, so the warm blood only tickled her face. Another blow was due, but it never came. Nina's eyes grew heavy, but for a moment she saw a mad whirling of lights and heard the sound of violence.

She was lying there, waiting to die, but she heard Purdue scuttling away into the dark like a cockroach to get away from the man standing just outside the reach of his light. He bent over Nina, gently lifting her into his arms. His touch hurt her blistered skin but she did not care. Half awake, half lifeless, Nina felt him carry her toward a bright light overhead. It reminded her of the accounts of dying people seeing white lights from heaven, but in the sharp whiteness of daylight from outside the well mouth Nina recognized her rescuer.

"Widower," she sighed.

"Hey sweetheart," he smiled. Her tattered hand caressed

241

his empty eye socket, where she had stabbed him, and she began to sob. "Don't worry," he said. "I lost the love of my life. An eye is nothing compared to that."

When he gave her fresh water outside, he explained that Sam had called him, having had no idea that he had no longer been with her and Purdue. Sam was safe, but he had asked Detlef to find her and Purdue. Detlef had used his security and surveillance training to triangulate radio signals coming from Nina's cell phone in the Volvo until he had been able to pin her location to Chernobyl.

"Milla broadcast again, and I used Kiril's CB to tell them that Sam was safely away from Kemper and his compound," he told her, while she was cradled in his arms. Nina smiled through cracked lips, her dusty face riddled with bruises, blisters and tears.

"Widower," she dragged the word with her swollen tongue.

"Yes?"

Nina was about to pass out, but she forced her apology. "I'm so sorry I used your credit cards."

~

KAZAKH STEPPE – 24 HOURS LATER

KEMPER WAS STILL NURSING his brutalized face, but he was hardly crying about it. With the Amber Room beautifully converted to an aquarium of decorative gold carvings and stunning bright yellow amber over wooden patterns. It was a substantial aquarium right in the middle of his desert fortress, about 50m in diameter and 70m high, dwarfing the tank Purdue had been kept in during his stay there. Well-dressed, as always, the refined monster sipped his champagne, waiting for his scientific staff to isolate the first organism to be implanted into his brain.

A storm was raging over the Black Sun compound for the second day. It was a freak storm, unusual for that time of year, but the occasional bolts of lightning that struck were majestic and powerful. Kemper looked up to the sky and smiled. "I am God now."

In the distance, Misha Svechin's IL 76-MD cargo plane appeared through the raging clouds. The 93-ton aircraft careened along the turbulence and fluctuating currents. Aboard were Sam Cleave and Marko Strensky to keep Misha company. Tucked and safely secured in the bowels of the plane there were thirty drum loads of sodium metal, covered with oil to prevent contact with air or water – for now. The highly volatile element used in reactors as a heat conductor and coolant had two naughty traits. On contact with air it combusted. On contact with water it exploded.

"There! Down there. You cannot miss it," Sam told Misha as the Black Sun compound came into view. "Even if his fish tank is out of reach this rain will do the job for us."

"Correct, Comrade!" Marko laughed. "I have never seen it done on large scale before. Only in laboratory with small pea size sodium chunk in beaker. This is going on YouTube." Marko always filmed everything he enjoyed. In fact, he had a questionable amount of video clips on his hard drive that had been recorded in his bedroom.

They circled the fortress. Sam winced with every flash of lightning, hoping it would not hit the plane, but the crazy Soviets seemed fearless and chirpy. "Will the drums break that steel roof?" he asked Marko, but Misha just rolled his eyes.

On the next turn, Sam and Marko cut loose the drums

one by one, rapidly pushing them out of the aircraft to fall hard and fast through the roof of the compound. The volatile metal would take a few seconds on contact with water to ignite and explode, breaking the sheeting over the Amber Room plates and exposing the Plutonium to the heat of the explosion.

Once they had dropped the first ten drums, the roof in the middle of the UFO-shaped fortress collapsed, exposing the tank in the middle of the circle.

"There you go! Aim the others at the tank and then we must get the fuck out of this place quickly!" Misha shouted. He looked down on the scattering men and heard Sam say, "I wish I could see Kemper's face one last time."

Laughing, Marko looked down as the dissolving sodium started to build up. "This one is for Yuri, you Nazi bitch!"

Misha piloted the giant steel beast as far away as he could in the short time they had so that they could land a few hundred miles north of the impact zone. He did not want to be in the air when the bomb went off. They landed just over 20 minutes later in Kazaly. From the hard Kazakh ground, they looked to the horizon, beer in hand.

Sam hoped Nina was still alive. He hoped that Detlef had managed to find her and that he had refrained from killing Purdue after Sam explained that Carrington had shot Gabi while being in a hypnotic state under the influence of Kemper's mind control.

The sky was yellow across the Kazakh landscape as Sam stared over the barren terrain of whipping gusts, just as in his vision. He had no idea that the well he had seen Purdue in had been significant, only not to the Kazakhstan portion of Sam's experience. At last, the final prophecy came true.

Lightning had struck the water in the Amber Room tank, igniting everything inside. The power of the thermonuclear explosion disintegrated everything within range, rendering the Kalihasa organism extinct – for good. As the bright flash turned into a pulse that shook the heavens, Misha, Sam and Marko watched the mushroom cloud reach up to the gods of the cosmos in terrible beauty.

Sam raised his beer. "To Nina."

THE END

Made in the USA
Coppell, TX
13 June 2020